# THE UNDERGROUND CITY

D0557493

# THE UNDERGROUND CITY

Book 2 of the Lily Harper series

## HP MALLORY

THE UNDERGROUND CITY
Book 2 of the Lily Harper series

By

# HP MALLORY

Copyright © 2013 by H.P. Mallory

This book is dedicated to the memory of one of my dearest friends, Anastasia Hahalis.

Anastasia, your gentle smile, your contagious laugh, your magnanimity and your sympathetic nature will never be forgotten. To have known you was a gift in and of itself. The joy and love with which you enriched our lives will continue living in those of us who were lucky enough to have called you our friend.

Sleep well, my beautiful friend.

**Music, When Soft Voices Die**
by Percy Bysshe Shelley

Music, when soft voices die,
Vibrates in the memory;
Odours, when sweet violets sicken,
Live within the sense they quicken.
Rose leaves, when the rose is dead,
Are heap'd for the beloved's bed;
And so thy thoughts, when thou art gone,
Love itself shall slumber on.

Acknowledgements:

To my husband: Thank you for always being there for me. I love you.

To my mother: Thank you for always being the first set of eyes on my books!

To Delilah Crespo: Thank you so much for entering my "Become a character in my next book" contest. I really hope you enjoy your character!

To my beta readers: Evie Amaro and TJ MacKay, thank you for all your input and your help!

To my editor, Teri, at www.editingfairy.com: thank you for an excellent job, as always.

To my personal trainer, Al, thanks for making your character so easy to write!

"New torments I behold, and new tormented
around me, whichsoever way I move, and
whichsoever way I turn, and gaze."
– Dante's *Inferno*

## ONE

It took me a moment or two before I could
accept that Tallis Black was standing in my living
room. Tallis, who was a two-thousand-year-old
Celtic Druid, didn't belong in my house, or, for
that matter, in the city of Edinburgh at all. No, he
should have been in the depths of the haunted
forest, where I'd first met him. Why? Because
Tallis wasn't civilized.

Well, civilized or not, I basically owed Tallis
my life. He'd accompanied me on my first mission
to the Underground City, a mission that certainly
would've been my last if not for Tallis's brawn
and brains. I'd been forced to go on the mission in
order to retrieve a soul who was mistakenly placed
in the Underground City during a Y2K glitch.
Although Y2K hadn't affected the natural order of
things here on Earth, it most definitely affected the
afterlife. Souls who were meant to go to the
Kingdom (think of Heaven) were instead
incorrectly routed to the Underground City and
vice versa.

As a Retriever employed by Afterlife Enterprises, the government of the hereafter, it was my responsibility to find those lost souls in the Underground and restore them to their proper places. And to say I needed Tallis's help was pure understatement. As a newly appointed Soul Retriever, I had no training on how to defend myself against the creatures of the Underground. Nope, instead, I was basically tossed into the deep end, which translated, meant I was battling demons. Given my lack of preparation, I was more than sure that Afterlife Enterprises assumed I'd have no chance in hell of surviving the Underground. Well, they'd been wrong. Courtesy of Tallis.

"Okay, yoze, I'm out," Bill, my short, squatty roommate declared before starting for the front door of our lavish apartment. He gave Tallis one last discouraging glance, making it known to all that Tallis was not to touch me. It didn't matter that Tallis had never displayed the slightest interest in doing so in the first place. "My belly's 'bout ta eat itself!" Bill finished as he closed the front door behind him, leaving me alone with Tallis.

Bill was my guardian angel, although I couldn't really say he was much of a guardian. It was on his watch that I'd been killed in a car accident a few weeks earlier simply because he'd been too busy "getting it on with a chick" (his words). His attention should have been focused on me, while I was driving in the rain, and paying too much attention to my cell phone. Bill was also an alcoholic, now in recovery and, as such, he was required to wear a monitor which equated to a narrow, black band around his wrist. The thing was supposed to alert Afterlife Enterprises if Bill ever strayed from the straight and narrow.

Since Bill was employed by Afterlife Enterprises and I'd died before it was my true time to go, they'd offered me the option of living again. The alternative was spending the next hundred years in a place called Shade, which was a lot like Limbo—a place which offered a whole lot of nothingness. It was sort of like a holding area for souls before they could move on to the Kingdom. In Shade there was nothing to look forward to, although there was also nothing to be frightened of. I imagined it was comparable to taking an open-ended vacation in Lancaster, California. Needless to say, I'd opted to live again. But as with most things in life, or in this case, the afterlife, beware the small print. My choice to live again required that I become a Soul Retriever. My full job description? *Enter the bowels of hell and rescue any misplaced souls found there, being very careful, in the process, not to become one, yourself.*

Along with my new line of work, I'd also had to choose a new body, seeing as how my old one perished when my soul had. The new body was the one fractionally good thing about this whole cluster f#%*. I went from being an overweight, unattractive, pale, plain redhead to an absolute knockout. While still maintaining my red hair, I now had large, round, green eyes, framed by inky black lashes. My face was a lovely oval with very high cheekbones that led down to a pouty mouth, and ended with lips like Cupid's bow. And my body? I was five foot eight, with stork-like legs and 34 D boobs, that were surprisingly real even though I was thin. Yes, I had the body that some women would kill for. The kicker of the whole thing, however, was that my body still didn't feel like it was mine. And I wasn't sure if it ever would.

The best part about this whole Soul Retriever business was that I was again alive and I was beautiful for the first time ever. The bad part, no, make that, the worst part, was that I couldn't contact anyone I knew from my previous life. And that was the sticking point because I'd been incredibly close to my mother and best friend, Miranda. Afterlife Enterprises were very strict and clear about making sure that all attachments to former family and friends were broken forever. And I guessed it made sense—I mean, how could I explain the new me to my mom or Miranda? They'd never believe it. In general, I tried to avoid thinking about my mom or Miranda because the end result was an overwhelming sadness that wouldn't do me any good. Things were how they were. Salman Rushdie got it right when he wrote: *When thought becomes excessively painful, action is the finest remedy.*

"Um, have a seat," I said to Tallis as I glanced around my apartment, noticing all the moving boxes that littered the floor. Luckily, my dining table had been one of the first pieces of furniture that Bill and I, well, make that *I,* assembled. We'd recently moved into a townhouse and were still in the process of unloading the furniture I'd ordered using the relocation allowance provided me by Afterlife Enterprises. There were some other benefits to being an employee of Afterlife Enterprises—I had a company-supplied Audi A5, a constantly full bank account, and a plush pad.

"Thank ye, lass," Tallis answered in his thick Scottish brogue. Taking a seat at my table, he dwarfed both the chair and the table. That was because Tallis was enormous and quite easily the largest man I'd ever seen. Standing at nearly seven feet tall, he was like looking up at an ancient redwood. Well, that is if a tree could have incredibly broad shoulders, bulky pecs and abs that were so defined you could trip over them. Tallis's face wasn't half bad either. Although I considered him "rugged," he was nonetheless handsome. Well, handsome might be too feminine a word to describe him. There was nothing feminine about Tallis at all. "Striking" would probably be more descriptive. His face was comprised of a chiseled, square jaw, a masculine nose, and piercing navy blue eyes. His full lips, in the rare instance that he smiled, parted to reveal very white, very large, but straight teeth. Having short, black hair and a tan complexion, most women would have considered him a looker except for the scar that ran down one side of his face and bisected his cheek. It started at the tip of his eyebrow and ended at his jawline. His scar only hinted at the hard life he'd led. Some people might have considered it a blemish, but to me, it embodied everything that was Tallis.

"So, going back to my training," I started, hoping to focus on the task at hand because Tallis had a way of making me anxious. Tallis had just arrived on my doorstep to remind me of my sword training which I'd completely forgotten about. Tallis was, by nature, a bladesmith—someone who forged swords from hot iron. He lived in the Dark Wood, a place that existed in its own plane, somewhere between Earth and the Underground City.

"Aye," he interrupted, nodding. "Time is wastin,' lass. Ye require skill an' knowledge on wieldin' yer blade."

"Okay," I answered, biting my lip, as I glanced around my house. "Um, so are we going to practice here?" I was trying to imagine a place inside my smallish apartment that would lend itself to sword play.

Tallis laughed a deep rumbling sound, which I found very attractive. Then he shook his head. "Nae, lass, there is naethin' here that would pose a threat to ye that ye would have ta defend yerself from," he answered. "Nae. We practice in the wood." He was referring to the forest where he lived. The same one that was rumored to be haunted and alive in its own right. The same one which could swallow up your tracks in the snow simply because it wanted you to lose your way.

"Great," I said with an unconvincing smile. "One small problem though," I started as I remembered having to drive all the way to Peterhead, a good two hours from Edinburgh, where Bill and I lived. From there, we'd managed to access the Dark Wood by entering an old shack which conveniently turned out to be a portal into the forest. "Peterhead isn't exactly close," I finished, thinking my training would have to be fairly regular in order for me to progress at a decent pace. The last thing I wanted to do was drive to Peterhead repeatedly. I still wasn't used to driving on the opposite side of the road.

Tallis nodded and reached inside his jeans pocket. He produced an iron blade, which was maybe two inches long. He handed it to me, and I accepted it, running the pads of my fingers over the marks on the blade where Tallis had pounded it into a serrated point. "Ye will use this blade ta cut yer way inta the wood," he answered as if his response made an ounce of sense to me.

"Um, what?" I asked, looking up at him and shaking my head to let him know I was lost.

"The blade will clear the pathway ta the wood," he added. Seeing my still concerned expression, he continued. "Ye simply hold the blade in the air, where ye want ta place yer pathway, an' then ye coot down. The blade coots the air in half, revealin' the wood."

"So it cuts right through thin air?" I asked, dubiously. I should have known better though. I wasn't sure if it was because Tallis was a Celtic Druid, or two thousand years old, or because he was possessed by the ghost of an ancient warrior, making him immortal, but Tallis possessed magic. He could do things that defied science—like healing himself. Well, and cutting portals through thin air.

"Aye, 'twill coot right through the air, lass," he answered matter-of-factly.

I glanced down at the blade in my hand and rotated it. As I studied it, I wondered how Tallis had imbued it with such magic. I didn't get the chance to inquire, however, because the front door suddenly burst open, exposing Bill who was balancing on one leg. The other leg had, presumably, just kicked the front door open. His arms were full with two large, white plastic bags. He also balanced two cups, of what I imagined was soda, beneath his chin.

"A lil' help'd be nice!" he growled out as I lurched forward from where I'd been leaning against the bar in the kitchen. I grabbed the two drinks from beneath his chin as he released a pent-up breath and I closed the door behind him. "Thanks, Conan," he remarked with raised brows at Tallis, apparently ticked off that Tallis hadn't made a move to assist him. To say the two men were as compatible as water and oil was an abject understatement.

*8*

Tallis didn't say anything, but I caught the corners of his lips lifting a bit. Apparently he found the whole situation amusing. Bill plopped the two bags onto the kitchen table and untied them. He pulled out a Styrofoam clamshell container, which he placed in front of me. "Chicken Tikka Masala for you, nips," he said, handing me one of the beverages. "An' a Diet Coke, since you're wantin' ta keep your bod 'do me' worthy." Then he handed me something wrapped in aluminum foil. "And the garlic naan, which you love so much, but makes your breath smell like ass."

"Thanks, Bill," I said with a reluctant smile.

"An' butter chicken for me," Bill continued. He placed the dish in front of his empty seat, which was next to me and across from Tallis. He set the other beverage in front of himself, as well as the only other package of naan. Then, reaching back into the plastic bag, he presented Tallis with the last dish. "An' this is Alpoo Mater or some shit I can't pronounce. It's vegetarian," he added, smiling wickedly at Tallis.

"Bill, you know Tallis isn't vegetarian?" I asked, frowning at him.

"'Course I know, bubble-butt, but the dude needs ta go on a diet," he explained with a shrug. It was a ridiculous thing to say. Tallis probably had less than 6 percent body fat, while Bill must've been pushing 30 percent. "An' that's the reason why Conan doesn't get a drink neither,"

Bill continued, facing Tallis. "Empty calories—they go right to your hips."

Tallis frowned at him, but didn't say anything. He simply opened his container and reached for one of the plastic forks, which Bill had taken from the bags. Tallis took a small bite of what looked like potatoes in some sort of curry sauce. Really, Tallis's quiet appreciation for the food was the best revenge. And based on Bill's ensuing frown, Tallis's approach was working.

"Do you want some of my chicken?" I asked Tallis, irritated at Bill's bad manners. But Tallis shook his head.

"Nae, this is fine, lass. Ah've supped oan far worse." He finished his bite and smiled at Bill as if to say the angel hadn't bested him. Bill glowered in response before spearing another piece of butter chicken, which he then popped into his already full mouth.

"Okay, so when did you want to start my training?" I asked Tallis.

"Oan the morrow, lass," Tallis answered. "Ah'll expect ye ta be at mah doorstep at first light."

"At first light?" Bill roared, bits of food flying out of his mouth. "We got shit ta do, yo! We ain't got time ta go trick-or-treatin' with your sorry ass!" Bill glanced around the room as if to say the unpacked boxes were our number one priority. As far as I was concerned, survival was my number one priority.

"Ah dinnae care," Tallis answered indifferently as he impaled another piece of potato and brought it to his mouth. "Find yer own time ta make yer nest," he finished, facing Bill.

"Okay, tomorrow at dawn," I said, not wanting to give Bill the chance to pursue the argument. I took a deep breath and forked a piece of chicken. None of us said anything for the next few minutes as I struggled for a new topic of conversation. Glancing over at Tallis, I took in his black sweater and dark blue jeans, and figured that was as good a place to start as any. "So, I'm surprised to see you dressed like that, Tallis," I began. "I'd imagined your wardrobe consisted only of kilts and the Roman sandals we always see you wearing."

He glanced at me and shook his head. "Aye, an' sooch is what Ah'm wearin' now, lass."

I frowned because he clearly wasn't wearing a kilt. Looking down at his feet, I noticed they were covered by black boots. "Um, it doesn't look like you are," I said with a nervous laugh. It was generally not a great idea to argue with the bladesmith, since he was about as unpredictable as a cornered feral animal.

He didn't say anything. Then he extended his arm out before him, holding his large palm directly in front of my eyes. He brought his hand downward, and when his palm no longer blocked my eyes, I noticed he was now sitting at my table clad in a blue and purple kilt and his sporran, which he wore around his waist. He wasn't wearing anything up top. Glancing down beneath the table, I found that, yes, his sandals were also present and accounted for.

"How did you do that?" I asked, shocked. I noticed that Bill didn't say anything. He was still too enthralled with finishing his meal.

Tallis raised his eyebrows at me and smiled in a self-impressed sort of way. "Druid magic, Besom," he answered. "Besom" was Tallis's nickname for me. In Gaelic, it meant "troublesome woman." It wasn't the most endearing nickname, but Tallis didn't strike me as the Hallmark type.

"Explain," I said.

He shrugged. "Ah dinnae like ta attract attention when Ah travel ta yer world, lass," he started. "Usin' the magic o' mah ancestry, Ah'm able ta disappear inta a crowd. People see meh as they choose ta."

"So you mean you look different to everyone?" I asked, always finding Tallis's magic far beyond interesting.

"Aye. Ah appear as inconspicuously as Ah can, dependin' oan how someone wants ta see meh." He took a deep breath. "How did ye see meh afore Ah released the magic?"

"You were wearing a black sweater and dark jeans," I answered, bringing another bite to my mouth.

He nodded. "An' was mah face an' height the same as ye see now?"

"Yes," I said as his eyebrows raised, showing surprise. A moment later, the expression was gone.

It was unusual for Tallis to look startled, although I had managed to take him unexpectedly maybe twice in the duration of our acquaintance. "Most people willna see meh as Ah am boot far shorter an' smaller." It made sense—if Tallis wanted to blend in, his immense height and build wouldn't be an asset.

"Wanna know how I see you, Tido?" Bill piped up, but didn't wait for Tallis to answer. "I see you as buck ass nekked," Bill finished, his mouth full of chicken. I had a sneaking suspicion it was my chicken because his plate was already licked clean.

"Naked?" I repeated, not meaning to sound aghast, but there it was. I felt my cheeks coloring. There were times when it wasn't so easy to be a twenty-two-year-old virgin.

Bill nodded and speared another morsel from my dinner. "That's right. Ol' Conan looks ta me as nekked as the day Medusa birthed him." He glanced at Tallis and smiled as if he'd just bested the Druid. Then he glanced down at Tallis's crotch. "An' the ol' bladesmith ain't packin' much penis heat, know's what I mean, Lil?" he asked, glancing over at me, and nudging me with his elbow. He shook his head like Tallis's lack of "penis heat" was a tragic shame.

"Bill," I started, now more than aware that he was making everything up.

"It's true," he continued as he nodded vehemently. "Conan ain't gotta lap hog, namsay?"

"No, I don't know what you're saying," I spat back at him. He exhausted me with the never ending rivalry he insisted upon displaying toward Tallis.

"Lap hog, babydoll, means someone's got a biggus dickus. In the case of Conan, though, he ain't sportin' a large rod." Bill took a sip of his Sprite as Tallis watched him patiently, without uttering a single sound. "But I will tell ya," Bill continued, taking my last bite of chicken and stuffing it into his mouth before waving the fork in time with his nodding head, "Conan is also sportin' a mean lookin' rash on his nads." He swallowed the bite and eyed Tallis's crotch again before shrugging. "Might be blisters actually." Narrowing his eyes, he added, "But I think it's Chlamydia."

"You can't see Chlamydia, Bill," I retorted with a frown, quickly tiring of his antics. "It's symptomless."

Bill shrugged and cocked his head to the side, his eyebrows reaching for the ceiling. "I'm just sayin'."

Tallis started to nod as if he were agreeing with the angel. "Och aye," he said before taking a deep breath. "Ah noticed mah region beginnin' ta itch right after Ah took the stookie angel from behind when he was sleepin'."

I watched Bill's mouth drop open in horror and realized he thought Tallis was actually serious. I threw my head back and laughed, fully enjoying the fact that Tallis could hold his own. "The look on your face is priceless, Bill!" I managed between laughs.

At the sound of a demanding knock on my front door, I immediately stopped laughing. I faced Tallis and Bill with an expression that conveyed that I wasn't expecting any other visitors. Tallis shot up to his feet, and without making a sound, walked to the door, standing behind it, and beside the wall. I pushed up from where I was sitting at the dining table and approached the door cautiously. As I reached for the handle, Tallis's steely voice stopped me.

"Open the door verra slowly, lass," he whispered.

"It's probably just a neighbor or someone selling something," I offered, wondering why Tallis was reacting so strangely.

He shook his head. "Ye can never be too careful, lass," he responded.

I didn't say anything, but simply nodded as I turned the handle in my palm and gently pulled the door a few inches toward me. "Can I help you?" I asked. There was a short, slender man on the other side of the door, holding a clipboard in his hands.

"Perhaps," he responded in a nasally, high-pitched tone. "Are you Lily Harper?"

I swallowed hard, doubting very much that this guy was from Publisher's Clearing House. I glanced over at Tallis and when he nodded at me encouragingly, I answered. "Yes."

"Then, yes, you can help me," the man replied. He must have been no taller than five foot six. "My name is Herbert Hooter and I represent Afterlife Enterprises. May I come in?"

Not knowing what else to say or do, I nodded and opened the door. The little man pranced into my apartment as if he were on a cat walk. Herbert Hooter had the face of a baby with big blue eyes, a pert little nose, and jowl-like cheeks. A mop of thick, blond hair sat on his head like a napkin.

As soon as I closed the door, Tallis intercepted him after approaching the man from behind. "Why are ye here?" he demanded, his voice sounding threatening and louder than necessary.

Herbert turned around on his heels quickly and his eyes immediately widened at seeing the enormous Scotsman looming above him. Apparently, after getting his bearings and not wanting to appear unsettled, Herbert cleared his throat and narrowed his eyes at Tallis. He seemed to be saying that brawn would not intimidate him. "Like I said," he started, throwing his hands on his hips, "I am here on Afterlife Enterprises business to speak with Ms. Harper regarding the deaths of," he started, referring to his clipboard and ten or so sheets of paper, "Ragur and Kipur, both residents of the Underground City."

"Bludy hell," Tallis said as he shook his head. I remembered the two clown demons who accosted us during our mission to the Underground City.

"Hey, Mr. Hooters," Bill started, his lips tight. "Them demons dyin' had nothin' ta do with reverse cowgirl over there," he said as he inclined his head in my direction.

Herbert Hooter scowled at Bill, apparently not appreciating Bill's attempt to make fun of his last name. Or maybe it was the reverse cowgirl statement he found offensive. Whatever the reason, it was clear that he wasn't interested in trifling with Bill. "Nonetheless, I have been sent here by Jason Streethorn to take down the account as you recall it," he finished, his eyes resting on me again. Jason Streethorn was one of the managers at Afterlife Enterprises. Coincidentally, he was also the one who offered me the position of Soul Retriever.

"We were attacked," I answered, shaking my head. "That's all there was to it. We were attacked by Kipur and Ragur, so we defended ourselves."

"Thanks, but I will need quite a bit more detail than that," Herbert continued, shaking his head as if to insinuate I was slow. "The more information you can give me, the better for your case."

"My case?" I repeated, not realizing I even had a case.

"Yes," Herbert responded. "The master of the Underground City notified us of the deaths of his employees and as the complaint came directly from him, we must treat it with the utmost delicacy and respect."

"Bludy Alaire," Tallis commented again, shaking his head, his lips tight as he faced Herbert. "Ye can tell Alaire ta take his bludy complaint an' shoove it where the darkness lies!" he roared.

"You mean shove it where the sun don't shine, Conan," Bill corrected him with a wink.

"Aye," Tallis responded, nodding at Herbert who appeared anything but impressed.

Herbert turned his attention from Tallis back to me as he took a deep breath. "Very well, Ms. Harper, shall we get down to brass tacks?"

"I guess so," I answered as I watched Herbert take a seat on one of my moving boxes. I glanced at Tallis who nodded, as if to say he would ensure I didn't say too much or say the wrong thing. Or maybe that was just my own wishful thinking.

"Please describe what occurred at the carnival called *Freak Show*, Ms. Harper," Herbert continued in a bored tone. He pulled his pen from underneath the clip and put it on the paper, obviously eager to get moving.

"Okay," I started as I tried to remember exactly what happened. "I was told to retrieve the soul of a woman who was being held captive in a hurricane in the *Freak Show* carnival," I started.

"Very good," Herbert answered in a monotone. "Who were you with?"

"My angel guardian, Bill," I started, eyeing Bill.

"Represent," Bill said with a nod as he fisted his hand, and bounced it against his chest twice, like he thought he was a gang member or something. I glanced up at Tallis who nodded, indicating that he was okay with my mentioning he was with me as well. "And I was also with Tallis Black."

"Anyone else?" Herbert demanded.

There was one other person: Sherita Eaton Landers. But when I glanced at Tallis, he shook his head. I took that to mean he didn't want me to mention Sherita's name. "No, no one else," I said, not exactly comfortable about lying to an Afterlife Enterprises employee. Actually, I wasn't really comfortable with lying in general.

"Okay, so then what happened?" Herbert asked.

I felt my heartbeat racing as I recalled the particulars. "Using the detection device Jason gave us, we followed the missing soul to a circus tent at the center of *Freak Show*," I started.

"So you've said," Herbert interrupted, waving his hand impatiently as if to say I needed to get on with it.

"Um, so once we entered the tent and made it through the hurricane of souls, one of the demons …"

"Kipur," Tallis corrected me.

"Kipur started giving us trouble with the soul," I continued. Herbert Hooter apparently still found my narration too slow because he waved his hand dismissively and even sighed. "So, once we got the soul into the glass vial that Tallis brought with him, we were ready to leave *Freak Show*," I persisted. "But on our way out, Ragur, the other clown, ambushed and attacked us."

"How did he do that?" Herbert asked, not looking up from his note taking.

In reality, Ragur jumped on Sherita and knocked her down, but seeing as how I wasn't supposed to mention her name, I opted for a little white lie of omission. "Um, he jumped on one of us."

"Which one of you?" Herbert demanded.

"I, uh, I can't recall now," I answered sheepishly, feeling heat beginning to build in my cheeks. For as much as I disliked lying, I also wasn't very good at it. Herbert looked unconvinced and I realized I had better explain myself. "Everything happened so quickly, some of it is still a little blurry."

"Okay," Herbert said with a sigh of irritation as he wrote my words down anyway. "Then what happened?"

"Then we defended ourselves against Ragur," I finished.

"The demon beset oos," Tallis interrupted. "Once it attacked oos, all bets were off."

"That's very nice, Mr. Black, but I can't put that in my document, now can I?" Herbert asked. "I need details here, people!" he exclaimed as he rolled his eyes and faced each one of us. "Details!"

"Ah severed Ragur's head with mah sword," Tallis interjected. I watched Herbert's jaw go tight as he wrote down Tallis's gruesome words. "Once

Ragur was dead, Kipur came at oos," Tallis continued. "He was goin' ta slit Lily's throat so she killed him with her sword." It was more truthful to say that Tallis actually killed Kipur with my sword. Tallis had previously bathed my sword in his own blood, ensuring it had a special connection to him. Using that connection, Tallis was able to manipulate my sword even when he wasn't holding it. The end result was that Kipur was dead and although I had been the one holding my sword, Tallis had been controlling it.

"Very good," Herbert said as he finished writing and faced me expectantly. "And the heads?" he asked, his eyebrows arched. "Alaire noted that the bodies were found, but the heads of the two clowns were missing?"

"Aye," Tallis responded. "Ah took them as trophies."

Herbert swallowed hard, writing the note in his document. Then he glanced up at Tallis with a hurried smile. "Trophies … how very barbaric of you, sir." Taking a deep breath, he turned to face me again. "Finally, what became of the soul you retrieved? Your computer file does not reflect the successful completion of your mission?"

That was because Sherita took off with the soul as revenge for an occasion when Tallis stole a soul from her. "Right," I said with a glance at Tallis because I wasn't sure what more to say, or not say, on that point.

"Was or wasna the soul returned ta Afterlife Enterprises?" Tallis demanded of Herbert.

29

"Yes, it was," Herbert answered, nonplussed.

"Then ye have yer answer," Tallis finished, his jaw tight. "Whether or not 'twas credited ta Lily, the soul was rightfully restored. End o' story."

Herbert just nodded hurriedly and tucked his pen back underneath the clip on his board, before standing up and looking at me. "I imagine this incident will result in a mere warning, Ms. Harper, rather than an actual infraction. Just be more careful next time; and do try to stay out of trouble." He cleared his throat. "Remember, three warnings equal an infraction; and two infractions means you're headed to Shade."

"What?" I demanded. This was the first time I'd ever heard this and I couldn't help the shiver that ran up my spine. Two infractions didn't sound like much when it came to leniency. "No one ever mentioned infractions or warnings."

"Well, then consider yourself lucky that I'm mentioning them now," Herbert responded.

"What's considered an infraction?" I continued, suddenly feeling worry bubbling up inside my stomach. It seemed like every time I turned around, there was some new bit of information regarding my post of Soul Retriever that Jason Streethorn had failed to mention.

"Killing residents of the Underground City, for one," Herbert responded with a frown. "Other infractions can include failing to retrieve a soul on two or more missions. Those are the big ones."

"Hmm," I grumbled as I wondered if I were destined for Shade no matter what. Herbert Hooter, apparently feeling his job here was done, started for the front door. He opened it, but before leaving, faced me again with a hurried and very counterfeit smile. "I am sure we will be in touch."

"In the third circle am I of the rain eternal,
maledict, and cold, and heavy."
– Dante's *Inferno*

## TWO

When my alarm went off the next morning, it was easy to get up because I wasn't able to sleep all night. I tossed and turned, afraid I might sleep right through the persistent buzzing of the alarm, which would, no doubt, awaken the wrath of the Titan known as Tallis Black. I stretched my arms over my head and noticed it was still dark outside. The nascent glow of the sun was just making itself known, peeking out from the horizon of the Meadows, the quaint area of Edinburgh where I lived.

Trying to avoid wasting any more time, I hopped out of bed and threw on my black yoga pants, socks, black-pink-and-green Asics tennies, a sports bra, and a loose-fitting, pink Roxy sweatshirt. Then I started for the bathroom. Before I forgot, though, I took a detour and stopped in front of Bill's door, which was slightly ajar. I could hear the gravelly sound of his melodic snoring, periodically interrupted by a snort and then a little whimper. It sounded like he was having a nightmare. I knocked on his door. "Bill,

it's time to get up!" I called out in a cheery voice.
I was already well aware that my guardian angel
was anything but a morning person.

"Bloosgghlsf," he muttered indistinctly before
rolling over and instigating a new wave of snoring
that interrupted the peaceful morning.

"Bill!" I yelled, knocking on the door more
urgently. "Get up! We have to get going! Tallis is
waiting for us!"

"Jesus!" Bill grumbled in a sleep-heavy voice.
The bed groaned again as he rolled over onto his
other side.

"Bill!" I screamed. "Wake up!"

"Why the hell are you bangin' on my door in
the middle of the friggin' night, woman?" he
shouted back. "Don't you know I got Sleepy Bear
Syndrome?"

"You've got what syndrome?" I snapped back,
shaking my head because I could just imagine
what random crap was about to spew forth from
his mouth.

"Sleepy Bear Syndrome," he responded with
a loud yawn. "It's when you get super flippin'
pissed off after someone wakes you up while
you're sound-the-shit asleep!"

"Boo-hoo," I called back. "And for your
information, it's not the middle of the night. It's
five a.m. and the sun is about to rise so we need to
get a move on," I finished, now starting for the
bathroom. "You better be up and dressed by the
time I wash my face and brush my teeth, or I'm
going to be pissed!"

"Yeah, yeah, yeah," he muttered and yawned again. I could hear the sound of the sheets rustling, though, so that must've meant he was probably getting up, or so I hoped. "Don't go all Tiger's wife mad on me, nips, I'm comin'."

"I'll be back to check on you in five minutes," I replied from my bedroom.

"Okay, Mom! Sheesh, you're like an alligator," he grumbled, adding to himself, "shit, I got nap mouth."

"An alligator?" I repeated curiously as I began brushing my teeth. I was fully aware that the sound of the water would drown out Bill's response but I couldn't say I cared.

"Yeah, one o' those big, cranky green things that wants ta bite my head off first thing in the friggin' mornin'," he said, having obviously waited for me to turn the water off so I wouldn't miss his puerile comment.

"You'll get over it," I answered with a laugh. I splashed my face with cold water and felt around for the Neutrogena face wash. After pumping a few squirts into my hand and lathering my face, I heard the sound of Bill's heavy footfalls entering my bathroom.

"'Kay, I'm ready," he announced as I dried off my face. He stood in the doorway, looking at me impatiently.

"Those are the same clothes you wore yesterday," I pointed out, noticing his camouflage shorts were wrinkled and didn't look clean. His Megadeath T-shirt was in an even worse state—

bearing the same ketchup spot that fell on it
yesterday morning.

"So the hell what?" Bill grumbled. He cupped
his hand in front of his mouth and breathed into it,
like he was checking to see if he had bad breath.
His eyes went wide as he shook his head,
indicating his breath was so foul, it could set an
all-time record. "We're just meetin' up with Tido.
Ain't like I gotta purty myself up for him."

"You could at least brush your teeth for me."

He shook his head. "No can do. You'll hafta
deal with my stank mouth in return for gettin' me
up so damn early."

Seeing that the sun had already begun its
ascent, I realized I didn't have any time to argue
with Bill about the merits of hygiene and
cleanliness. "Okay," I said, reaching for the iron
blade Tallis gave me. Then I started for the living
room. Being the largest room in the house, I
figured it would offer us the most space for
incising a portal into the haunted forest.

"How in the hell is that thing s'posed ta
work?" Bill asked as he followed me.

I shrugged, having no experience with portal-
cutting iron blades at all and had no clue if the
thing would work at all. I was only going on what
Tallis told me. "Tallis said I'm supposed to just
hold it out straight in front of me, like this," I said,
before standing with my feet shoulder-width apart
and holding the blade out. "Then, I guess I just
slice in a downward motion, and the blade should
open a portal in the air." Obeying my own words,

I was amazed when the blade actually did what it was supposed to do.

"Holy guacamole," Bill whispered, also visibly in awe. We both watched the air separate as if it were a piece of paper that had just been cut in half. The image of my living room was divided by a sliver, maybe two feet long and one foot wide. Inside the sliver, I glimpsed the darkness of a forest, the Dark Wood, where Tallis lived.

"Now, I guess we go in," I said. Just then, I noticed that I cut the portal a little too high up in the air, meaning Bill and I would have a hard time climbing through it. Hoping to remedy the situation, I brought the iron blade to the bottom of the cut I'd already made, and continued slicing through the air in a downward motion to lower the portal and give us easier access. "Now we go in," I corrected myself with a smug smile.

"Chicks first," Bill announced and I responded with a frown. Placing the blade into the pocket of my sweatshirt, while my heart hammered with anxiety as well as adrenaline, I stepped into the open portal. The prick of cold air chilled me as soon as my leg made contact with the forest, but I forced myself onward. When my foot touched down on the forest floor, I balanced my weight and maneuvered the rest of my body through the opening.

"Everything okay in there?" Bill called out, sounding nervous.

"Yes, hurry up!" I responded, feeling irritated by his incessant cowardice. "You can't be killed so what are you worried about?"

"Just 'cause I can't be killed doesn't mean I like scary-ass shit jumpin' out at me," he yelled back. Eventually, I watched his pudgy leg entering the portal. It was followed by his equally fleshy arm. His fingers were stretched out and he kept moving his hand around, as if he were trying to locate something. Assuming we were already late, I grabbed Bill's hand and pulled him toward me, watching as he collapsed onto the forest floor. The portal instantly zipped itself shut behind us.

"'Tis aboot bludy time," Tallis's voice bellowed through the tranquil air.

Turning around, I found him standing behind Bill and me. He was wearing a black kilt, with a sporran around his waist, and his sword strapped securely in a scabbard across his naked chest. His eyes narrowed and his face took on an expression that said he wasn't pleased. "Hi," I said, smiling sheepishly. I couldn't deny feeling intimidated around Tallis.

"Hi yerself," the Scotsman ground out.

"How the hell did you know we were comin' through here, He-Man?" Bill asked, planting his plump hands on his ample hips.

"Whenever the blade moves," Tallis replied as he gestured toward my pocket, "Ah am alerted."

"Coolio," Bill responded. "It's like: Beam me up, Tally." Then he laughed at his own joke and added, "Tally-ho!"

Tallis frowned at the much smaller man before turning his scowl towards me. "Ah told ye ta arrive at first light." He glanced up at the sun, which was now beaming brightly at the top of the sky. He stared at me with a sour expression before turning on his heel and walking away, without waiting for either of us.

"Nice ta see you too, Shrek!" Bill called out behind Tallis, but the grumpy giant didn't respond. He just marched forward, with enormous strides that Bill and I struggled to follow. At the sound of rustling in the bushes nearby, I glanced over and barely caught sight of two or three Grevels.

Grevels were demons; and even though it was forbidden by Afterlife Enterprises, Tallis kept a handful of them as pets. Unlike tame, friendly dogs, however, Grevels were, by nature, ferocious. They stood about as tall as a Labrador retriever, but that's where the similarities ended. Unlike a Lab, Grevels were hideous to look at. Hunched over with misshapen bodies, shiny, rust-colored scales covered most of their bodies and their limbs terminated into cloven hooves. As if their figures weren't frightening enough, their faces appeared even worse. Rows of miniature, razor-sharp teeth filled their mouths and hot steam blew from their muzzles. Their eyes glowed red.

"Dude, I think Bubba is canine whipped," Bill whispered to me.

"Grevel whipped," I corrected him. "Demon whipped."

"True dat," Bill said with a nod before clearing his throat. "An' you better keep them ugly sons o' bitches away from me, Hercules!" Bill yelled out to Tallis, who still had a good lead on us. Bill had gotten into a few run-ins with the Grevels the last time we traveled through the Dark Wood.

Tallis, as expected, didn't respond, but continued plodding forward, while we remained maybe four or five paces behind him. He weaved through the trees, over the rocks and through a few shallow puddles, with no pathway to follow. If I hadn't known better, I might have thought he was lost …

After hiking through an open meadow and taking a right around an enormous oak tree, I recognized Tallis's home. It was a humble dwelling—more like a shanty than a house. The Grevels dispersed, and like tired dogs, lay down on the ground beneath the lush foliage. I stopped walking and watched Tallis remove the scabbard from his chest as he laid his sword against the log wall of his cabin.

"Dude, you got anythin' ta eat in that mansion o' yours?" Bill asked as he scratched his head and his stomach growled audibly. "Pollyanna over here didn't feed me breakfast this mornin'."

Tallis narrowed his eyes at Bill, but didn't respond. Instead, he faced me. "Have ye broken yer fast, lass?"

I swallowed hard, knowing Tallis wouldn't approve of my response. "We didn't have time to eat this morning." Then I glanced over at Bill. "We were running late."

"What?" Bill asked innocently, shaking his head as he threw his hands into the air. "Way to row me downstream, sugar lips." I assumed that phrase had something to do with selling him down the river, but wasn't interested enough to ask. "Dude, all this mission shit we're on is bogus. I'm startin' ta get volunteer's remorse."

"You didn't volunteer for anything, Bill," I pointed out. "You're here because you have to be."

"Whatevs," Bill said before frowning at me as if my point wasn't a good one.

Tallis glanced over with his jaw tight. "Ye have a long day ahead o' ye, lass. Ye cannae expect yer body ta perform withoot givin' it nutrients." Opening the door to his home, his eyes remained on me. "Coome," he said simply.

"Damn right," Bill interrupted as he started for Tallis's cabin and I brought up the rear. "You got any o' that squirrel stew, Conan?" Bill inquired once we were inside. Then, addressing me, he asked, "Was it squirrel stew last time? Maybe gopher?" He shrugged. "It was some little rodent with screwed up teeth."

Tallis ignored Bill and started a fire in the hearth by merely looking at it. I wondered if I would ever get accustomed to his acumen with magic. Probably not. I scanned his house, taking stock of everything and concluding it looked exactly the same as it had the last time I was here.

It smelled of earth, water and trees—like the forest, itself. All the furniture, which was comprised of a table and two chairs, a couch and Tallis's bed, was constructed of hand-hewn logs. The bed and the couch were covered with animal furs, while the mattress and pillows were filled with straw. Other animal hides were scattered on the ground directly in front of the fire. I was familiar enough with Tallis's cabin after spending the night here on more than one occasion, with Bill, of course.

"Looks like you're in luck, Bill," I said as we both watched Tallis carry an iron pot to the fire and place it into the flames. "Although I'll bet it isn't squirrel or gopher." As far as I knew, creatures in the Dark Wood weren't the same as you'd find in an Earth forest. The only experience I had with any creatures in the Dark Wood were enormous, flying spiders. The spiders, which we'd encountered during our first mission into the Underground City, were gargantuan. They stood as high as my knees and were dangerous because they squirted out venom, which could kill you. And they hunted in packs.

"Nice," Bill responded, patting his stomach as it growled again. "Although I will admit that the last time we ate Conan's food, I got major meat sweats for like a week. Then I had such rancid farts, when we went grocery shopping at Tesco, people started lookin' around and sayin' there must have been a sewage problem."

"God, Bill," I said, shaking my head.

"Swear!" Bill replied, even crossing his heart. "I was blastin' the most disgustin', rotten, shit-smellin' farts. The worst of my entire life! I nearly made myself pass out."

"Yer trainin' will be in two parts, lass," Tallis suddenly announced. He lifted the cover off the pot and stirred its contents, apparently not overly concerned about Bill's intestinal discomfort.

"Okay," I said, taking a seat on one of the animal furs I found on the floor. Bill chose to sit in one of the chairs beside the table.

"The first half o' the day will be spent oan trainin' ye how ta wield yer sword," Tallis continued. It was actually the second lesson he would give me on sword fighting. Because I was so hopeless when it came to fencing or using my sword, I figured I needed all the practice and guidance I could get. "The second half o' the day will be spent oan trainin' yer body."

"Training my body?" I repeated, with a frown, unaware of his gist.

Tallis nodded. "Jist as ye moost possess knowledge an' skill ta wield yer sword, so moost yer body be in tip-top condition ta deal with the trials an' tribulations o' bein' a Retriever."

"So, you mean ... I'll be lifting weights or something?" I asked, still confused.

"You *are* skinny fat, Lil," Bill pointed out, his eyebrows raised as he pointed at my stomach. "I mean, you look skinny but you're all flabby an' shit." I glared at him until he shut up.

"Aye, weights an' cardio trainin' ta ensure yer swiftness oan yer feet," Tallis answered as he stirred the contents of the pot again.

"Conan's gonna turn you into that Terminator chick," Bill piped up with a wink at me. "I totally wanted ta bone her when that movie came out." A few moments of silence ensued as he, no doubt, was picturing Linda Hamilton's naked body in his mind. "'Course, she's prolly too old an' loose now." Then he shook his head. "Nah, I'll bet she's a Freddy Cougar—an old chick who can totally rock her slutty Halloween costume."

I rolled my eyes at Bill before I addressed Tallis. "So you want me to join a gym or what?"

Tallis shook his head. "Nae. Ah've already consigned someone Ah troost ta train ye. Yer first session will begin at midday, today. Then, Ah expect ye ta train at least three times a week. With a proper diet, ye should be in fightin' mode in two fortnights."

"Okay," I said, heaving a sigh. I'd never enjoyed diets and, consequently, wasn't very good at maintaining them.

Tallis took the pot of stew off the fire using only his bare hands. His jaw seemed tight and his eyes narrowed. I wondered if he was feeling any pain from touching the incredibly hot handle, but he didn't make a sound. It struck me that he was probably intentionally hurting himself as some form of punishment. About a week ago or so, I discovered him bare-chested in the freezing snow, whipping himself with a cat o' nine tails until blood streamed down his back. After quite a bit of prodding, he'd admitted that he was punishing himself for past transgressions. Tallis Black was seriously messed up.

Taking out two wooden bowls, Tallis divvied up the stew and placed the pot in his sink, which was no more than a large metal tub that sat on the floor. Beside it were a jug of water and a bar of soap. He glanced down at his palm with curiosity, as if taking stock of the damage done by the scalding pot. From where I stood, I could see that his entire palm was bright red. As I watched, the angry redness began to vanish into his tan skin. Tallis could heal himself because of the warrior spirit who possessed his body. I didn't know much more about the warrior, because Tallis wasn't too forthcoming when it came to talking about himself.

He handed one of the stew-filled bowls to me and the other to Bill. Bill immediately stood up and inspected the contents of my bowl before addressing Tallis and claiming, "Dude, she got more than I did."

"Aye," Tallis answered as he faced Bill squarely. "An' as Besom has a full day planned, she needs every bit o' energy."

Bill frowned. "I thought you just said she was going on a diet?"

"Bill," I chastised him while shaking my head in an attempt to get him to stop whining. I worried that Tallis would freak out on Bill because the angel could be, in a word … annoying. Bill pouted and frowned, but returned to his place at Tallis's table and ate his stew, making slurping sounds with every spoonful.

"So tell me about my physical training," I said to Tallis, who was standing near the front door. I sat in the other chair at his table, across from Bill. Placing my bowl on the roughly hewn wood, I turned my chair around until I was facing Tallis. "I'll have a personal trainer?"

"Aye."

"What's his story?" I continued.

"He is a demon," Tallis answered nonchalantly.

"A demon?" I repeated, with anxiety emerging in my voice. "I thought our main goal was to avoid demons?"

But Tallis shook his head. "He doesna reside in the Oonderground City."

"Where does he live?" I asked.

"Here," Tallis answered. "In the Haunted Wood."

"And he's a personal trainer?" I asked, my tone growing dubious. It sounded like the prelude to a bad joke.

"Aye. He has made it his business ta train Retrievers. An' he is verra good at what he does." He paused for a moment or two, but watched me. "Ye are loocky, lass. Not everybody has connections ta Ael."

"Ael is his name?" I asked, pronouncing it "Al."

"Aye," he answered.

"Al don't sound like no demon's name to me," Bill piped up with a mouthful of potatoes.

"An' does Bill sound like ah name o' an angel?" Tallis asked, raising his eyebrows with a lofty expression.

"Ha-ha, very funny, Shrek," Bill answered, frowning at Tallis. After slurping his last spoonful and swallowing it down, Bill put the bowl and spoon on top of the table. "Done!" he exclaimed as if he'd just won an eating contest. "Any seconds?" he asked Tallis.

"Nae," Tallis answered before shaking his head and muttering something about Bill's appetite being more like that of a pregnant sow.

Since they were both waiting for me to finish my stew, I shoveled down the last three bites and put Bill's bowl and my own into Tallis's "sink." Picking up the jug of water, I intended to wash our dirty dishes, but Tallis's hand on my arm stopped me. At his touch, I felt goose bumps break out all over my skin. It was very unusual for Tallis to actually touch me.

"We've wasted enough time," Tallis announced. "Ah can wash oop later. Now, we practice yer sword fightin'."

"Hey, Tido, you mind if I hang back an' get me a little shuteye?" Bill asked, eyeing Tallis's bed with undisguised interest. "I'm prexhausted."

"What?" I demanded, throwing my hands on my hips. "How can you be exhausted? You haven't done anything today except eat!"

"Duh!" Bill responded, shaking his head like I was the one who was slow. "That's why I said I'm prexhausted, not *exhausted* or *post exhausted*. Just thinkin' about everything we gotta do today has exhausted me."

"Aye, ye can remain 'ere," Tallis replied. "Boot yer not ta sleep oan mah bed."

"Blewdy hell," Bill answered, doing a poor imitation of Tallis. With a shrug, he headed for the fireplace and sat down on one of the animal furs. Stretching out, he covered himself with another fur before looking up at me. "Since I just ate whatever the hell that shit was, I get Farte Blanche," he said as he eyed me knowingly. "You hear me, Lil? I get unrestricted power to fart at my own discretion, got it?"

I just shook my head and looked at Tallis, who faced me. "Yer sword is leanin' 'gainst the wall, lass," he said, pointing to a long, narrow object, which was wrapped up in muslin. Tallis had disallowed me from taking my sword back with me to Edinburgh after our last mission. His explanation was that I knew just enough about wielding it to be a danger to myself and others.

Picking up my sword, I followed Tallis outside. He closed the door behind us and grabbed his own sword from where he'd left it leaning against his house. Heading for the rear of the house with me following closely on his heels, along with the herd of Grevels, I asked, "Where are we going?"

"We cannae parry here," he answered as he plodded forward, without offering any more information. Trying to interact with Tallis was what I liked least about him. He wasn't a talker by any stretch of the imagination. The incessant silence between us always made me uncomfortable. Trying to look at the bright side, I pasted on a smile and started humming "Do I Wanna Know?" by the Arctic Monkeys. Tallis glanced back at me with a furrowed brow that said he didn't appreciate my humming, but I didn't care. If he couldn't politely engage in some form of conversation, then he'd have to tolerate my humming.

When we reached the same clearing where we'd practiced the first time around, Tallis stopped walking. Some of the Grevels disappeared into the undergrowth, no doubt scouting for God-only-knew what, while the others collapsed beneath the cool shade offered by the nearby trees, and watched us both curiously.

"Ye can oonbind yer sword from its swathe," Tallis announced as he pulled the scabbard from his chest and took out his own sword. I, meanwhile, fumbled while trying to unwind the muslin wrap that swaddled my sword, not finding it particularly easy. I heard Tallis's chuckle and looked over at him in surprise. He rarely smiled or laughed. "Jist stand the sword oop straight, an' the cloth will drop, Besom."

I did as he instructed and, as usual, he was right. The sunlight glinted off the polished blade of my sword and as I held the hilt, a strange feeling overcame me, as if I were being reunited with an old friend. "What type of sword did you say this was again?" I asked Tallis.

"A Claymore."

"No, I mean in Gaelic," I clarified. "You called it something else."

"A claidheamh mhor."

I nodded. "Yeah, that was it." Fastening my eyes on the sword's undeniable beauty, I allowed my gaze to absorb the essence of it. The sword was long, maybe four feet or so, and featured two handles at the top of the blade. Each handle curved into a honeycomb shape. The hilt was created of wood, which I assumed must've come from this very forest. I gripped the hilt tightly and examined the flawless beauty of the blade, unable to restrain my smile.

"Ye have missed her," Tallis said. I found him studying me with an expression of curiosity.

"Yes," I said, nodding as I beheld my sword again. "It's beautiful."

"Aye," Tallis said as he nodded. "Boot the look in yer eyes was not one o' admiration, lass, boot pride."

"Maybe," I said with a shrug. "I am proud of it."

Tallis actually smiled. "It pleases meh ta hear it, lass." I didn't respond or have to. "We shall begin," Tallis continued. "Do ye recall yer lessons?"

"I think so," I replied while gripping my sword with my right hand, the dominant one. Then I took hold of the pommel, using three fingers: my ring, middle and pinky fingers. I pointed the tip of the sword right between my sternum and my throat, just like Tallis taught me.

"Aye," Tallis said while nodding to let me know that my stance was correct. "Is the pommel jist above yer belly booton, lass?"

I glanced down and saw that it was. My stance was correct. "Yes."

"Strike," he ordered. Bringing my left hand up past my eye, I aimed for the sky. Then I brought the sword down, using my right hand to guide it while my left hand provided the force. "Good, lass, good," Tallis said. "Again!"

This time, I focused on my footwork. With my left foot behind my right, I stood on the ball of my foot and pushed off, being careful to place my left foot down before sliding my right one along the ground to ensure my balance. When I was ready to strike, I brought my left foot back into position and lashed out with my sword.

"Ye appear a wee bit unbalanced, lass," Tallis said as he studied me. "Boot all in all, not bad. Ah daresay ye've been practicin'?"

I wasn't sure if he would have wanted me to practice without him, seeing as how he'd kept my sword rather than allowing me to take it with me. But there was no use in lying. "Yes, I have."

"With what?" he asked, suppressing a smile. He appeared to be amused, or maybe he was actually pleased with me. Tallis was such an enigma, it was extremely hard to tell.

"A long stick," I answered and remembered how ridiculous I looked when practicing in my room and jabbing at the air with my pointed stick. I started to laugh.

"Ye have done well, lass," Tallis said as he stepped away from me, bracing himself with his feet shoulder-width apart. He assumed the same position I had when I demonstrated proper striking stance. "Now, ye will fight meh."

"Huge hail, and water sombre-hued, and snow,
athwart the tenebrous air pour down amain."
– Dante's *Inferno*

# THREE

"Um," I started, prepared to argue the reasons why I shouldn't fight Tallis, namely because he was a practiced warrior and I was a nobody; but he was already coming at me, his sword raised high in the air, and the maniacal look of a crazy person in his eyes. I was as good as dead.

Bracing myself, I held my sword out in a defensive stance before me. When the blade of his sword struck mine, it felt like an earthquake rocked my entire body, with the epicenter in my right arm. After the initial, jarring blow, my arms felt like jelly but, amazingly enough, I managed to maintain my grip on my sword. My brain, however, still felt like it was rattling around in my head. "Are you trying to take my arm off?" I yelled at him. "Not so freaking hard!"

Tallis raised his sword into the air again, clearly continuing his assault. "Demons o' the Oonderground wilna be lenient oan ye, lass," he explained as he rushed toward me again. "Ye moost learn ta defend yerself, come what may!" I experienced a few seconds of intense déjà vu, but then figured I'd just seen *Braveheart* one too many times.

I deflected the blow in the same way as before, but a split second later, the blade-wielding Scotsman circled around and charged me once more, his sword held high again. Before I could even fathom what was happening, Tallis held the tip of his blade against my throat. I clutched my sword in my left hand with the tip of it just skimming the ground, realizing it wasn't doing me a whole lot of good. Tallis walked a few paces forward, and forced me to walk backwards to avoid being run through.

"If Ah were a demon, mah sword would be buried in yer head by now," he said calmly. "Och aye, perhaps then Ah'd sever yer head an' later, it'd be mounted oan mah wall."

"Ha-ha," I said with little or no humor. I fought to take a deep breath and calm my heart, which, even now, suggested I was having an attack.

Tallis shrugged. "Ye shoulda blocked meh, lass," he finished in a deep voice, his eyes riveted on mine.

I didn't respond until I backed up against the rough bark of a tree and realized I was cornered. "You can't expect me to defend myself from you when you've had over two thousand years of practice!" I yelled, not liking the feeling of being trapped. "And what's more, I'm not possessed by the ghost of some dead warrior! So this isn't exactly fair!"

"Do ye wanna survive the Oonderground?" he asked rhetorically. His tone remained casual and calm, which only irritated me more.

"Of course I do!" I railed back at him, craning my neck to the side as he held me captive beneath his blade. "What are you doing?" I demanded. But he didn't remove the sword. He held it in place, while staring at me like he'd lost his mind. "Take your sword away from my throat!" I ground out as burgeoning fear tried to overcome me. Tallis was always unpredictable, which was, by nature, intimidating.

My voice was abruptly cut short when he pushed ever so slightly on his sword and I felt the cold metal riding up my larynx, its keen point threatening my neck, yet still not piercing my skin. Without a clue of what was going on, I looked into Tallis's eyes and what I saw there worried me. A lot. His standard, midnight blue gaze was gone and replaced by a dark, inky blackness. His eyes were so dark and shadowy, I couldn't distinguish his pupils from his irises. I'd seen his eyes eclipsed like this before—usually in moments of combat or after his anger was incited. I'd always figured it was just the warrior spirit within him suddenly overtaking his body. But why would the warrior feel threatened by me? I had no idea why. All I could hope was that I'd survive long enough to find out.

Tallis continued to stand there, silently watching me, his sword still precariously aimed on my neck. His eyes were completely engulfed by the strange blackness. They no longer resembled the eyes of a human ...

"Tallis," I whispered. "You're scaring me."

My comment seemed to thrill him because his lips parted into a smile. But he still didn't say anything. Instead, he continued staring right through me with enigmatic eyes that revealed nothing. He continued to smile as he studied me, though, appearing amused by the fact that he had me where he wanted me, amused that I was his captive. And that was when I realized he intended to kill me.

"Ta ... Tallis," I gasped before moving my arm toward his blade, with the hope of pushing it out from underneath my chin. There was a strange gleam in his eyes that matched his bizarre smile. "Don't do this," I said as my heartbeat began to pound loudly through me. I could feel sweat breaking out along my hairline as the gravity of my predicament overcame me. "You said yourself that you were looking for salvation," I started. "If you kill me, it's not going to help you find it."

"Kill ye?" he repeated, suddenly frowning. All at once, the black pitch of Tallis's eyes disappeared altogether. In a matter of seconds, it simply dissolved into the navy blue I'd come to know so well. His eyes widened as if he were surprised, as he instantly dropped his sword on the ground beside me. Looking up at him, I shook my head, feeling the rush of heat in my cheeks as I witnessed how powerful Tallis could be and, more importantly, how completely unpredictable.

"What the hell was that all about?" I yelled as I pushed myself away from the tree and touched my neck, examining my fingers for any signs of blood. Although I found none, it didn't alleviate how pissed off I was. "What the hell just happened?"

Tallis shook his head and looked confused. He started to explain, "Ah dinnae …" but I interrupted him.

"You were about to kill me," I continued, my voice angrily accusatory. There was no way I was going to buy this act. I was more than convinced that whatever had just gone on in his head had nearly cost me my life.

"Nae, lass, ye are wrong," he replied immediately.

But I vigorously shook my head. There was no way he could talk his way out of this one. "I actually saw it in your eyes!" I railed back at him. "You were just about to run me straight through with your sword right before you suddenly came to your senses." I took a deep breath, trying to slow my frantic heartbeat. "Bill and I are leaving," I tersely announced, wanting nothing more than to get as far away from him as I could. "I'm heading back to your house right now!" I added as I started forward. Then I thought better of it and turned back around to face him. "And when Bill finds out what just happened, you bet your ass he's going to be furious, mister!" I knew Bill couldn't do anything at all to Tallis or anyone else for that matter, since angels were prohibited from inflicting physical pain, but there it was.

"Nae," Tallis repeated, but this time, his jaw seemed tighter and he looked more stressed than a moment ago.

"Nae yourself!" I screamed before turning around again and starting for Tallis's house. Yes, I had no clue where the house was, but I didn't intend to let that stop me! I planned to just continue marching, with my head held high, and be damned grateful that I still had one. My only hope was that the forest wouldn't pull a Rubik's Cube on me and make me lose my way.

"Lass," Tallis muttered as he caught up with me and gripped my upper arm before yanking me to a stop. He so rarely touched me that I was immediately taken aback. "You'll nae retreat 'til Ah've had mah say."

"Then have your say!" I yelled at him, throwing my hands on my hips as I dared him to come up with a good enough excuse as to why he'd nearly lopped my head off.

"Ah wasna goin' ta kill ye, lass," he said before grunting and taking a deep breath. Whatever he had on his mind was obviously not easy for him to spit out.

"So you've said," I muttered.

"Aye," he began and seemed like he had something more to say before he firmly shut his mouth again and ran his enormous hand over the back of his neck, looking frustrated.

"Is that your best defense?" I asked in disbelief, frowning at the enormous man. "Because it's pretty lame!"

"Nae!" he thundered at me, his eyebrows meeting in the middle of his forehead in undisguised frustration. "This isnae easy fer meh, lass!"

"I'll bet it isn't easy! How do you tell someone you were just about to cut her throat, even if you are possessed by a warrior ghost!" I railed back at him.

"Fer the last bludy time, Ah wasna goin' ta kill ye, ye daft woman!" he yelled, his patience clearly failing. "Ah was tryin' ta keep mahself from tearin' yer clothes off an' plantin' mah face 'tween yer thighs!"

"Well!" I replied, biting my lip because my thoughts suddenly crashed headlong into a wall and now bits and pieces of them were strewn all over, never to be made into a coherent whole again. "Well," I repeated, shaking my head. My first battle was wrapping my mind around the knowledge that Tallis not only possessed a libido, but, apparently, harbored sexual attraction toward me.

"See? 'Twas noot an easy feat fer meh ta tell ye," he grumbled, shaking his head like he was both embarrassed and angry with himself.

"Well," I said again, for the third time, which turned out to be the charm because my words didn't fail me this time. "I guess that's better than thinking you were trying to kill me."

He glanced at me and raised one brow. "Aye, Ah'd agree with ye, lass."

"So," I began while studying him curiously. "Was that … response coming from Donald or was it from … you?"

"Doonald?" he repeated, shaking his head, clearly at a loss.

"The warrior ghost inside you," I prompted before rolling my eyes as if to infer he should have figured out whom I was referencing, even if Donald wasn't the ghost's actual name. The real name sounded like something close enough …

Tallis shook his head. "Ah dinnae know, lass," he answered, raising both eyebrows. "Donnchadh has been a part o' meh fer so long, I dinnae know where he ends an' Ah begin."

"Donnchadh, that's right," I said with a little smile, feeling relieved. Now that I knew Tallis hadn't wanted to kill me but was only after a little tongue action, I was a little more relaxed. Although I had to admit I was still finding it difficult to come to terms with the fact that Tallis was lusting after me even if the information did thrill me. It really didn't make sense because it wasn't like I felt any romantic feelings for the guy. I mean, he was practically a hop, skip and jump from being a wild animal. He probably had much more in common with the Grevels than with me…

After studying me for a moment or two, Tallis seemed to get his wits back about him. "We are finished with our practicin' fer today," he announced, placing his sword back into the scabbard before fastening it across his chest. It wasn't lost on me that the practice lasted only what? Twenty minutes, max. It was fairly obvious that the whole image of cunnilingus threw a hiccup in Tallis's giddyup because he was definitely acting very weird. He refused to look at me and I thought his cheeks seemed a little redder than normal.

"I thought my personal training appointment was at noon," I said with a scowl. "And I don't know what time it is, but I'll bet it's nowhere close to noon."

"Aye," Tallis answered indifferently as he started toward the forest from where we'd just emerged. The Grevels hurried out from the undergrowth and trotted behind him, happy as demons could be now that they were headed home. Lacking another option, I caught up with him.

"So?" I prodded.

"So we are goona be a wee bit early," he answered and stiffly shook his head to discourage further questions.

"Okay," I said before falling silent and stepping in line with him. But silence was not one of my virtues. It never had been. Instead, I was one of those people who hated awkward pauses. I would have rather filled the gaps with meaningless conversation than to endure silence. 'Course, in this case, the conversation on my mind wasn't exactly meaningless. "You surprise me, Tallis."

He glanced over and raised his left brow, but his expression indicated that he wished he didn't have me as a companion. "Surprised, Besom?"

"Yes," I said just as I spotted a fallen tree branch, and had to carefully sidestep it. It was difficult to keep up with Tallis's breakneck stride. "For a while there, I thought you might be asexual." Then I shrugged. "Well, that's not entirely true. At first, I thought maybe you were gay, but ..."

"Gay?" he repeated, scowling at me and shaking his head. "Ah mayna carry oan mooch o' a social life, boot Ah also dinnae care ta dally with the menfolk."

"Right," I said, nodding. "After convincing myself that you weren't gay, I just figured you were asexual."

Tallis glanced at me again and raised the other eyebrow, as if to say he was either amused or offended by my conclusion. "Ah am a man, lass."

I nodded. "Right, that's true." Yep, that was very true. In fact, Tallis was the manliest man I'd ever met. He almost defined the word "man." Maybe his title should have been "superman" or "man and a half." Yes, I definitely knew that he was a man. "But that doesn't change the fact that maybe some men aren't necessarily swayed ... sexually. You know?"

He shook his head and eyed me with a frown. "Nae, Ah dinnae know, lass." Then he sighed. "Ah dinnae even profess ta know what goes oan in that daft head o' yers." Then he inhaled deeply. "Boot what Ah can tell ye is that a man cannae go without thinkin' aboot a woman more than a day." He exhaled. "Ah dinnae care who he is. A man has undeniable needs."

That was a surprise. I couldn't imagine Tallis thinking about anything except survival. "Hmm," I started.

"An' whether 'twas meh or Donnchadh that was thinkin' loostful thoughts 'bout ye, lass, Ah cannae say."

"Your eyes were completely black," I said as I faced him, intimating that I figured Donnchadh had been steering the lust boat.

Tallis nodded and then exhaled heavily as he looked at me. "Ah wouldna be surprised ta find 'twas both o' oos." Then he smirked, as if to imply that was most likely the truth. This side of him almost seemed playful, and his candidness made him appear years younger. It took me by surprise.

"So, uh," I started, taking a deep breath because my question wasn't an easy one to ask. "So, then, I guess that means you *are* attracted to me?"

He chuckled deeply, while shaking his head. "Didnae ye hear me when Ah said Ah had ta keep mahself from tastin' ye?" I gulped down the frog in my throat at Tallis's reminder of wanting to taste me. Somehow, I sensed he wasn't referring to my mouth. Meanwhile, he continued to shake his head. "Ah doona appreciate yer fishin', lass."

What? He thought I was fishing for compliments? "I wasn't fishing!" I retorted. "I was merely asking you because your response doesn't make any logical sense to me."

"It doesna make sense ta ye?" he scoffed, but stopped walking. Turning to face me, he threw his hands on his hips and made me very aware of how incredibly large he was. "Ye are a woman. Do ye think Ah'm not aware o' that?" he asked with frustration as his eyes continued to spear me with a narrowed expression. "Yer body is equipped, designed an' built ta accommodate a man … physically."

"Yeah, I get that part," I interrupted, fully aware that my cheeks were on fire. I was so embarrassed, and yet also turned on at the very same time. Even though sex was still a new realm to me, I was suddenly consumed by the idea of what sex with Tallis might be like. I imagined he probably wouldn't be gentle, given his overbearing personality, but at the same time, I didn't think he'd be rough. It was an idea I found captivating, but it also made me feel deeply mortified to even consider sex with Tallis. Especially during his lecture on the birds and the bees.

"Ah am a man, lass," he continued as his eyes traveled from my face to my bust. A shiver raced down my spine as he brought his gaze back to my face again. "An' 'tis in mah nature, mah instincts, ta want ta bed ye." His eyes settled back on my breasts before he huffed a sigh and started forward again. "Ye will find that most folk cannae deny nature's instincts, lass. Sooner or later, yer instincts catch oop with ye."

"That wasn't my question," I yelled at his retreating back. It both irritated me that I couldn't restrain my feelings of lust toward him and it was equally irritating that he'd commandeered the conversation and totally missed my point. He stopped walking and turned back around to face me as I caught up with him.

"Jist what is yer bludy question, lass?" He sounded exasperated.

Well, I was just as exasperated. "If you're so obviously attracted to me, and your instincts want to have sex with me, then why didn't you when you had the chance?"

"Why didnae I?" he repeated, obviously confused.

"Stop answering my question by repeating it!" I yelled back at him. "I'm talking about the time when I asked you to have sex with me before we entered the Underground City? Remember?" Since I was a virgin, in the eyes of the Underground City, I was considered innocent. And as Tallis had explained to me and I'd experienced firsthand when I'd set foot in the Underground, my innocence had nearly cost me my life. In my mind, if Tallis had taken my virginity, I would have been much safer in the Underground.

Tallis shook his head. "'Tis nae as simple ah question as that, Besom," he said as he started forward again. I had to move more quickly to keep up with him. And keeping up with him was paramount because I wanted to understand where he was coming from. My question deserved an honest response. As far as I was concerned, Tallis's refusal to have sex with me indirectly risked my life.

"Why not?"

He didn't turn to look at me but kept his eyes trained on the rough wilderness that lay ahead of us. "As Ah told ye before, Ah carry mah own weight oopon mah shoulders, lass. Ah cannae add ye to it."

I frowned at him, and his argument, which made no sense to me. "But you wanted to have sex with me? Even then?"

He nodded and slowly breathed out deeply, becoming clearly irritated. "'Course Ah did! Any man would."

"You make no sense at all!" I said, crossing my arms over my chest defensively. If Tallis could have pulled the stick out of his ass (as Bill would say) and taken my virginity, I would have been much safer in the Underground City. As it stood now, my virginity was a dangerous commodity.

"Ah am atonin'," he said, glancing over at me with a shrug. "Ah am makin' amends fer the wrongs Ah've committed, lass. An' in mah mind, takin' yer virginity would be addin' ta an already long list."

"Even though it could actually save me?"

"Aye." He nodded. "'Tis not mah place."
Then he sighed. "An' if ye recall, mah blood did a
damned good job o' savin' ye anyway."

He was referring to the first time we went into
the Underground, and because of my innocence,
my body immediately began dying. Tallis had to
cut himself and force me to swallow his blood in
order to pollute me with his lack of innocence
which had, in turn, allowed me safe passage
through the Underground City and kept me from
dying. So I guessed he had a point.

We walked the remainder of the way to
Tallis's house in silence. When we reached the
shack, the Grevels disappeared into the
undergrowth. Tallis opened his front door and we
both walked inside. Bill was asleep in front of the
fireplace, snoring.

\*\*\*

I didn't really know what to expect of my first
visit with my personal trainer, but I certainly never
foresaw the situation that now faced me. Tallis,
Bill, and I stood at the entry of what seemed to be
a warehouse. The room was maybe forty feet wide
by thirty feet long and the ceiling had to be twenty
feet tall. The room featured a roll-up garage door-
like opening at the opposite end from where we
stood which revealed the forest scenery on the
other side. Yes, the structure was randomly
located right in the middle of the Dark Wood, with

nothing but trees on either side of it and not even a road to access it.

Tallis strode into the room, stepping over a man who appeared to be passed out in the doorway. At first, I thought he was dead, but the gentle rolling of his chest told me he wasn't. The extent of Tallis's interest in him was no more than a quick glance as he stepped over the man. I followed him, and figured the guy must have been okay because no one else seemed concerned.

"Looks like someone partied too hard," Bill said with a chuckle as he glanced down at the man. "Carpe noctem, eh, dude?" he asked with another chuckle before looking up at me again. "I don't know 'bout him, but I got me a hang under," he continued as I frowned and he decided to explain. "That's like when you haven't had too much to drink the night before, and instead o' havin' a shit-tastic mornin', you feel better than normal."

"Nice, Bill," I said shaking my head, and figuring I had much better things to focus on. Scanning the room, I noticed it was comprised of some exercise machines, lots of free weights, and other contraptions I didn't recognize. A few machines looked somewhat familiar even though I'd never really been a gym zealot. Several New Year's resolutions were about the only occasions that got me into a gym, and I lasted maybe a month or so before the call of the elliptical, or the treadmill, fell on deaf ears.

"Dude looks like he's gonna pass the hell out," Bill whispered, pointing to a guy who was running at breakneck speed on the treadmill, the sweat pouring off his forehead and onto his already saturated clothes. "Calm that shit down, man," he called out. "You're gonna give yourself a heart attack, yo." But the man didn't respond. Instead, he continued to stare straight ahead without breaking his gait. Bill looked back at me and shrugged. "He's a beardo anyway."

"He's a what?" I whispered, afraid the man might overhear us.

"A weirdo with a beard," Bill answered. I could only shake my head with wonder at where he came up with this stuff.

"Bladesmith," a man said in a deep voice as he approached Tallis. Neither of them smiled, although Tallis nodded his head in a weak semblance of a greeting. The man was probably six foot three inches and must've weighed two hundred ten pounds or so. But none of it was fat. The guy was ripped—as in, his biceps were as big as my head. His skin was the color of dark chocolate and if I had to guess his age, I would've said he was in his early thirties. He was dressed in a dark grey T-shirt and black shorts that ended just below his knees.

"Ael," Tallis said.

Ael nodded, turning his attention first to me and then to Bill. That was when I noticed his red eyes appeared to glow. His hair was cut short and on one side shaved close to his head in a flame pattern. After studying Bill, he glanced back at Tallis. "Who am I trainin'? Red or Jack Black?"

he asked. I noticed his canines were long and sharp.

Bill immediately started chuckling as soon as he realized Ael was referring to him. "Shit, that's a good one. Jack Black is like my hero, yo!"

Ael eyed him, but frowned and crossed his arms against his chest while looking at Tallis for a response.

"Ye will be trainin' Lily," Tallis answered as he inclined his head in my direction.

Ael nodded, turning his full attention to me, as if he were taking stock of me. Then he addressed Tallis. "Twelve to fifteen weeks tops before she's in shape. We'll plan on addin' six ta eight pounds of muscle an' I expect her here three times a week." Then he took a breath. "You bring them shoes, Bladesmith? I require payment up front."

Tallis nodded and removed the pack he'd been carrying over his shoulder. He loosened the knot but kept the bag closed as he searched inside it, before producing a box of shoes. He handed the shoes to Ael who eagerly accepted them. Ael opened the box and pulled out a pair of red, white, and black argyle Air Jordans. He nodded, obviously pleased to see them as he inspected the sides of the shoes where the letters "AEL" stood out in block type. A smile brightened his face. "You got 'em right, Bladesmith," he said before facing Tallis again.

"Aye," the taciturn Scotsman responded.

"I want them Team Jordans next time I train Red; an' the Come Fly With Me's the time after that; you got it?" Ael continued, eyeing Tallis with more interest. "I gotta check my inventory an' see what else I'm missin' but for now, that's good."

"Aye," Tallis said again.

Then Ael's attention returned to me. "She gotta be on sixteen hundred calories a day," he said. I was beginning to get irritated by him continually referring to me in the third person.

"I am standing right here, you know?" I barked out, surprising myself. "You don't have to keep referring to me as 'her' or 'she.'"

Ael's eyebrows lifted as if my ability to speak surprised him. Then a grimace took over his features. "An' I ain't about ta put up with no attitudes, got it?"

I frowned at him as Bill erupted into a fit of chuckles which better resembled giggles, while pointing at me and indicating that I just had my ego handed over to me on a plate. Then, apparently losing interest in the three of us, Bill scanned the room and eyed a large-breasted blond woman who was doing squats with a loaded barbell beside us. He waddled over to her.

"Hey, baby, you come here often?" Bill asked as he leaned against the wall and eyed her up and down. She just ignored him. "You know, I'm on a mastabbatical," Bill continued while nodding as if she should understand what he was talking about. "If you ain't in the know, a mastabbatical is an abstinence period, free from masturbation. I'm tryin' to improve my productivity in other parts of my life, ya know?" She didn't so much as glance in his direction, but that didn't seem to concern him. "You know how dangerous a mastabbatical is? Way dangerous … doctors compare it to some of the worst health hazards around." He nodded again, apparently not realizing that he was basically having a conversation with himself. "Anyhows, my mastabbatical's nearly over, which means one lucky lady is gonna have her whole world rocked very shortly." Then he winked at her. "Feelin' lucky, baby?"

"Athwart the tenebrous air pour down amain"
– Dante's *Inferno*

## FOUR

"Ain't nothin' wrong with you!" Ael yelled out to one of his clients. She was on the stair climber, bent over and clinging to the railing as if for dear life. Meanwhile, her legs were forced to take the stairs so quickly, it looked like they were on fast forward.

"My legs are going numb!" she managed to exclaim.

Truth be told, she looked like she was about to pass out. I'd never seen anyone climb stairs so fast. Gingerly placing the box of shoes Tallis had just given him as payment to train me in the corner of the room, Ael reached for a coiled whip that was leaning against the wall. "Complain, complain, complain," he muttered as he shook his head and continued grumbling to himself. "Just wait 'til she comes across one o' them Pintry demons an' gets away from it, thanks ta my trainin' … then we'll see how much complainin' we hear."

Pulling his arm back, he released the whip, which had to be twenty feet long, cracking the air around the woman's left calf. "Get back to work an' be happy for it! This place could save your life!" he called out to her, as she, in turn, jumped at the snapping of the whip. However, to Ael's credit, she did stop complaining.

Returning the whip to the corner of the room, Ael took stock of the rest of his clients. He eyed each one suspiciously, as if to ensure that they were working to their full potential. His eyes narrowed as he watched a guy taking a few deep breaths before attempting a bench press. His barbell was obscenely overloaded with weights as big as tires. "It ain't gonna lift itself!" Ael yelled at the man. In flustered response, the guy quickly pumped out ten consecutive presses.

"Ah will be back ta collect ye later, lass," Tallis said as I turned to face him. He nodded to me and Ael before his attention fell back on me again. At hearing he planned to leave me here, by myself, I suddenly felt horribly nervous like a scared kid on her first day of school. 'Course, instead of a matronly, sweet kindergarten teacher, I was assigned to Ael, who appeared possibly homicidal.

"Okay," I said, trying to smile confidently as I watched Tallis turn around and abandon me to my fate. At least I still had Bill. Speaking of whom, after giving up any chance of conversing with the large-breasted blond, he was now making his rounds to the various machines and mats, pausing here and there to assess whether any of the remaining women might be interested in celebrating the end of his mastabbatical. His gall was inexhaustible.

"It's too quiet in here!" a handsome man called out from the corner of the room where he'd been jumping rope. "Ael, how about some tunes?" Dropping the jump rope on the floor, he approached a bench where two fifty-pound free weights sat.

"Demands, demands, demands," Ael responded, shaking his head with a frown.

That only made the man's smile broader. "And none of that Luther Vandross, easy-listening shit either!"

Ael glanced at the man and shook his head again while crossing his enormous arms over his chest. "Don't be talkin' no smack 'bout Luther!" he retorted, appearing even more rankled than previously. He went to the opposite side of the room, where a lone CD player stood on a shelf made from cinder blocks and some two-by-fours. I glanced at Ael, then back to the man who made the Luther Vandross comment and noticed he was making his way over to me, smiling all the while.

"I'm Saxon," he introduced himself with a large grin, extending his hand. Then, as if thinking better of it, he wiped the sweat from his palm onto his pants before offering his hand to me again, with a slightly embarrassed chuckle.

"Hi," I said, grateful to find at least someone in the place who appeared to be friendly. "I'm Lily Harper," I added with a smile as I shook his hand, noticing how my much smaller mine was and how it disappeared into his.

Saxon was tall, maybe as tall as Ael, but not as buff, and nowhere near as enormous as Tallis. Saxon had more of a swimmer's physique—broad shoulders that tapered down to a narrow waist and a pair of very long, lean legs. Facially, he had a boyish sort of charm that came from the combination of his dark brown hair (in need of a haircut), his wide brown eyes, and his contagious smile. The firm, square jaw, perfectly straight nose, and plump, full lips collaborated to result in a handsome, boy-next-door friendly appearance. I would have guessed him to be in his late twenties or early thirties, but no older than thirty-two.

"You're new here," Saxon pointed out with another big grin as his unkempt hair fell into his face and he pushed it out of the way again.

"Yeah," I said, before frowning with concern. A man, who was previously going full bore on the elliptical machine, while also practicing overhead shoulder presses with two large free weights, suddenly tripped. He instantly fell off the elliptical and dropped both of the weights. One banged into the elliptical, while the other landed right next to the man. He just collapsed into a large heap on the floor. I looked for Ael who was still fiddling with the CD player. Sparing the man a furtive glance, which lasted all of three seconds, Ael returned his attention to the CD player. And everyone else in the room? Not one person seemed even slightly concerned. "I don't think he's getting up," I said to Saxon.

Saxon just shrugged. "Yeah, I'm sure he'll be fine. People pass out in here all the time." Then he added, "Just another day of training with Ael." I couldn't hide the shock on my face as I wondered what awaited me at Ael's instruction. But I didn't get to ponder that subject for long because Saxon had already changed it. "Are you a new Retriever?" he asked with real interest.

"Yeah, I am," I answered with a shy smile. As a rule, I wasn't very comfortable talking to handsome men. "Are you a Retriever too?"

Saxon nodded. "Yep and have been for about," he started and then glanced up at the ceiling for a few seconds as he, apparently, tried to remember. Then he looked at me again with another big grin. "Twenty years today, I think."

"Twenty years?" I repeated, frowning as I shook my head. "How is that possible unless you became a Retriever at age ten or something?"

He chuckled. "Ah, so you aren't in the know?" I shook my head immediately, very well aware that when it came to my new life, I wasn't even in the same zip code as "in the know." He nodded as he gazed at me. "As a Soul Retriever, you won't age, Lily," he answered. "That's why I'm so well preserved." Then he laughed again.

"So I can die but I won't age?" I questioned, just to make sure I had it right.

"Yep," Saxon responded.

I glanced around at all the people who were working out in the gym before looking back at Saxon again, only to find he was already gazing at me. I felt myself immediately start blushing. "And all these people are Soul Retrievers too?"

He simply nodded as I focused on the woman beside me. She was lying down on a bench with a weighted bar clutched tightly in both hands. On either end of the bar was what looked like an orange, furry ball. As she lifted the bar, and struggled a bit, one of the furry balls unwound itself. It appeared to be a rather bizarre-looking ferret or weasel of some sort. It had a long, narrow snout with a large, wet nose like a dog's, although the teeth were more comparable to a crocodile's. The body was long, thin, and covered in soft-looking fur with an equally lengthy tail that looked like a raccoon's. It stood no higher than a foot tall, but had to be at least three feet long. "I'm either imagining things or two very bizarre-looking creatures are hanging onto that woman's barbell," I said while indicating the creatures in question.

"Handrels," Saxon responded without further concern.

Meanwhile, the woman's arms began to waver and tremble because the Handrel's movement was throwing off the balance of the bar, I assumed. As soon as it appeared that she couldn't lift the barbell all the way up, the nasty little thing bit her right on the thumb. "Oh my God!" I said with a quick, shocked glance back at Saxon. "It just bit her!"

Saxon, again, didn't look surprised. "Yeah, they have razor-sharp teeth so Ael keeps them to make sure his clients balance the bars."

"Handrels?" I repeated, looking back at the woman, only to find that the other Handrel had unraveled itself and bitten her other hand. "Are they demons?" I couldn't imagine they might be anything else.

Saxon nodded. "Yep, and they aren't the only demons here. Ael considers the demons a good way to keep us motivated." The plinking of a piano started up in the background which was quickly followed by the mournful tones of a man's voice, which I assumed was Luther Vandross. Saxon shook his head and moaned something unintelligible before smiling again at me. "Now that crap is definitely anti-motivational." Then he turned to face Ael who was already heading to us. "Come on, Ael, I can't take any more of that sappy ass, slow shit! How do you expect us to work out to such crap? It puts me to sleep instead!"

"You don't like it? You know where the door is!" Ael responded as his red eyes began glowing a bit brighter.

"Calm down," Saxon said with another winning smile aimed my way. "I guess I shouldn't complain since we had to listen to R. Kelly nonstop all last week."

Ael frowned at Saxon before addressing me. "That's R. Kelly, as in pre-pedophile, by the way." I didn't say anything but the lyrics to Dave Chapelle's R. Kelly parody song, *I want to piss on you*, were already playing through my head. "Now stop flirtin' with my client an' get them bicep curls done," Ael said to Saxon and then, shaking his head, added, "You a time waster, boy."

"Yeah, yeah," Saxon replied before turning back to me. "Nice to meet you, Lily. Maybe I'll see you around?"

I wasn't sure how that could be possible unless he meant at Ael's gym. Not wanting to be rude, though, I nodded and said, "Yeah, I hope so. Good luck with your workout."

He raised one brow and smirked. "Famous last words."

"Enough o' you both wastin' time," Ael interrupted as he steered me away from Saxon. We headed to the far side of the gym. I spotted Bill who was lounging on the front of someone's treadmill. All I could see of the woman on the treadmill was that she had long, dark hair and a pretty trim body. Bill smiled at her just as she yanked her iPod out of her pocket and plopped an ear phone into each of her ears. Bill sighed as he pulled back from the treadmill and turned to face me. "Cockblocked by Steve Jobs," he muttered as he walked over to join Ael and me.

Ael looked at him from head to toe and shook his head again, no doubt discouraged at Bill's overall slovenly appearance. His shoelaces were untied, and he was wearing two different socks. The hem was pulled out of his shorts on one side, and his knees were so dry, the skin was bright red, crusty, and flaking off, looking like psoriasis. There were so many different colored stains on his Megadeath T-shirt, which was also two sizes too small, that I wasn't even sure what the original color might have been.

"An' you makin' my gym look bad," Ael finished.

Bill glanced over at me and shrugged, not showing the least bit of concern. "Haters gonna hate." Then he looked back at Ael and threw his pudgy hands on his hips. "So, we gonna get this shiznit on the road or what, yo? Nips needs ta be turned into a lethal ninja like ... yesterday."

Ael studied him with interest before he glanced back at me. "You two friends?" he asked and then alternated pointing his finger from Bill to me and then to Bill again.

"Fo shizzle," Bill answered. "I'm poindextrous."

"You what?" Ael asked, frowning.

Bill shrugged. "I'm able ta communicate equally well with nerds," at which time he glanced over at me, "and normal people," at which time he glanced back at Ael, smiling smugly. I decided not to take offense because I had too much other stuff on my mind.

"Are you plannin' on stayin'?" Ael asked, eyeing Bill with morbid resignation. "'Cause you gonna irritate me, I can already tell."

Bill shrugged again. "I'm Nerdlet's guardian angel. Where she goes, I go." Then he crossed his flaccid arms over his bulbous chest and glared at Ael until the demon simply looked over at me in exasperation, his eyebrows meeting in the middle. He obviously didn't know what to make of

Bill. 'Course, most people didn't. "Dude, you gotta place for me ta take a piss?" Bill asked as he cupped himself. "'Cause I gots ta go real bad."

Ael didn't say anything, but pointed to a door in the far right corner of the room. Bill nodded with an uneasy smile and left us. Ael studied me for a few moments before a large smile curved his lips, revealing his extremely pointed canines. "That's your guardian angel?" he asked with a laugh. "Girl, you musta done somethin' real bad in your past life."

I didn't say anything, but sighed. I often wondered the same thing, myself. For as much as I loved Bill as a friend, he wasn't the ideal guardian. And I really couldn't see him as being much of an ideal angel either, for that matter. "He grows on you," I answered with a hesitant smile.

Ael frowned and raised his eyebrows as high as they'd go, in an incredulous expression of utter doubt. Then he shook his head. "We gonna start with some skull crushers," he abruptly announced in a getting-down-to-business tone.

"Of course we are," I said underneath my breath while following him to an unoccupied bench. Beside it stood multiple barbells, some with bent handles and others that were just straight across. Next to that was a large white bucket. Ael reached inside the bucket and grabbed two Handrels by the scruff of their necks before pulling them out. Addressing me, he said, "Grab one o' them twenty pound bars," and motioned to the bar rack.

Never having held a barbell before, I wasn't sure which one was a twenty-pounder; but luckily for me, they were labeled. I gripped the one he requested and lifted it up with both hands, carrying it to the bench. I rested one end of the bar against the bench seat while eyeing the Handrels with sincere concern. Ael dropped each of them onto the bench and they scurried toward the bar, one nipping at the other when it inadvertently cut him off. The other one growled a response, but dutifully got in line behind the first one. They both climbed up the barbell, their tiny rat-like claws making a scratching sound as they did. "Um, are you sure I need to use those on my very first workout?" I asked, frowning up at Ael.

"Who's the trainer? Me or you?" he growled back.

"Um, you are," I said with an equal amount of hesitation.

"That's what I thought," he said with a nod while making his lips tight. "Now lay down with the back of your head on the end o' the bench." I did as I was instructed and Ael placed the bar in my hands. The Handrels clung to either end of it, curled around the metal in orange, furry balls. "Keep your elbows tucked in; an' then you're gonna lower the bar directly over your face by bendin' only at the elbow," Ael continued. "Keep the bar level, else you're gonna end up with some sore ass fingers." I figured he was referring to the bite of the Handrels. Fearing for my fingers, I gritted my teeth and lowered the bar, being extra careful to keep it perfectly balanced. But it wasn't as easy as Ael made it sound, and consequently, the bar slumped to the right. In no time, the balled up little bastard rushed over and bit me right on the knuckle.

"Ow!" I yelled.

"Keep the bar straight, or else you're gonna get it from the other one!" Ael warned me. I immediately righted the bar. "Now keep yer elbows tucked in!" he continued. I tucked in my elbows as far as they'd go. "Lower the bar over your face!" I lowered it and felt a burning pain in my triceps. But I figured that was where I was supposed to feel it. Better there than on my poor knuckles. "Now bring your arms back ta the front!" Ael demanded. I did so and finished the first exercise of my set, with my fingers all the worse for wear. I breathed out a sigh of relief … a sigh which was short-lived. "Now, you gotta do fourteen more!"

"What?" I ground out, the bar starting to slope again. I immediately straightened it and resumed my set, promising myself that somehow, someway, I would get even with Tallis over this.

"Number two, come on!" Ael yelled. "I ain't got all day, woman!" I busted out my next skull crusher, glaring at the Handrels as I did so. I kept the bar straight. "Number three!" Taking a breath, I brought the bar back over my head again.

"Dude!" Bill's voice suddenly exclaimed as he appeared directly over me. Consequently, I lost control of the bar and not one, but both Handrels bit my index fingers at exactly the same time.

"Son of a bitch!" I wailed, glaring at Bill as soon as I straightened the bar again. "Bill, can't you see I'm busy?!"

Bill nodded, giving a two-second glance to the Handrels before facing me again. "Sorry, Lils, but I totally just experienced peehicular manslaughter in the men's room."

"What the hell you talkin' 'bout?" Ael asked, his voice as irritated as mine must've been.

Bill nodded with glee, seeming incredibly anxious to enlighten us both, using his hands dramatically like he was planning to mime his story. "I was usin' the urinal, an' this freakin' dude comes up next ta me an' starts pissin'; an' next thing I know, his piss is splashin' out o' the toilet an' all over me!" he continued nodding vehemently, like it was too unbelievable to be true. "So I'm like: dafuq, yo? Right?" But Bill didn't wait for anyone to respond. "Right!" Then he shook his head. "So now I'm stuck with some other dude's piss all over my leg an' Demon Bright here," he glanced over at Ael, "don't have a single goddamned shower in this shitbox." He shook his head again. "Fuuck." Then he looked at me. "The dude was totally sportin' Eau de Douche anyway. Could smell him a mile away."

"You done lost your damn mind," Ael replied, shaking his head, before looking at me. "I got no idea what the hell …"

"I know," I interrupted as I rolled my eyes, staring back at Bill as I shook my head. "No one ever knows what he's talking about!"

"Eau de Douche!" Bill repeated like we were both dumb. "You know, that obnoxious, headache causin' cologne cloud that always hangs over those beefy, tight-ass shirt-wearin' dudes who are really just total douche bags." He nodded at both of us, like he'd just made a really good point. "An' they're such posers too! Freakin' frauders! They wanna come off like they're loaded, but the truth is they're nothin' but a bunch of fake Armani-wearin' Splenda daddies 'cause they ain't got the funds to pull off bein' a real sugar daddy!"

Ael pointed to the front of the gym and said with no slack in his jaw at all, "You're not allowed back here no more. You stay up front an' keep yourself occupied 'cause you're gonna make me lose mah shit."

"I'm just sayin'!" Bill frowned as he held up his arms in submission. "CTFD yo … Calm the fuck down!"

"Outta here!" Ael yelled at him as Bill shrugged once more and started for the front of the gym. Then looking back, first at Ael, then at me, before taking stock of the entire gym, he asked, "Anyone got one o' them handheld Nintendos? 'Cause I got a whole bucket o' nothin' ta do right now." No one responded and he shook his head. "Shit, this is totally gonna suck."

***

I'm not sure if our gym visit really sucked for Bill, but it definitely sucked for me. I couldn't remember a time that I'd ever attempted to do anything so physical. And now, as Bill and I followed Tallis back through the woods, I had half a mind to ask Tallis to carry me the rest of the way.

After three sets of fifteen reps of skull crushers, which coincidentally hurt my fingers more than my skull, we moved on to dips and chest presses. The chest presses equated to a straight bar with the burdensome head of a demon on either end. Apparently, Tallis wasn't the only one fond of killing demons and keeping their heads. However, as far as I knew, Tallis didn't go so far as to use them for chest pressing...

After the demonic head chest presses, we practiced bicep curls and seated rows. From there, we ventured into lower body territory, which included so many squats, my butt felt like it might fall off. But Ael, just as expected, didn't offer any sympathy at all. Instead, we then began three sets of fifteen reps of lunges. After the lunges came the leg extensions, and then, the leg curls. By that time, I felt like I'd been hit by a Mack truck.

"But the worst had to be the deadlift," I said as I glanced over at Bill and shook my head. I felt like I'd earned the opportunity to feel sorry for myself. Tallis was already five or so paces ahead of us, which seemed to be the rule, rather than the exception. "Or maybe the burpees."

"You mean vurpees," Bill said with a smug smile and a chuckle. "Anytime I watch people doing those, I vomit a little in my mouth."

I shook my head. "You were totally reaching with that one, Bill."

"What?" he demanded, puffing out his chest in defense of his pride and acting like I was being completely unreasonable. "Reaching? What you talkin' 'bout, Willis?"

"Burpees and a vurp have nothing in common."

He frowned at me. "An' tell me just how in the hell you would even know that? It's not like you speak cool."

"Because I can figure it out!" I railed back at him. I was tired and sore so my temper had a very short leash. "A vurp clearly is a burp laced with vomit. And a burp laced with vomit has absolutely nothing to do with a burpee, aside from the fact that they rhyme." I raised an eyebrow at him. "But nice try."

"Well excuse the shit outta me for makin' a funny-ass joke even if it doesn't meet Your Royal Hostess's joke standards!" Bill said as he frowned at me.

"It's Royal Highness," I corrected him. "Hostess makes Twinkies and Ding Dongs."

"Whatevs," he mumbled as he rubbed his stomach. "What I wouldn't do for a Twinkie." Then he glanced up at Tallis who was still ahead of us by about ten feet and frowned. "I'm sick of eatin' Shrek food."

I smiled and patted his arm in a feeble attempt to make amends. Then I took a deep breath and let it out, realizing I shouldn't have jumped down Bill's throat. Especially after he'd been a good friend and hung out in the front of the gym with nothing to do for two hours. "Sorry, Bill. I'm just really exhausted."

"It's okay, sugar nipples," Bill responded with a big grin, his hurt feelings suddenly forgotten which made me wonder if they were really ever genuine in the first place. "So you were saying the deadlift was the worst," he started, clearly attempting to mend our little rift. "How come?"

I smiled at him, grateful he was my friend and someone to keep me company in this godforsaken place because Tallis definitely wasn't the sociable type. I sighed and tried to remember the worst part of my training. Ah, yes, the deadlifts …"Because it was so difficult to lift up the Intonker, and the thing looked scary as hell."

An Intonker was yet another species of demon. Somehow, and I imagined it was probably against Afterlife Enterprises policy, Ael managed to collect ten demons of different species. Some of the more domesticated ones, i.e., the Handrels, were allowed to roam somewhat freely inside the gym. Because Intonkers were, apparently, easily angered and possessed foul tempers in general, all three of them were hogtied and used for exercises like the deadlift. The only other type of demon I saw was tethered outside the gym. It was tied to a tree, but had a long enough rope to allow it to chase people, thereby improving their running speeds.

As to the proper procedure for doing an Intonker deadlift, Ael ordered me to bend over with a straight back, then reach down and grab the ropes binding the creature before simply standing up again. But my grip on the ropes had to be wide enough that the demon couldn't crane its neck around and sink its unlimited fangs into my arm.

Unlike the Handrels, that were somewhat harmless since they could only take a small bite out of you, the Intonkers weren't. They were much larger, about the size of a boar, and just as thick. They were the color of deep swamp water and the texture of their skin felt like rough leather. Their faces were the worst part about them—completely hideous. Their squarish heads had jaws that were very angular and pronounced, with exaggerated underbites. Their fleshy jowls hung all the way down to their necks, sort of resembling a bulldog's muzzle, but only slightly. They certainly didn't share any of the bulldog's charm though. Their myriad, razor-sharp teeth protruded every which way, filling their mouths until they looked like they were sucking on a cluster of white quartz. Their upturned noses were wide with broad, flaring nostrils. Their small, narrow, slit-like eyes glowed yellow and were very intimidating, to say the least.

"Shit, when I saw you pick that thing up, I thought for sure it was gonna bust through those ropes and swallow you whole," Bill said with a nod.

"Oh really? Nice to know that your main concern was finding a Nintendo to play with."

Bill was about to respond when the words faltered on his lips. Instead, he reached into his pocket and pulled out his cell phone which was currently vibrating with a text message. He flipped the phone open, a feat in and of itself, considering it was covered in duct tape from being dropped one too many times. His eyes went wide as he glanced up at me. "It's from Skeletor Horn," he said (his pet name for Jason Streethorn, the general manager of Afterlife Enterprises). I felt my heart drop.

"What … what did he say?" I asked, breathlessly.

Bill shrugged. "Looks like we're headed back to the Underground."

"Noisome the earth is, that receiveth this"
– Dante's *Inferno*

# FIVE

*Looks like we're headed back to the Underground.*

They were eight words that I could honestly say I hoped to never hear again. But as a Soul Retriever working for Afterlife Enterprises, I also knew better.

"Yep, shit just got real," Bill said, shaking his head as he sighed, letting it be known that he didn't like the news any more than I did. But because Bill couldn't be killed, the risks to him were nothing like what they were for me.

"Why is Jason ordering us to go back to the Underground now?" I inquired, angry and worried at the same time. "We just got back!" I yelled at Bill as I shook my head. My stomach had already plummeted to the ground. "Does Jason expect us to leave right now? Tonight? Tomorrow? What?" I didn't wait for Bill to respond, but started vigorously shaking my head again as I started to seriously freak out. "I'm nowhere near ready to go there again! I still can't defend myself!" My voice sounded panicky as I turned to face Tallis who was already looking my way, his face expressionless, as usual. "My training has barely even begun! I mean, shouldn't Jason know that?" I threw my hands up in the air as I railed at Bill again. "What does his text even mean?" But Bill just shrugged as if to say he was just the messenger and didn't appreciate being shot.

"I would take it to mean that we're goin' back to the Underground," he said with another shrug and a sigh.

"Lemme see," Tallis ordered as he motioned for Bill's cell phone. Bill didn't say anything as he handed the phone over to Tallis who studied it for a few moments. He was, no doubt, trying to figure out where the soul who needed retrieval was located. Mission texts from Afterlife Enterprises always included a live map of whatever area of the Underground City the soul happened to be in. The map acted like a homing device by reporting the soul's current location in real time. So that way, no matter where the soul went, we would be able to track it … er, him or her.

"Circle Two," Tallis said with a nod as if he were familiar with that area of the Underground City.

"What's in Circle Two?" I asked. I was annoyed that I couldn't recall the answer myself from Dante's *Inferno*. Dante's book was given to me by Afterlife Enterprises upon my acceptance of the position of Soul Retriever. The book was intended to serve as my guide through the Underground City, even though it was way outdated, and definitely slanted to Dante's own prejudices at the time, i.e., the fourteenth century. Bill and I had a tough time sifting through Dante's explanations of each level of the Underground because the Underground City wasn't comprised of levels at all. Rather, it was laid out just like a city, with buildings, streets, and various "citizens" walking about. Tallis explained the discrepancy by comparing it to our own world—just as Earth evolved over time, so did the Underground City. So today, it was just that—a city. After surviving my first mission, which took us to the Underground City's carnival of nightmares, I could only wonder what lay in store for us now.

As to Circle Two and what awaited us there, panic started to breed inside my stomach and made me feel like I might throw up. Not to mention the sweat that was already beading along the small of my back and hairline. I not only felt sick, but also clammy and wet. Images of our previous trip to the Underground City suddenly overtook me as memories of the demon clowns, Ragur and Kipur, flashed through my mind. To make a long story short, I'd come very close to losing my life on that trip.

I started to feel faint.

"The sewer," Tallis replied as he handed the phone back to Bill, although his facial expression was still unreadable. "Circle Two is the sewer aqueduct o' the Oonderground City."

"Great," Bill grumbled as he shook his head. "Love me some shit smell."

Tallis crossed his arms over his chest and looked my way, appearing preoccupied, like he was pondering something. Then he started to nod as if something were suddenly occurring to him. "The good news is Ah know a shortcoot inta the sewers," he started.

I frowned, not seeing why he seemed so pleased with that information. Shortcuts into a death by sewer didn't exactly cheer me up very much. "Why is that good news?" I asked.

"Aye, 'twill give oos some time," Tallis responded. "Streethorn believes we have ta traverse the River Acheron ta the aqueduct, a four-day's journey at the verra least."

"Four days?" I repeated, my mouth dropping open. The memories of our last voyage through the haunted forest reappeared in my mind. Suffice to say, the expedition to the Underground City was almost as bad as the Underground City itself ...

Tallis shook his head. "Ah can git oos there in one day."

I was quiet for a moment. Stifling the ray of hope that suddenly blossomed, as Tallis's words started to register, I cautiously asked, "Does ... does that mean you're going to go back down there with us again?" I asked, trying not to sound too hopeful. I was deathly afraid any hopefulness I harbored might suddenly be smashed to smithereens if Tallis said that I'd misunderstood him and he had no plans to escort us anywhere.

Tallis frowned at me. "Aye, lass, ye are hardly prepared ta go; ye jist said so yerself."

"Thank you," I answered automatically, completely ignoring the fact that Tallis was regarding me like I was a halfwit. "Just add that cost on to my list of what I already owe you," I said, reminding myself and Tallis, for that matter, that we still had to account for the ton of money I already owed him. That ton of money had come about because Tallis wasn't particularly charitable, and therefore, didn't work for nothing. Instead, we'd agreed to the sum of fifty thousand pounds that I would pay Tallis to accompany Bill and me to the Underground City the first time around. I also promised to pay Tallis for training me in the art of sword fighting, the sum of which now escaped my mind. At any rate, I was sure that the total well exceeded fifty thousand pounds. Luckily for me, Afterlife Enterprises had to foot the bill. And, no, Afterlife Enterprises hadn't exactly been informed of their involvement in this arrangement, but I didn't care. After being granted a constantly full bank account as part of my benefits package when I accepted the job, I planned to use that benefit to the nth degree.

"We can discoos the particulars later," Tallis announced. "For now, we have three days in which ye will do naethin' boot train with yer sword."

I swallowed hard and nodded to show my agreement. Even though training with Tallis was no walk in the park, by any stretch of the imagination, at least I'd be spared Ael's torturous physical boot camp for a few days. Seeing how every one of my muscles was already aching, any reprieve from Ael was a relief in and of itself. Although spending so much time with Tallis didn't exactly thrill me either. It wasn't that I didn't like Tallis … well, sometimes I didn't— when he was being a jerk, for example. But there were also times when he seemed like he wanted to let me in, as a friend. Still, most often, whenever Tallis and I spent too much time together, we got on one another's nerves. Big time.

"Shit," Bill announced with a sigh as he eyed Tallis and frowned. "That means we're gonna hafta stay in your shitbox accommodations again, doesn't it?"

Surprisingly enough, a smile broke across Tallis's face as he turned to me and answered. "Aye, it does."

\*\*\*

For the next three days, I trained, and trained, and trained some more. Bill and I stayed in Tallis's shack and Bill acted like he was on vacation by sleeping in late every morning and going to bed even later. I was up at dawn every day with Tallis's sword in my face. At the end of the three days, even though I was no master of the sword, I was certainly much better off than before.

The first lesson Tallis taught me, which took me a while to grasp, was simply relaxing. Tallis explained the perils of being tense while in combat and taught me how to control my nerves so I could remain cool and calm at all times. He showed me how to keep my muscles loose by teaching me how to control my breathing. It was like a form of meditation, but meditation for combat purposes. As Tallis explained, if I was too wound up and tight while fighting, I wouldn't be able to act with speed. And slow reactions could be fatal. I thought about it, and it made sense because when it came to Tallis and his skills, speed was probably number one on the list.

After my lesson in relaxation techniques, we worked on maintaining balance and quick footwork. Tallis taught me to always keep my feet shoulder-width apart, and move with my legs spread without allowing my feet to come close together. My stance was imperative to my equilibrium because without balance, I was as good as dead. Tallis showed me how to slide my feet, rather than lift them, and to keep my posture straight and my chest and torso forward. That was to help me keep my balance whenever I took a swing. We must have practiced the correct fighting posture for half a day.

My next lesson was becoming aware of my surroundings and taking stock of everything around me. Tallis referred to surroundings as my assets and my liabilities. Was the sun behind me or in front of me? Could I use the angle of the sun to blind my enemy? And speaking of the enemy, Tallis told me to watch whomever I was fighting and to take mental notes. Was my opponent cautious or boastful in his attacks? Was he skilled in his approach? Or a novice? Tallis believed that everyone had a fatal weakness and my responsibility was to figure out what that weakness was ...

But perhaps the most important factor in assessing my situation was speediness. I would only have a few seconds to make critical judgments that might doom or save me. After assessing the situation properly, my next lesson was to engage the enemy with care. In general, Tallis thought it best that I wait to be attacked, rather than vice versa. Because I was inexperienced and Tallis would be along for the ride (at least for my next mission), I focused mainly on defensive moves, rather than offensive ones. By engaging defensively, I would be able to maintain control and focus. Tallis spent the first full day of our training just teaching me how to dodge his blows. If that sounds easy, believe me, it wasn't. I ended up with a vast array of bruises up and down my legs to match the ones on my arms.

Once we reviewed all the defensive strategies until I was blue in the face, we moved on to the offensive ones. Tallis taught me how to keep my opponent "on point," which meant learning how to extend my sword in a short, quick movement toward my enemy's throat or eyes. The movement had to be fluid and done in a split second because the goal was to take my enemy by surprise. As Tallis often reiterated, surprise was always an ally in a fight.

When on the defense or the offense, I kept my elbows bent and close to my sides. Tallis explained that inexperienced fighters often stretched their arms out, which only impaired their ability to thrust and parry quickly. It was my sword that needed to be extended toward my enemy, never my arms.

"Measure twice, coot once," Tallis reminded me as we walked through the Dark Wood. We were now on our way to the sewer aqueduct of the Underground City. After walking for at least four hours, my legs already felt like jelly. The landscape had also changed—the lushness of the forest where Tallis lived having given way to the charcoaled remains of long dead trees.

"Is that like sayin' two birds in your hand is better than a big ol' bush?" Bill piped up, chuckling to himself. "Or maybe it's like killin' two pigs with one bird?"

I frowned at him and my eyebrows knotted in the middle. "You mean, killing two birds with one stone?"

"Um, no, I don't," he answered in a high-pitched, girly voice while fluttering his eyelashes. I had no idea whom he was pretending to be. "I'm talkin' Angry Birds, yo."

"Historically speakin', a sword fight ended with the first blow stroock. It could take only thirty seconds, lass," Tallis continued as if Bill never interrupted him. "Boot fightin' demons can be even quicker, Besom, because they possess abilities ye dinnae. Ye moost be quick an' skilled."

"Okay," I said, sighing over the enormous obstacles ahead of me. "Does, um, Donald or Donnchad or whatever his name is, have any immortal friends who might want to possess me?" I asked jokingly, but then didn't think it was such a bad idea.

Tallis frowned at me, which, I guessed, meant no. "Ye moost be certain o' yer aim, fer 'tis verra likely that if ye miss yer first strike, yer enemy will take advantage," he continued.

"Which means, your enemy will knock you the fuck out!" Bill added before he started punching the air like he was a boxer. "I'm gonna knock you out," he sang, not sounding a bit like LL Cool J. "Bill said knock you out!"

"Thanks, Bill," I grumbled as I scanned the forest of dead trees on either side of us. I wanted to make sure that none of the enormous spiders that attacked us the last time were scheduling another visit.

"Seriously, Lils, what is up with Tido and his Jesus shoes?" Bill asked as he indicated Tallis's brown leather homemade sandals. I was spared the need to answer when Tallis interrupted.

"We have arrived." He stopped walking and ran his hands over his sword, which was still in its scabbard, looped around his chest. Then he patted his sporran with both hands before dropping his attention to my sword, which was also looped around my chest, in the scabbard Tallis lent me.

"Um, where's here?" Bill asked with a glance around himself, probably taking note that the forest was exactly the same on both sides as it was a few feet away. Nothing but the hollowed remains of what once appeared to be a thriving forest. As to how the Dark Wood became the Dark Wood, I wasn't sure. But Dante also referred to it, so I imagined it always looked this way, even back in the fourteenth century.

"The entry ta the short coot," Tallis answered in an annoyed tone. Without another word, he turned around and walked a few paces forward, his strides long and purposeful, as if he were counting his steps. Dropping down on his haunches, he dug up two palms full of dirt, rising as the soft earth sifted through his fingers. Then he reached beneath his kilt, unintentionally giving me a glimpse of his muscular upper thigh, as he retrieved a blade. He dropped down to his knees and held his right arm out. With no hesitation, he sliced his forearm and blood gushed out, dripping from his arm and sinking into the ground below.

Bill frowned at the sight warily. "Conan should prolly look into gettin' some counselin'," he remarked as he pointed to Tallis. Meantime, Tallis was too busy with his ministrations to notice we were talking about him, or maybe he just didn't care. "Methinks he might be a cutter."

I didn't respond as I watched Tallis lean forward and push a huge mound of earth into the same spot where his blood had just fallen. As soon as he did, the earth suddenly started falling into some sort of vortex, as if there were a hole right beneath it.

"Lass," Tallis barked as I stepped forward. He gripped my arm and pulled me next to him. I noticed there was a passageway beneath the dirt. It looked like a huge pipe and was maybe four feet tall by three feet wide. The metal gleamed in what little light the moon provided. Tallis faced Bill. "Angel, ye will go first."

"Like shit I'll go first," Bill snapped back, his hands on his hips. He took a quick look down the tunnel before glaring at Tallis again. "I'm not into gettin' inta no tight places unless a woman's involved, namsay?"

"Bill!" I started.

"Hush, nips," he interrupted, while glaring at Tallis. "An' I'm also claustrophobic."

"Ye will havta declaustrophobe yerself 'cause we are goin' in," Tallis answered, his lips tight. "An' ta do so, ye will havta go oan yer belly."

"What?" Bill erupted, shaking his head and throwing his hands in the air as he glanced over at me. "Shrek has lost his mother-freakin' mind, yo! There is no flippin' way I'm gettin' into that shit tunnel and crawlin' through with rats an' whatever the hell else in my face." He shook his head again, this time more decidedly. "Homey definitely don't play that."

"Bill, you can't be killed," I reminded him, my lips pursing as my temper started to flare. I was already beyond stressed out and Bill's cowardice was the furthest thing from my mind.

"So man up and deal with it because there's no alternative."

He opened his mouth like he was about to say something else, but wisely clapped his lips together and glanced down the tunnel again before looking back up at Tallis. "How long are we gonna hafta crawl through that?"

Tallis shrugged, wearing the same grin he had been throughout the entirety of Bill's fit. Tallis seemed to enjoy seeing the angel in uncomfortable situations. Usually, the two of them could tolerate one another, but there were moments when their irritation with the other manifested. "Long enooff."

"Go!" I ordered Bill as I pointed to the tunnel. He muttered something unintelligible before getting down on his hands and knees and crawling into the tunnel. "Smells like shit!" he complained, his voice echoing.

Tallis chuckled and looked at me. "Ye will go next, lass, an' Ah will be jist behind ye. That way, ye are protected on either end."

I just nodded and took a deep breath, looking down at the pipe and hoping I wasn't claustrophobic. I got onto my hands and knees and started forward, preferring the soft dirt to the hard cold metal of the tunnel. As soon as I stuck my head inside the tunnel, the smell of rotten feces nearly gagged me. My eyes watered as I plugged my nose and suddenly felt nauseous.

"Breathe through yer mouth, lass," Tallis ordered. I nodded and opened my mouth, inching farther inside the pipe. As soon as my eyes adjusted to the pitch darkness, a bright light momentarily blinded me. "What is that?" I yelled out, putting my hand up to shield my eyes.

"That's my halo," Bill answered from where he was crawling ahead of me. He was maybe a mere two feet in front. "I just turned the shit up so I can see where the frick I'm goin'."

Removing my hand from my eyes, I allowed them to adjust to Bill's brightly lit halo, which became a white glow that encapsulated his entire body. I continued forward, now able to see Tallis's hands just behind my legs. He was already in the tunnel, which basically meant his face was at the same level as my butt. Somehow, that information created a flurry of anxious bubbles in my stomach and I shook my head, hoping the bizarre feelings would go away.

"Good thinking on the halo light, Bill," I said, directing my attention to anything besides being on all fours with Tallis only a few inches behind me.

"You're tellin' me, hot cheeks," Bill responded. He seemed to be taking his sweet time as he baby crawled through the pipe, moving forward, inch by inch. "You should be damn happy you've got me with you, that's all I'm sayin'."

"I am happy you're with me, but you really need to crawl faster, Bill, otherwise we'll never get through this thing," I replied. I felt cold wetness under my hands and knees and realized we were now crawling through water. Flashing on what the water might possibly contain, I decided I didn't want to know. Instead, I kept reminding myself to breathe through my mouth while hoping whatever organisms survived in this tunnel weren't airborne.

"Easy for you to say!" Bill called back. "You're not up front, blazin' the goddamned fart-reduction trail!"

"What is a fart-reduction trail?" I asked, not because I really wanted to know, but I figured it would help me get through the foul tunnel more easily if I focused on Bill's inane language. I was still having a hard time trying not to smell the noxious sewage fumes in the tunnel.

"It's what happens in the process of repeatedly farting in a super confined space, which then infuses the space with the pure essence of fart," Bill answered.

"But this isn't farts," I argued.

"Thanks for pointin' that out, Sweetcheeks," Bill grumbled. "Whatever it is, it's cold and wet and freakin' rank." Then he screamed in such a high pitch, I briefly thought a little girl had just joined our crew.

"What?" I demanded, right as my head rammed into Bill's ass.

"There's bones in here, yo!" Bill yelled as he suddenly sped up, maybe because I'd just prodded him in the butt with my head. Anyway, he passed over the "bone" and I was right behind him. The "bone" wasn't a bone at all, and looked more like the head of a fish, with rows of incredibly sharp teeth. Its jaw was a yellowish color.

"What is that?" I asked Tallis, as I glanced back and saw he was now basically right on top of me. I could actually feel the heat of his breath through my yoga pants. And, yes, it did strike me as incredibly odd that I was traipsing through shitty water, my face basically in Bill's butt, while trying to avoid dead piranha heads and, yet, I had to remind myself not to get turned on! There was something seriously wrong with me…

"'Tis a Flain demon's skull," Tallis replied indifferently. "Keep a move oan!" he yelled out, presumably addressing Bill. His voice was extra loud as it bounced off the tunnel walls. "We still have a long ways ta goo, jist ta reach the aqueduct."

"You mean this ain't the aqueduct?" Bill asked, his voice breaking.

"Nae," Tallis responded. "The aqueduct isnae fer another quarter mile."

"Fuck!" Bill squealed. "We gotta 'nother quarter mile in this shit water?" Then he shook his head. "What lives in here anyway?"

"Naethin' in here is alive, save oos," Tallis responded.

"But who the hell knows how long that's gonna last?" Bill grumbled.

I took small comfort in the news that whatever was inside this sewer tunnel wasn't alive. I was also somewhat pleased to find that the water we were crawling through wasn't getting any deeper. *The little things are infinitely the most important,* I reminded myself, quoting Arthur Conan Doyle. Then it suddenly dawned on me that I hadn't been quoting the advice of my self-help books lately. Usually, I lived my life by clinging to the wisdom and knowledge of people who had training in helping other people find their life's path. For the last few days, I hadn't really been bothered with inspirational quotes, which was beyond bizarre since my mind was usually cluttered with them.

"Are we there yet?" Bill's voice interrupted my brief epiphany. "How much longer, yoze? My freakin' knees hurt like bitches, Conan!"

"We are almost there," Tallis answered, without irritation or anything else really. Tallis was a master in the art of speaking without any inflection.

"Dude, you shoulda told us ta bring knee pads!" Bill persisted. Then he was struck silent and I looked beyond him and noticed our tunnel had simply ended. "Um," Bill started.

"We have reached the aqueduct," Tallis announced.

"Cerberus, monster cruel and uncouth"
– Dante's *Inferno*

# SIX

"How in the hells are we 'sposed ta get down, Bruno?" Bill demanded from Tallis as he faced me with his hands in the air like the question he just asked was a clue in Charades.

Pushing past him, I glanced over the edge of the pipe, and noticed that not only did our tunnel end, but there was also a pretty precarious drop that appeared to plummet us right into what looked like a vast pool of sewage. The cesspool was the size of an Olympic pool and lay smack dab in the middle of a dome-shaped cavern. The walls of the cavern were completely constructed from red bricks, which were crumbling and faded with age. The only way I could make out any of the scenery was from the ten or so oil-burning sconces that hung on the circular walls. Atop each of the sconces was a two-foot flame, lending a jaundiced appearance to the cavern. From the center of the pool of sewage were four brick tunnels that led in different directions. At the base of each tunnel was a platform, probably used for docking boats at some point. Each one had that kind of look.

"We joomp," Tallis answered. Apparently, sewage didn't bother him more than any other horrible thing did. Well, good for him! As for me, I could honestly say that I was far beyond grossed out at the prospect of submerging myself in poo water. I was also scared to death, and I think I *had* managed to make myself claustrophobic somewhere along the way.

"You want us to jump into that pool of sewage?" I asked, my voice riddled with doubt.

"The pool is naethin' more than shit an' piss," Tallis responded.

"Okay ... so let me repeat myself," I continued, shaking my head as I wondered if these trips to the Underground would ever become any easier. "You want us to jump directly into that cesspool?"

"Did ye see a better way down, Besom?" Tallis asked, his eyebrows meeting in the middle of his forehead as he waited for my response. Looking back over the precipice, I realized that unless a twenty-foot ladder magically appeared, Tallis was absolutely right; there was no other way. If we wanted to continue forward, we had no choice but to jump.

"Is it deep?" I asked with a sigh. The realization that I was about to be submerged in feces, urine, and God only knew what else could not have been more depressing. Any way I looked at it, I knew today would not be one of my best.

"Aye, verra deep," Tallis answered. "Ah have traversed these toonnels many times," he added, as if to say I should just trust him at his word and be done with it.

"This is screwed, yoze," Bill said, shaking his head and glaring at me. "Why the hell didn't you just take the offer ta go to Shade? At least you wouldn't hafta crawl around in demon shit an' now be swimmin' in it!"

"Because Shade meant one hundred years of nothingness!" I yelled back at him. "At least this way, I still have my own life to lead and things I can look forward to!" He continued to frown as I shook my head. "Bill, why don't you just materialize yourself down there? Then you wouldn't have to jump at all!" I asked, with my jaw tight because I wasn't in any mood to argue with him. "Then one of us won't have to swim through it." Bill had already demonstrated how he could materialize from one place to another when we were en route to the Underground City the first time around.

He shook his head. "I'm not sure I can do it if we're actually in the Underground. I think this place kinda sucks my powers up." Then he turned to address Tallis. "Hey, Yeti, are we in Underground proper?" Tallis frowned at his nickname but simply nodded. Bill looked at me and shrugged. "Yeah, prolly ain't gonna work."

"Well, it's worth a try, right?" I pressed.

Bill sighed with a quick glance over the cliff again. "Yeah, I guess so." Then he looked back at Tallis. "Which tunnel we takin'?"

"The one ta the right," Tallis answered, without even a fleeting glimpse over the edge of our pipe. Apparently, he did know these sewer tunnels pretty well.

Bill nodded as he then leaned over the edge of our tube and eyed the tunnel in question, probably in order to judge how far away it was. He pulled himself back into our tunnel again and closed his eyes. A second or so later, he squeezed them even tighter. Then he pursed his lips together and looked like he was suffering from constipation. When he reopened them, he said, "So the hell much for that."

I sighed with a smile of consolation. "Guess we're all going swimming then."

"Ye will joomp an' then swim ta the corridor off ta the right," Tallis instructed Bill, clearly anxious to get a move on. "Ye *can* swim?"

Bill rolled his eyes. "Dafuq, dude? 'Course I can swim." Bill looked over the edge of the pipe again before answering Tallis. "You swear on that dead dude who's possessin' you that I'm not gonna get attacked by some enormous, freakin' shit alligator? Or some monster that's made outta demon turds?"

"Ah swear," Tallis replied calmly.

"You can't be killed, Bill," I reminded him.

"Yeah, but that ain't to say that it wouldn't seriously suck to be some demon's chew toy!" Bill replied with another whine. "It's been real, Lils," he said as he scooched himself to the end of the pipe and closed his eyes while pinching his nose.

He sort of plopped/rolled off the ledge of the
tunnel, cannon-balling into the sewage below.

"Bill!" I called out once his body was entirely
submerged. "Bill, are you okay?"

When he surfaced a second or so later, he
looked like he was treading water as he cleared the
muck from his eyes. He started spitting, and
shaking his head as more and more droplets of
sewage water dripped off his hair and slid down
his face. "Dude! I think I just drank some!" he
yelled as he continued to cough and spit. "I think I
just freakin' swallowed a gulp of demon shit an'
piss!"

Looking back at Tallis, I half-smiled. "Looks
like he's okay."

Tallis smiled in return and leaned over the
edge of the pipe, calling out, "Swim ta yer right!"
Then, facing me again, he muttered: "Bludy
stookie angel," while shaking his head. A few
moments later, he nodded at me. "'Tis yer turn,
lass." I nodded and crawled to the edge of the pipe
as I took a deep breath. At the feel of Tallis's hand
on mine, I looked back at him. "Doona be afeared,
Besom," he said in a hushed tone. "Ah will make
it mah mission ta keep ye safe."

"Thank you, Tallis," I whispered, genuinely
taking comfort in his words, although at the same
time, they surprised me. In general, Tallis wasn't
exactly demonstrative about caring, or showing
compassion of any sort, so moments like these
really threw me for a loop.

I didn't say anything more as I sat back on my butt and let my legs dangle off the edge of the pipe. I had to readjust my sword in its scabbard which was strapped across my chest, so the tip wouldn't scratch the pipe. Then I took another deep breath, reminding myself not to open my mouth, and pushed off the ledge. I was airborne for a few seconds, my mouth clamped shut tightly before the icy water engulfed me. I pawed through the water, kicking my legs at the same time to force myself upward. When my head cleared the water's surface, I wiped the disgusting sediment from my eyes and spat out several times to ensure that nothing seeped into my mouth. Then I started swimming for the tunnel on the right, where Bill was standing and leaning down with his hand extended to me. The tunnel was a bit higher than the cesspool, by about three feet, so thankfully, there wasn't any sewer water in it at all.

"Give me your hand, Babydoll," Bill said as soon as I got close enough. I nodded as I reached for him, using the edge of the brick platform beside the tunnel to heave myself out of the water. As soon as I stood up, I looked back to find Tallis already swimming our way. As for the aqueduct: from my new vantage point, I could see it in its entirety. The cavern was completely comprised of bricks and the ceiling was maybe forty feet high. The walls became concave as they rose up to meet the ceiling. The pipe we'd just traveled through was located about halfway up the side of one of the brick walls.

"Do you need help?" I asked Tallis once he reached us.

"Nae," he answered, gripping the sides of the brick platform and hoisting himself up. He shook himself off before checking his sword, which didn't look any the worse for wear. It reflected the yellow light provided by the wall sconces that illuminated the entire cavern. That was when something occurred to me.

"Tallis," I began as he cleared the brown water from his eyes and shook his hair out, wiping the hideous sewer water from his face. I wasn't sure why, but suddenly the scar that ran down one side of his face seemed more pronounced somehow. It almost appeared to be glowing. Maybe it was just a trick of the light.

"Aye?"

"If we are actually in the Underground now, why am I not having the same reaction that I did when we traveled to the Underground previously?" The first time I set foot in the Underground, I basically started dying.

"Ye still carry mah blood in yer veins," Tallis answered nonchalantly, walking past Bill and me and starting for the entryway to the brick tunnel. Luckily, this tunnel was a good ten feet high so we wouldn't have to crawl again.

"Oh," I answered, as I wondered how long Tallis's blood could survive in my body. Tallis didn't seem to be in a very conversational mood, though, so I figured I'd file the question away for later. For now, we just had to get through the sewer tunnels.

"Shit!" Bill yelled out as he palmed his shorts and reached inside his pocket, pulling out his phone which was dripping with sewer water. "My phone is soaking wet!" he said as I felt my heart skip a beat. Without Bill's phone, we didn't have a snowball's chance in hell of locating the misplaced soul. That meant our entire trip down here would be for nothing. And who knew if we could even manage to make it back out of here alive? Well, who knew if *I'd* make it out of here alive, anyway?

"'Twill work," Tallis said, showing little interest in the phone or Bill's complaint.

"Um, not sure how well you did in science class, slick, but submergin' electronics in shit water ain't good for 'em." Then he glanced over at me and frowned. "I bet the frickin' thing's broke."

"It isna broken," Tallis responded calmly before he stopped walking and turned to face us. "The Oonderground has a verra strong electric force field surroundin' it, which enables anythin' electrical."

"That's great an' all, Einstein, but when you put a phone in water, the thing shorts out," Bill insisted.

Tallis frowned at Bill who was already scowling back at him. "If ye doona believe me, look at yer phone."

Skeptically, Bill flipped open the top of his phone, pressed a few buttons, and a huge smile lit up his face. "Shit, Tido's right!" he announced, looking at me. "Frickin' thing ain't broke." He studied the phone for a little while longer before nodding. "An' looks like our soul in question ain't too far away." Then he addressed Tallis. "Thanks for the science lesson, yoze. Shit, maybe you will turn out to be my mantor after all."

"Yer what?" Tallis asked even as he faced forward again and started walking, with Bill and me right behind him.

"Like mentor, only mantor," Bill started, but Tallis shook his head as if to say he still didn't get it. Bill sighed. "Like the man I aspire ta be. Like the ideal dude, ya know?"

"Aye," Tallis responded but then shook his head again. "I doona wanna be yer mantor."

"Yeah," Bill answered. "Now that the moment's passed, I'm startin' ta think of you as the Yeti again," he finished while looking over at me with a shrug. "It was good while it lasted, nips."

"What does Dante say about this level?" I interrupted, my mind wholly obsessed with what awaited us in the sewer system. Although Tallis and Bill could discuss such trivial things like whether or not to be a mantor, I couldn't. As the only one of us who risked being killed, I guessed it only made sense that I would take our mission the most seriously.

"Ah, shit balls," Bill answered with a scrunched up face, which I assumed meant that he'd forgotten Dante's book.

"Bill, the book was your responsibility!" I chastised him. "We agreed to that!"

"I know, I know; my bad," he answered as he shook his head. "I totally forgot the damn thing on Conan's table." Then he cocked his head to the side and studied me. "I actually did us a big ol' favor though 'cause phones might not get screwed up in vortex land, but books ain't gonna fare well in water."

"I guess you have a point," I conceded with a sigh of frustration. "But how are we going to find out what's lying in wait for us in this part of the Underground now?"

"Cerberus," Tallis answered, glancing back at Bill and motioning for Bill's phone, which the angel was carrying in his right hand. Bill didn't say anything as he handed it to Tallis, who flipped it open and studied it for a few moments. He flipped it closed again and passed it back to Bill. "The soul is at the apex o' the sewer," he answered. "Nae doubt, bein' guarded by Cerberus."

"Cerberus?" I repeated. "As in the three-headed dog?" I could feel fear as it spiraled up inside me when I uttered the words.

"He doesna have three heads," Tallis responded.

"Then why did Dante say Cerberus had three heads?" I inquired, although I should have probably known better, seeing how familiar Tallis was with this place.

"'Tis jist another detail 'twas incorrect," Tallis responded. "Cerberus doesna have three heads, though he is ta be reckoned with, all the same." He took a breath and then looked back at me from over his shoulder. "He is the leader o' the pack o' demon dogs."

"What the hell kind o' dogs?" Bill asked.

"Demon dogs," Tallis answered. "They patrol the sewer an' tear at the damned."

"How much longer until we reach them?" I asked, my voice beginning to quake. I tried to remember my lesson from Tallis on how to remain calm. *Demon dogs, just like demon clowns, could be defeated*, I reminded myself. I breathed in for a few counts and out again for a few counts, remembering Tallis's instruction. But I wasn't sure if it helped.

"They patrol these toonnels," Tallis answered.

"So we could come across them anytime?" I asked.

He nodded. "Ah'd advise ye ta be prepared though the threat isnae so great as 'twill be at the center o' the aqueduct, where the souls o' the damned reside."

"An' how much further 'til we come across that fun little party?" Bill asked, kicking something in his way. It bounced off the brick wall with an echo.

"Bill, don't make so much noise!" I reprimanded him. "We don't want to broadcast our arrival!"

"Aye, we dinnae," Tallis concurred as he eyed us both. "The water level deepens here. Ye'd do well ta take plenty o' caution." The tunnel went downhill, and as I watched, the water level began to rise. I continued following Tallis with Bill behind me and tried to ignore the freezing temperature of the water as it rose up to my ankles, then my knees and finally, my upper thighs. The tunnel began to straighten out again and when it did, the water level was waist-high.

"How long is it going to be this high?" I whispered, but Tallis suddenly stopped walking and stood stock-still as he turned his head and appeared to be listening to something. He held up his right hand, indicating he didn't want either of us to continue forward or to say another word. I felt my heart drop all the way to my feet.

I doubt if I even had the chance to take one quick breath before the water in front of Tallis began to ripple. It looked as if something were swimming around in circles, directly in front of him. Tallis drew his blade and stood with it poised over his head. Moments later, something grey and circular burst through the water, and as I watched in horror, a creature emerged from the cesspool. The water dripped off its light grey, slimy skin, which looked like it was peeling off the creature's body in rivulets. The creature was nowhere near as tall as Tallis, but seemed about my height or maybe a few inches taller. It didn't have any hair, just a round orb for a head with two large, black cavities for eyes. Inside the black orbs, I could faintly detect two small pupils, which seemed to glow grey.

"Son of a bitch!" Bill screamed as soon as the thing fully revealed itself from beneath the water. "It's Aquaman! Aquademon!"

"We're oan Afterlife Enterprises business," Tallis announced, his voice steely, but calm. "We dinnae want any difficulties."

*I know who you are,* the creature responded even though it didn't have a visible mouth. It must have communicated with its thoughts, because I heard its voice in my head. I guessed its voice was sounding in Tallis's head too because his body language showed that he was listening to something. The thing's voice sounded strange— almost robotic.

"I think I'm gonna shit myself," Bill whispered. "I think I'm gonna shit myself. I think I'm gonna shit myself."

"Then grant oos passage," Tallis requested from the thing.

The thought that I probably should have been prepared for battle crossed my mind, and I drew my sword from its scabbard and held it aloft, ready to strike. I mean, who knew how many of these water creatures lived in the tunnel? The creature inclined its head toward my direction.

*I will not harm you,* it said in my mind before turning back to face Tallis again. *I have been sent by the keeper of the Underground City,* it continued. *He requests the favor of your company.*

"Like fuck we're gonna go visit the devil!"
Bill roared back. "You musta swallowed too much
o' this piss water, yo, 'cause this shit's messin'
with yer head!"

The creature simply glanced at Bill but said
nothing.

"We are here oan a mission," Tallis replied
tersely, in a controlled but annoyed tone. He was
still holding his sword although he was no longer
in striking stance. He must have believed to some
extent what the creature was saying.

*The master is aware, Bladesmith,* the creature
responded. *He will allow you to capture the soul
in peace, if, afterwards, you will agree to visit him
in his headquarters.*

Tallis was quiet for a few seconds. "As long
as Alaire will allow mah friends ta return ta the
Dark Wood oonharmed," he answered. "Then Ah
will go with ye."

The creature shook its head and looked at me.
*The master also requests an introduction to the
woman.*

"Nae," Tallis responded immediately. "Alaire
has nae business with her."

"That's right," Bill suddenly piped up. "Both
you and the devil want nothin' ta do with us.
We're just here ta get in and get out. We don't
want no trouble."

*The master is not interested in you,* the
creature responded before settling its attention on
me again, as if to say, Alaire was mostly interested
in meeting me. Why? I had no clue. Maybe he was

pissed off that his two clowns got killed during my first trip down here. Actually, the more I thought about it, the more that line of thinking made sense. Maybe Alaire was going to kill me in revenge for the deaths of his two henchmen?

*The master does not want to harm you,* the creature said as it stared at me. It was starting to freak me out because I wasn't sure if it had just read my mind and was now responding to my thoughts or what.

"Well, the maestro really shouldn't be too thrilled over Bubble Butt neither," Bill interrupted, shrugging. "She's just a touron," he continued. Then he glanced at me, nodding. "She's a mix 'tween a tourist and a moron. Girl's so dumb, she can't do nothin' to save her life. Seriously, the master dude wouldn't be missin' a single thing by not meetin' nips." He cocked his head to the side and his eyebrows reached for the ceiling as he started nodding again. "She reeeeeal dumb; know what I'm sayin'?"

*I am merely repeating the master's orders,* the creature announced, as if it had no interest in whether I was intelligent or not. The creature faced Tallis again. *I am to inform you that he will not harm her. He wishes only to make her acquaintance.*

"Why?" Tallis demanded.

The creature shook its head. *I was not entrusted with that information,* it responded.

"An' if Ah dinnae agree, what then?" Tallis barked.

*122*

*Then we cannot guarantee your protection or safety during your mission.* The thing glanced back at me. *Nor that of your fellow travelers.*

Tallis was quiet for a few seconds before he took a deep breath and simply nodded to the creature, indicating his consent. The creature turned around and started forward, moving through the sewage water as if it were swimming. I caught up with Tallis and gripped his forearm. "Why did you agree for us to meet Alaire?" I demanded.

"Yeah, that didn't sound like such a great idea to me neither," Bill piped up from behind me.

Tallis leaned down and whispered in my ear, "'Twas the only way ta guarantee yer safety, lass."

"You think meeting Alaire will guarantee our safety?" I repeated in a hushed tone, shaking my head. "You think we'll be any safer than if we just fulfilled our mission and got out, like our original plan?" I continued, clearly unconvinced. Bill, apparently disinterested in our conversation, lagged behind a few paces and I could hear him humming something I didn't recognize.

"Och aye," Tallis whispered back at me. "Alaire is merely curious 'bout ye, lass. We can troost his word."

"The word of the devil?" I snapped back at him. My eyes narrowed with skepticism as I shook my head, not getting how he could place any trust in someone who ruled the Underground.

Tallis shook his head as he studied me, a slight smile pulling at his lips. His smile made him downright handsome. "Alaire isnae the devil, Besom. He is merely the keeper o' the Oonderground. They are two verra different things."

"Regardless of what he is, are you sure he isn't going to want to get even with me? Don't forget, Ragur and Kipur were killed during my mission!" I responded, paranoia beginning to occupy my entire body. I just couldn't understand why Alaire, supposedly a pretty important person as head of the Underground, could be bothered with me, a nobody.

"Alaire doesnae care 'bout either o' the clowns, lass," Tallis answered while shaking his head. He stared at the creature in front of him, then on either side of the tunnel before focusing on me again.

"Then why did Alaire contact Afterlife Enterprises to report it?" I asked, keeping my eye on the water creature who was now a few strokes ahead of us. It was apparently leading the way to the apex of the sewer, where we would encounter Cerberus and the souls of the damned, or so I imagined.

"'Twas policy, Besom," Tallis responded. "Alaire reported it 'cause he had ta, 'tis all."

I shook my head, suspicious that there was more to the situation than what Tallis seemed to believe. "There's no reason for him to want to make my acquaintance," I continued. "I'm just another Regulator, interloping in his affairs and territory. I'm just another thorn in his backside and someone who should be of zero interest to him."

"Ye are innocent, lass," Tallis argued and shook his head as if I just wasn't getting it. "Alaire is as tainted as they come."

"So why the interest in someone innocent?" I continued.

"Aye, 'cause he is fascinated with anythin' ootside o' what he's used ta. Ye would simply be a plaything ta him, an amusement," Tallis finished.

"That's it?" I asked, my tone still doubtful. "You think he simply wants to meet me for that reason?"

"Aye."

"How would he even know who I am? Or that I'm … innocent in the first place? It's not like I've ever met the guy." It still seemed like Tallis was keeping something from me. His answer was too simple for it to be the whole truth.

"The Watchers," Tallis replied. Then I remembered the strange creatures that patrolled the Underground City and looked like businessmen wearing suits. They were Alaire's eyes, and reported back to him everything that happened in his city. They were comparable to the Underground's version of Big Brother.

"Oh, shit!" Bill called out. We had just emerged from the tunnel and found ourselves standing in the center of another enormous cavern. This, too, was made of brick and was circular, like the cesspool we'd just left.

But that's where the similarities ended.

Instead of an empty pool of sewage, now we faced hundreds of damned souls who were wallowing in sewage that was up to their waists. Meanwhile, a ceaseless barrage of rain bled from the brick ceiling and showered everyone below with putrid sewer water in droplets the size of quarters. The damned souls beneath could only writhe and scream as if suffering excruciating agony from the rain above. The main focus of my attention, however, was centered on the three snarling "dogs" that were headed toward us.

"What the hell are those?" Bill wailed out.

"With his three gullets like a dog is barking over
the people that are there submerged."
– Dante's *Inferno*

## SEVEN

"Demon dogs," Tallis replied as he held his
sword up in a defensive stance and pushed me
directly behind him. Reminding myself of Tallis's
lessons again, I breathed in for a few counts,
trying to calm my frantic heart and scan my
surroundings.

*Demon water creature directly in front of
Tallis*, I thought to myself. *Three demon dogs
standing in front of the water creature and all
seem lethal.* Glancing to my right and left, I
realized there was no way to escape the cavernous
room. I looked at the demon dogs again and
figured Tallis would go for the largest one in front,
leaving me to defend myself against the other two.
*If the need arises, Lily, just retreat until your back
is against the brick wall; then lash out at anything
that approaches you with your sword,* I strategized.
Tightening the grip on my sword, I breathed in
slowly for another few counts, readying myself for
the battle that was sure to ensue any minute.

The demon water creature that had led us thus
far faced the three demon dogs and held its watery,
grey arms open wide. Even though I couldn't hear

its voice in my head, I believed it was imparting its message and warning them that we must be left alone per Alaire's fiat. The two smaller demon dogs continued to snarl at us, but soon dropped behind the largest one that appeared to be the leader, and the one, which I supposed, was Cerberus.

It stood on all fours and was maybe the size of a Great Dane, although much leaner. It didn't have any ears that I could see, but its eyes glowed orange and its snout was long and very fierce looking. Its hideous mouth flashed enormous incisors. And its body was so thin, I could see every vertebra of its spine protruding from its back. It didn't have any fur at all, but rather, a light purplish-colored skin that was darker in some spots than others. There were areas on its ribs where the skin was either missing or translucent, revealing the redness of its flesh and muscle, as well as its bones, which glowed yellow.

The two demon dogs behind the larger one looked nothing like it. Both were smaller in stature and the one on the right had ears that stuck straight up from its head like a German shepherd. It was a greyish-brown color and its skin looked loose and pillowy, like it was wearing a bodysuit that was maybe two sizes too big. It also had no hair or fur, but its skin looked leathery, like an armadillo's, and its snout was long, terminating into a triangular, black nose between two glowing red eyes. Its fangs were just as enormous on both its lower and upper jaws.

The third demon dog looked least like a dog and more like a lizard. Its skin was a hide of scales that reflected all the colors of the rainbow, depending on how the low light of the cavern reflected off them. This creature also had sharply pointed ears and glowing eyes like the other smaller one, but its eyes were blue, not red. I could barely make out its nose because the scales were so prominent in its face that the lines of its nose just sort of faded away. Its mouth, however, was every bit as intimidating and sharp-fanged as its brethren.

The largest of the demon dogs, which finally stopped snarling, now examined each of us with keen interest as it took a few paces forward, studying us with large, strange, glowing orange eyes.

"I do not appreciate interruptions, Grashnelle," the dog suddenly announced to the water creature who still stood in front of Tallis and me.

"You can talk?" Bill cried out, sounding mildly amused. "Rad! I feel like we're in a Disney movie!" I gave him a look, shaking my head as I wondered if he'd ever seen a Disney movie. Judging by the hideous creatures standing before us, which were anything but charming and lovable, I'd say no. Bill sighed and shrugged. "Well, a screwed-up Disney movie, but whatevs."

The dog glared at Bill, its glowing orange eyes adopting a deeper ginger hue. "And I definitely don't appreciate angels in my territory,"

it said with a snarl as it looked over at Grashnelle.
I supposed that was the water creature's name. Of
course, Grashnelle didn't say anything that was
audible, and again, I figured he must've been
conversing in thought, rather than speech, because
there were long, silent pauses where no one said
anything at all.

"I don't care what Alaire wants!" the demon
dog suddenly barked out angrily, in response to
whatever Grashnelle said, albeit silently. "He
should have shown me the respect to inform me of
this himself!" he continued. The dog's voice was
deep, gravelly, and very enraged. When it spoke, it
vacillated between words and barks, as if it were
speaking two different languages at the same time.

"We dinnae want any trouble, Cerberus,"
Tallis announced, his tone low, but hard as steel.
The enormous demon dog looked at him and
narrowed its eyes as its canine mouth lifted into a
warped smile that instantly caused my stomach to
turn on itself.

"I know you well enough to know that isn't
the case, Bladesmith," Cerberus responded, its
eyes narrowing as soon as they rested on Tallis. A
spark of recognition flashed through its gaze, and
immediately, they seemed to cloud with anger.
"Trouble always finds you, no matter how hard
you try to avoid it."

Tallis's posture went suddenly rigid and he
tightened his grasp on his sword. He didn't say
anything, but he didn't have to—his body

language conveyed that he was obviously bothered by Cerberus's comment.

My attention shifted to Grashnelle when the creature lifted its hands in the air almost in frustration. It was, presumably, still explaining to Cerberus that we had permission to do our business without threat of being harmed per Alaire's orders. Cerberus just listened to the watery, grey creature while eyeing each of us skeptically. A low growl sounded from its mouth. Then it looked at Tallis again. "Bladesmith, as I seem to have little choice in the matter, I give you permission to retrieve your soul," it spat out. Then, its lips peeled back into a snarl as it showed off multiple rows of sharp teeth. It glared at Tallis for another few seconds before the snarl vanished from its face. "I am not pleased to do so."

"Cerberus," Tallis responded as he lowered his head slightly in what I imagined was his way of saying "thank you." He resheathed his sword, turning to face me as he nodded, indicating that it was okay to put my sword away as well.

Cerberus barked at his canine companions a few times before they turned around and padded back into the muck of sewage at the center of the room from which they'd emerged. Cerberus made no sign to retreat, but continued standing where he was, blocking our path to the sewer's vortex.

Tallis faced Bill. "Yer phone," he said. Bill handed Tallis the phone and the much larger man studied it for a few moments before handing it back to Bill again. Then he faced Cerberus. "The soul is in the vestibule," he announced as he crossed his arms over his chest. Apparently, he was waiting for Cerberus to step aside.

Cerberus, however, made no motion to step aside, but merely nodded stiffly before turning around and trotting down the brick path that led to the cesspool. The raining sewage continued to pelt the damned, who whined and cried as they swam through the pool of feces, moaning pitifully. When Cerberus reached the sewage, he growled at two souls who were in his way. The souls, in response, doubled over on themselves in their attempt to get away from him. But since the muck in the pool was so viscous and gluey, they didn't get very far.

Cerberus didn't seem to notice though, but discourteously pushed past the two souls before simply jumping into the cesspool and demon dog-paddling to the center. I watched the damned as they attempted to clear a path for him, pushing and pulling at each other in the sticky goo, all the while trying to get away. But, as with the other two souls, none of them could manage to get very far; and seemed mired in place, getting stung by the disgusting rain overhead as the tar-like sewage held them captive.

Cerberus paid them little attention. Once reaching the center of the cesspool, he simply dove into the putrid water, his head fully disappearing under the dark brown muck. Unlike the souls, Cerberus appeared to move fluidly through the sewage, as if its tackiness didn't affect him. The other two demon dogs continued to

patrol the cesspool from the brick pathway beside
it, where they could escape from the pelting rain
overhead. Whenever a soul moved too close to
one of them, the demon dogs lashed out with
gnashing teeth and long, pointed claws.

Despite searching the tumultuous sea of
sewage for any sign of Cerberus, I didn't see him.
The seconds seemed to drag on as I watched the
demon dogs continue making their rounds,
harassing the damned. Meanwhile, Grashnelle
stood in front of us silently, apparently waiting for
us to retrieve the lost soul so he could lead us
directly to Alaire.

Cerberus finally appeared above the sewage
again, seemingly minutes later. He paddled
through the feces pool and shook himself off as
soon as he climbed out of the muck and onto the
brick pathway. I wondered why the noxious sewer
fumes no longer bothered me and could only
deduce that maybe I was just growing accustomed
to them. At any rate, my attention was rerouted to
Cerberus's mouth when I noticed his jaws were
slightly open. It almost looked like he was panting.
As soon as he came closer to us, though, I realized
something was inside his mouth, glowing. When
he reached Tallis, he sat back on his haunches and
Tallis pulled a vial from his sporran. Tallis popped
the cap of the vial and held it in front of Cerberus,
who poked his snout into the tip of it, opening his
mouth as widely as he could. The white light,
which turned out to be our lost soul, gladly moved

into the vial as Tallis replaced the cork cap and returned the vial into his sporran.

One of the riddles I was unable to solve was why the souls who were mistakenly routed to the Underground City appeared as small, white, glowing balls; while the souls of the damned were very detailed, making it easy to distinguish their faces and even some of their features. It was another question I had to add on my long list for Tallis. But now was clearly not the time.

"Thank ye, Cerberus," Tallis said as he nodded toward the enormous, ugly dog.

Cerberus eyed Tallis narrowly, but didn't say anything more as he trotted back down the pathway, still growling at the damned souls closest to him.

*Very well, we shall now travel on to the master*, Grashnelle's voice suddenly sounded in my head.

None of us said anything, but Tallis silently nodded and started forward, pushing me behind him with his right arm. Bill followed me and pretty soon, the four of us were walking single-file like kids on a field trip. The water was still up to my thighs, which made walking a little more difficult.

The tunnel continued straight for maybe a quarter of a mile. When it finally turned slightly to the right, I noticed it led into an expansive, open area where there was nothing but vast brick floors and walls. There wasn't any water in this area at all. It was almost as if the sewage water in the

tunnel was restrained by an invisible dam. The
water level went from being thigh-high to
completely nonexistent as soon as we entered the
open breadth of the cavern.

Looking ahead of us, I noticed a fairly large
pipe sticking out from the center of the cavern's
wall. It was to our left and the entrance into the
pipe was probably five feet above ground level. A
ladder leaned against the opening of the pipe, and
I had the sinking feeling that this was our exiting
point.

*That tunnel will lead you out of the sewer and
onto the mainland*, Grashnelle said, affirming my
hunch. *I am not able to continue as your guide*, he
finished while motioning to his lower body, which
was still submerged in the foul sewer water, right
up to his waist. I supposed he meant that since his
bottom half was basically a fish, he couldn't
continue to guide us over the land. *Bladesmith, are
you familiar enough with the Underground City to
find your way to the master's headquarters?*

"Aye," Tallis responded quickly, as if he were
uncomfortable with his familiarity with the
Underground City. Whatever the reason, his
discomfort seemed strange to me—if he'd been
retrieving souls for a while in the Underground
(which he obviously had been,) why would he be
uncomfortable? Without another glance at
Grashnelle, Tallis started for the tunnel pipe,
which, apparently, led out of the sewer aqueduct.

"It's been real, yo," Bill piped up behind me,
addressing Grashnelle. The water creature didn't

respond, but simply spun around until it was facing the way that we'd just come. It dove down, disappearing into the murky sewage water below. "That was a cool dude," Bill continued, glancing back at me as he nodded. "I mean, his skin's a little messed up, but I bet a dermatologist could fix that."

"Um, he was a demon, Bill," I pointed out.

Bill frowned and waved a pudgy hand dismissively. "You gotta be an equal opportunist, hot cheeks. Demons need love too, ya know?"

"Besom," Tallis interrupted, grabbing my attention as I faced forward again. He'd already reached the tunnel leading out of the sewer and climbed up the ladder. Now, he stood facing me expectantly, just beyond the opening to the tunnel.

"How'd you get up there so fast?" I asked, shaking my head in wonder.

"Ah choose not ta dilly-dally," Tallis responded, frowning at Bill and me in turn.

I ran the full length of the cavern that separated us. When I reached him, Tallis leaned over, placing both of his hands on either side of my waist and lifted me up to the level of the pipe. When he set me on my feet, he didn't release me right away and we just sort of looked at one another … awkwardly. "Thanks," I said, not really knowing what else to say, but the longer he held onto me, the more uncomfortable I felt. Tallis cleared his throat, seemingly remembering that his hands were still on my hips, and released me immediately. Then, without another word, he turned around and dropped down on his hands and knees as he entered the tunnel. Yep, it was another small one that required us to crawl.

"What about me?" Bill demanded, whistling and waving at Tallis before looking up at me wistfully. "Isn't Tido Swayze gonna Jennifer Grey me too?"

I figured he must have been referring to the finale of the dance sequence in *Dirty Dancing*. I glanced ahead at Tallis, who was already making his way into the tunnel before turning back to Bill while shaking my head. "I don't think so."

Bill sighed deeply as if it were a big shame, but started for the ladder leading up to the tunnel. "Nobody puts Billy in the corner," he muttered as he hoisted himself up the rungs. The ladder creaked beneath his burdensome weight. Taking a whiff of his underarms, he faced me with his eyes widened and his eyebrows reaching for the brick ceiling. "I thought I'd never say this, but shit, I'm really lookin' forward to bathin'."

"You're telling me," I mumbled as I started for the inside of the pipe, getting onto my hands and knees with Bill just behind me.

"Nice ass, Lils!" he said and catcalled behind me as his halo lit the inside of the tunnel. There wasn't any sewer water to speak of, thankfully.

"Bill, really?" I asked as I tried not to focus on how sore my palms and knees were from the seemingly incessant tunnel crawl.

"You know," Bill continued, "you could friend flash me?"

"Oh my God," I retorted.

"That's not against the rules," he argued. "Gimme a little flash of your big ol' titties or maybe even some ..."

"Enough!" I interrupted him. When I heard Tallis chuckling, I swatted him right on the butt. "And you quit it! You're just encouraging him!"

"Ah apologize, lass," he said, a laugh still evident in his voice.

I wasn't sure how long the three of us crawled through the pipe, but probably not as long as it seemed. Maybe ten minutes, although it felt more like an hour. Bill's halo continued to light our way and I had to admit I was more than happy for it. Navigating the tunnels would have been a thousand times worse if we had to crawl through them in the pitch black.

"Are ye all right, Besom?" Tallis asked in a soft voice.

"I think so," I replied, although I wasn't sure if I were being completely honest. The strain of my emotional responses to everything we'd experienced thus far was definitely taking its toll on me. I was exhausted; and it was a type of fatigue which wouldn't permit my body to unwind. Instead, my instincts were still on full alert, only taxing my weary body even more. It was difficult to stay ready for anything—and constantly be "on" just in case some hideous creature or creatures ambushed us.

Tallis suddenly stopped moving, and I must not have been paying attention because my head rammed right into his backside. His wool kilt felt like it gave my cheek a rug burn.

"Besom, watch where yer goin'!" he railed at me without any real anger in his tone. It seemed more as if it were just for show. I didn't say anything when I noticed that our pipe was blocked by an enormous iron plate that occupied the end of the tunnel. Tallis, seemingly unconcerned that our path suddenly ended, reached for what looked like a giant handle, which popped out from the top of the plate. It reminded me of the steel plates you often see on roads in the middle of construction.

"Is the way to the mainland through there?" I asked, deciding to ignore the fact that I'd very nearly sodomized Tallis with the end of my sword.

"Aye," he answered, and it was plainly obvious that all of his focus was currently on turning the handle on the iron cover in order to open it. He gritted his teeth, his lips going white as he pulled against the handle as hard as he could. The veins in his neck looked like they were about to burst. But when the plate suddenly made a popping sound, I realized Tallis was successful.

"Hmm, seems your brawn is good for something," I said with a teasing laugh. Tallis looked at me and seemed surprised that I was joking with him. 'Course, having never joked around with or teased him in the past, I wasn't sure why I was doing so now.

"Aye, an' Ah am still waitin' ta see what benefit yer constant blabbin' will offer oos," he responded as he reached higher and slid the top of the plate off. I was so intrigued to learn where we now were that I didn't even stop to ponder Tallis's lack of social graces, specifically flirting. Instead, I watched him push himself through the opening before disappearing from the tunnel. His hand reappeared in the pipe when he reached down for me, and I took it. With that, he pulled me up and out of the tunnel, right back into the dark night of the Underground City.

Glancing around, I realized I didn't recognize our whereabouts. We were standing in the middle of a street with nothing but pavement and nondescript buildings on either side of us. There wasn't a sign of greenery—no plants or trees—because nothing could grow in the Underground City.

As soon as Bill poked his head out of the tunnel, huffing and puffing as he pulled himself up to street level, I heard the rumblings of what sounded like a motor. I spun around and noticed an electric blue, sporty-looking car that pulled up alongside us. Its windows were tinted so dark that I couldn't make out who or what the driver was. It probably also didn't help that there was no daylight in the Underground. It was always and perpetually night.

"Shit!" Bill called out with a whoop as he noticed the car. "That's a Jag XKR-S! That's sick!" he said, shaking his head in wonder. "That shit's easily over a hundred thousand clams!"

In response, the car, a two-door coupe that reminded me of a Porsche, opened both of its doors. As soon as it did, I noticed that there was no one sitting in the driver's seat. "Um," I said, eyeing Tallis, and wondering what we were supposed to do.

"Shit's haunted!" Bill screamed, taking a few steps back, and shaking his head. Then he held his hands out straight in front of him, as if he wanted to keep the car at bay. When Tallis took a few steps towards the car and we realized that he intended to get in, Bill started shaking his head furiously. "There's no way in hell I'm gettin' in ta some haunted ass car. I've already seen *Christine*, thank you very much. I ain't interested in experiencin' it!"

Seemingly in response, the Jag revved its engine and rolled forward about a foot. It was pretty obvious that the vehicle wanted us to get inside it. I looked up at Tallis and swallowed hard as I wondered what his reaction would be. He simply nodded as if to say the car wasn't a threat; and then as if to prove his point, knelt down and adjusted his sword so it wouldn't get in his way. Then he took his seat behind the wheel. "Git in," he said to Bill who continued to shake his head.

"Bill, it's either that or we walk to wherever Alaire's headquarters are," I started as I crossed my arms against my chest. "Shall I describe all the scary things that live in the Underground City for you?"

Bill cocked his head to the side as if he were considering my comment before nodding with a deep sigh and approaching the car with keener interest. Without saying a word, he climbed over the center console and sort of rolled into the backseat. Holding the end of my sword out, so it wouldn't get stuck as I sat down, I took the passenger seat. The doors on the Jag immediately closed, and before I could take another breath, the motor revved and we were off. I glanced over to see if Tallis was driving the car, but it didn't appear that he was. Instead, he leaned back into his seat and crossed his arms over his chest. His legs were spread wide and his knees pulled all the way up to his chin in order to fit behind the seat. He actually looked pretty ridiculous because the tiny sports car was way too confining for him.

The car seemed to go from zero to sixty in only a few seconds. I watched the speedometer hike from sixty to seventy to eighty and then ninety. It gripped the road remarkably well as it took a few turns, and the scenery outside my window faded into a blur.

"Seatbelt, nips!" Bill called out from the backseat as I heard him buckling himself in. I immediately nodded and reached for the belt, securing it across my chest and lap, just as the car came to a screeching halt and smoke wafted up from the tires. With my heart in my throat, I glanced over at Tallis to make sure he was okay, and caught him already looking at me with a smile on his face.

"Aye, perhaps Ah will git one o' these fer mahself," he said with a chuckle as he ran his hands around the leather-wrapped steering wheel.

"To drive in your forest?" Bill piped up, shaking his head. "You need a four-by, dude." Then he started nodding vigorously. "Screw that; you know what you need? You need ta move!" Then he started rubbing his chest as if it were sore. "Dude, this frickin' car gave me niplash."

The doors to the Jag suddenly opened, indicating that we'd arrived at our destination. I unbuckled myself and stood up, pulling my seat forward so Bill wouldn't have to climb over the center console again. Then I turned around and noticed we were now parked in front of another high-rise building, surrounded by more concrete and asphalt. This part of the Underground looked exactly like the part we'd just left. Now, however, I noticed there were many more Watchers, walking back and forth, paying particular attention to us.

Watchers looked like mummies, well, that is if someone were to unwrap a mummy from its cocoon. They didn't have any hair and the skin on their faces looked like spaghetti. They dressed in business suits and patrolled the Underground, and were generally considered to be Alaire's eyes.

The moonlight overhead seemed to spotlight us as Tallis reached for my hand and pulled me up close behind him. Then we started for the building directly ahead of us. It was a good six stories high and the only lights that were on came from the very top floor.

"Besom, dinnae show any weakness when ye meet Alaire," Tallis whispered down to me, tucking me in tightly beside him.

"We passed across the shadows, which subdues
the heavy rain-storm."
– Dante's *Inferno*

# EIGHT

As to Alaire's "headquarters," it looked like
some sort of high-end office building. When we
walked through the front doors, I immediately
noticed the circular interior of the building and
then the floors. They looked like a checkerboard,
courtesy of alternating black and white marble
tiles. In the center of the room were six concrete
columns that formed a circle around what I
supposed was the lobby desk. The columns
extended all the way up to the sixth and top floor.
We continued past the lobby desk which,
coincidentally, wasn't being manned by anyone.
The fluorescent lights overhead bathed the room
in a strange, unnatural glow and the fake plants
decorating the walkway to the bank of elevators
added a level of plastic to the room. The walls in
the hallway were painted blue and interrupted with
white, wispy brush strokes which reminded me of
clouds. I couldn't shake the feeling that whoever
was in charge of the interior design of the building
clearly missed foliage and warm summer days.
This was merely a cheap reproduction.

Tallis pushed the button to call the elevator, looking completely out of place in his kilt, sporran, and "Jesus" shoes. With his sword strapped across his chest, he looked more like a Highlander birthday gram sent to some lucky lady.

"Where the hell is everybody?" Bill asked as he glanced around and shrugged. "It's like we just walked into the *Twilight Zone* or some shit."

Bill had a good point. We hadn't seen one person, creature, or demon inside the building since stepping foot into it. No one was working behind the desk in the lobby, and so far, the only "people" we encountered were the Watchers who continued to patrol outside. Tallis didn't respond and just stared straight ahead, expressionless.

"Is this an office building?" I asked Tallis after I couldn't stand his silence any longer. My nerves were on high alert and my heart was beating so quickly, I was afraid it might shut down from fatigue.

"Aye," he answered finally, his jaw so tight it looked like he might crack a molar. His eyes were narrowed and troubled as he stared straight ahead while we awaited the elevator. I almost felt like Tallis had forgotten that Bill and I were even there. His entire posture was completely rigid, which put me on edge. Whenever Tallis seemed uncomfortable about something, there was usually a very good reason for it.

The elevator doors dinged as they opened wide and the three of us stepped inside. Tallis hit the button for the sixth floor and none of us said another word as we passed all the floors, ending on the sixth. I was too nervous and anxious to speak, and instead, just focused on the interior of the elevator, feeling strangely detached from myself. It was almost as if I were watching a movie of someone who looked like the new Lily Harper as she rode the elevator in silence, wondering what possible fate awaited her on the sixth floor. I figured that was due to the intense stress my body was experiencing.

"Dudes, my gut's startin' ta feel funny," Bill said as he frowned at me and rubbed his stomach. "It's all rumbling like it's cranky an' shit."

"You're probably just nervous," I said, feeling something similar in my own stomach. I tried to smile at Bill in order to console him, but my lips were twitching with uncontrollable nervousness so I was pretty sure my smile came out as more of a wince.

"Pro'lly right," Bill responded as he swallowed hard and faced me again. "I guess meetin' the head honcho of hell makes you feel all bloated almost like you got the shit sweats, ya know?"

I just nodded, trying to ignore the "shit sweats" as well as my own unraveling sanity. I decided to ask Tallis more about the building again. "If this is an office building, how come no one is working here?" I asked. "Is it nighttime or something?"

"'Tis always night," he answered stonily, still facing forward and giving off the appearance of someone who didn't want to be bothered answering silly questions. Well, I was two steps away from having a mental breakdown because I was so tense about this meeting with Alaire, so I didn't care if Tallis didn't want to talk to me.

"Right," I said as I wondered if there was a better way to phrase my question. "Well, is it past working hours right now or something?"

"Noo one works in headquarters, lass, as Alaire has verra few visitors," Tallis replied quickly as he turned to face me with an expression of impatience. Clearly, he was preoccupied with other things.

"Hmm," I said with a frown. "Then why does he have his own office at the top of the building if no one works here? That seems a little strange to me."

"Ye an' yer bludy questions," Tallis grumbled before eyeing me quickly with a discouraging frown. Facing the elevator doors again, the elevator stopped and a second or so later, it dinged, indicating that we'd reached the sixth floor. "Alaire is naethin' boot pomp an' circumstance, lass," he answered hurriedly as he started forward with Bill and me following close behind him. He glanced back at me and his jaw was tighter than before. "Remember, Besom, show nae weakness."

I inhaled deeply without responding to his warning because I was too busy trying to calm my frantically beating heart. Taking deep breaths, I reminded myself of Tallis's lessons, breathing in deeply for a count of five and exhaling deeply for a count of five. Amazingly enough, my breathing exercises did manage to alleviate some of the anxiety now flowing through me.

Bill and I followed Tallis out of the elevator and down the hallway, which led to a pair of double doors painted glossy black. The hallway was about six feet wide with charcoal grey walls and black lacquered hardwood flooring. It gave the place a clean, modern sort of look. Very obviously lacking, however, was any artwork on the walls, or any windows.

When we reached the double doors, Tallis took a breath and rapped on one door with his knuckles. His shoulders were so tight, they actually appeared narrower than usual. "Alaire," he called out. His tone seemed caustic, almost abrasive.

There wasn't a response right away, but a few seconds later, the right door began to open on its own accord. Tallis stood up straight and placed his hand on the hilt of his sword, but didn't unsheathe it. With the other hand, he gripped my arm and pulled me closely behind him. I had the sudden desire to unsheathe my sword. So, figuring I should go with my gut instinct, I pulled my sword out. I held it with the tip facing down as I followed Tallis through the door, with Bill just behind me.

"Ah, the Bladesmith," a man's voice rang out from the far side of the room as soon as we entered it. The voice was deep and slightly accented, sounding almost Scandinavian.

"Alaire," Tallis said without inclining his head. His tone of voice was flat; and judging by the way he was holding his shoulders, he appeared to be very uncomfortable.

"It has been too long," Alaire said as he stood up from his Henry Miller-looking swivel chair. He was sitting behind a large, black desk in a room that shared the same dark tones as the hallway. The walls were painted the same dark charcoal, and the only thing brightening the space was the spotlighting that was inlaid into the ceiling. Two large, black couches sat before Alaire's desk, and just beyond them was an enormous pool table. It, too, was painted black and had black felt lining. Above the pool table hung three crystal chandeliers. But what I found most interesting were the framed prints hanging on the wall. They were images of 1940's pin-up girls. The other three walls didn't display any pictures because they were comprised of multiple floor-to-ceiling windows that revealed panoramic views of most of the Underground City.

"You're the devil?" Bill asked, in a tone of voice that echoed the doubt in my own mind. Even though Alaire obviously wasn't the devil, he didn't exactly look as though he were the keeper of the Underground either. He had blond hair, which was cut short, large blue eyes, tan skin, freckles on the bridge of his nose, and dimples on either side of his mouth that made him look decidedly handsome. There was a charming youthfulness about him as well, and I guessed he couldn't be much older than thirty-five. His height was impressive (standing almost as tall as Tallis) and his body was trim and muscular, judging by the swell of his biceps when he crossed his arms over his chest. He was wearing dark black slacks and a crisp, dark grey, collared shirt that contrasted nicely with his bright hair and white teeth. The first few buttons of his collar were unbuttoned, exposing his tan skin beneath.

"I am hardly the devil," Alaire answered, his voice sounding amused. With another practiced smile, his gaze settled on me. "And you must be Ms. Harper," he said the words softly as he strode up toward me and reached for my hand. As I beheld the smooth skin of his fingers, something inside me cracked. Before I even understood what I was doing, I drew my sword in a fraction of a second, resting it right at Alaire's throat. Apparently, I had deftly perfected the art of putting my enemy "on point." The surprised expression that registered in Alaire's eyes was priceless.

"What the hell, Lily!" Bill railed out at me, his tone revealing his shock. "You've lost your flippin' mind!"

However, my attention wasn't on Bill, but it was narrowed on Alaire as he speared me with his gaze, his mouth lifting up into a smile. His smile conveyed that he wasn't threatened by the fact that I could run my sword him through at any minute. It was a smile that promised he had other tricks up his sleeve. I didn't drop my sword, but continued to hold it at his throat. As smooth and handsome as this man was, he was also the embodiment of corruption and malevolence. He symbolized everything the Underground City stood for, and because of that, I hated him.

"My, my," he started in a low pitch as he studied me, his smile growing wider. "She is even lovelier than the preliminary reports alleged," he started as he studied my face. "Isn't that so, Black?" he asked Tallis, although his attention never left my face.

When Tallis didn't respond, I did. "I don't know why you ordered us here," I said, in an acidic tone. I was surprised by my own courage and rather proud of myself, even though I was well aware that this moment could be my last. I was pretty sure that Alaire wasn't accustomed to being addressed in such an impudent manner.

He chuckled, seemingly uncaring that my blade was resting on his carotid artery. "I thought Grashnelle informed you, my beautiful lady, that I wished only to make your acquaintance." He smiled even more broadly as he brought his hand to the blade of my sword. "As we are both civilized individuals, perhaps we can continue this dance without your sword pressed against my throat?" Without waiting for a response, he simply pushed the blade down. I allowed the tip of the sword to drop onto the floor, but wondered what Alaire's next move would be, and whether or not I'd live through it. For all I knew, maybe he was really an *uber*demon that could destroy me with no more than a glance.

"Please don't kill her, dude," Bill said as he took a step forward and stuck out his lower lip, looking like he was about to cry. "She's completely lost it, yo! Either that or she's like channelin' the ghost of Xena or some shit." He glanced at me and shook his head, as if he still couldn't believe the stunt I just pulled. "I ain't never seen her do nothin' like this before, man."

Alaire reached for my hand again, and this time was quick and firm as he took it. His eyes never left mine as he brought my hand to his face. "I have no plans to kill her," Alaire answered Bill, although his attention remained on me. "On the contrary, I quite enjoy her ... gumption."

"Oh," Bill said. "Then, Lils, pretend ta slice his throat off again so's we can get the hells outta here, for chrissake!"

"We've done what you asked," I said to Alaire between my clenched teeth.

"Yes, you have," he said while continuing to study me as if I were a rare painting. He brought my hand to his mouth, but instead of kissing it, just closed his eyes and inhaled the scent of my skin. A smile glossed over his lips as he did so, giving him the expression of someone high on drugs. "She smells of the ocean air and warm sunshine." He opened his eyes and studied me. All I wanted to do was yank my hand away from him. "That is a scent I have not experienced, in ... oh, a good three thousand years at the very least."

I gulped, unable to form another response.

"Alaire, we've done yer biddin'," Tallis suddenly piped up, apparently ill at ease with Alaire's affectionate ministrations. Perhaps, nearly as much as I was.

"Yes, you have, Black," Alaire answered as he seemed to gather his senses about him again. Dropping my hand, he turned to face Tallis.

"Then we will be oan our way," Tallis finished, eyeing Alaire narrowly.

"Tallis Black, is that any way to treat an old friend?" Alaire asked with a counterfeit smile.

"Ye are nae friend o' mine," Tallis responded as he folded his gargantuan arms across his chest and frowned.

"Perhaps not now, but you and I share a similar past, one which you cannot deny," Alaire continued as he approached the pool table and pulled a cue stick off the wall. He picked up the cue chalk, which was sitting on the edge of the pool table, and chalked the tip of his cue, the blue chalk powdering into a small pile of debris between his feet. "Much though you do not wish to admit it, Black, you and I are cut from the same cloth."

"You and the Yeti know each other?" Bill demanded, his face contorting into a confused frown.

Alaire faced Tallis and chuckled. "Yeti?" Then he cocked his head to the side and nodded. "Original." He put the cue chalk down and faced Tallis again. "One game of billiards, old friend, and you and your comrades can proceed on your way."

"Ah dinnae care ta play with ye," Tallis responded, shaking his head as he eyed me with what appeared to be intense concern.

Alaire nodded and faced me. "Perhaps you, Ms. Harper, would care to join me then, in lieu of your fellow traveler?"

Tallis took a few steps forward and gripped one of the cue sticks from the wall, apparently wanting to play more than he wanted me to. "One game," he announced tersely.

Alaire simply nodded, his attention still riveted on me. "I must admit, Ms. Harper, that I am curious as to the nature of your … acquaintanceship with the so-called Yeti."

"'Tis none o' yer business," Tallis piped up.

But Alaire didn't drop his gaze from my face. Instead, he pretended like he didn't hear Tallis. "Please enlighten me, Ms. Harper. Is the Bladesmith your guardian? Or perhaps … your lover?"

I swallowed hard and didn't respond because I didn't know what Tallis expected me to say. Well, referring to the guardian part, that is.

"Aye, Ah'm the guardian o' the lass," Tallis announced firmly.

Alaire shook his head, but the smug smile didn't vanish from his mouth. "Hmm, based on your reaction, Ms. Harper, I do not know if such is truly the case." Then he inhaled for a few counts. "Of course, I was merely teasing you about the lover bit." The smile dropped right off his face then. "I could sense that your pristine innocence is still very much intact."

My stomach felt like it dropped to the floor; and suddenly, I became unnaturally self-conscious. Alaire chuckled, apparently at my clumsy silence, and then smiled at me again. "Although I do find it interesting that an innocent, such as yourself, is able to breathe the tainted air of my city without experiencing a very … uncomfortable death?" He narrowed his eyes as he studied me. "I can only hypothesize that you must have contaminated yourself with the blood of one who is not quite so innocent?" Then he glanced at Tallis before his eyes found mine again. I chose not to respond and, with a shrug, Alaire refocused on Tallis. "Why don't you break, Bladesmith?"

Tallis didn't say anything as he pulled the scabbard holding his sword over his head and leaned it against the wall. Then he approached the pool table and began racking up the balls. He reached for the cue ball, and standing with his left foot forward, I noticed he held the cue with his left hand. He turned his body slightly away from the table and leaned into the shot. He hit the rack of balls and they all scattered in different directions over the table before the solid yellow "1" ball sunk into a pocket.

Alaire nodded and when it was his turn, he eyed the table meticulously for a few seconds before leaning into his shot and sinking the orange and white "13" ball. Then he nodded with pleasure as he walked around to the other side of the table. As he did so, he glanced at Bill. "To answer your question, angel, yes, the 'Yeti' as you so irreverently refer to our mutual friend, and I come from a similar background."

"And what background would that be?" I demanded, throwing my hands on my hips. I couldn't understand what Alaire wanted from us, or why he was insisting that Tallis play pool when it was obvious the Scotsman didn't want to play. That and I was still uncomfortable about the fact that he'd basically smelled my virginity and had the gall to announce it.

"I am pleased you asked, my very lovely guest," Alaire said as he stood up. Even though he'd been about to take his next shot, he rotated his body so he could face me. He studied me for a few moments with an undeniable expression of lust in his eyes. It made me feel sick to my stomach. "Both the Bladesmith and I were warriors once upon a time," Alaire started. "Though Tallis came from present day Scotland, I am of Swedish descent." So, I was correct in my hunch that his barely there accent was of Scandinavian ancestry.

"So, dude, you were like, what? A Viking?" Bill asked, awe suffusing his tone.

Alaire smiled as he faced the pool table again and took his shot, this time sinking the red and white striped "11" ball. He chalked his cue before continuing with his story. "Quite so, angel, quite so."

"That's rad!" Bill said with a wide smile. "I just saw that movie *Thor* like a few weeks ago. Bad ass!"

Alaire didn't respond, but raised his eyebrows as he returned to his game of pool. Taking another shot, he promptly sunk the yellow and white "9" ball.

"So you were a raider and a marauder," I piped up, irritated to find Bill looking at Alaire like he was some kind of hero. He wasn't. "So what? Why should that have anything to do with Tallis at all?" Then I frowned at Bill. "And for your information, Bill, *Thor* had absolutely nothing to do with Vikings."

Alaire turned around to face me with a wide grin. "So much anger for such a small, pretty creature!" Then he chuckled. "Yes, you are quite right, Ms. Harper, I was not a noble savage, by any stretch of the imagination. Instead, it is fair to say that I plundered, raped, and killed; and what was more, I enjoyed every minute of it." His arrogant smile suddenly sickened me. "Perhaps it was that very training that prepared me for this post," he finished. I figured he must've been referring to his title of Keeper of the Underground City. "Would you agree, Black?" he made a point of asking Tallis, who suddenly seemed uncomfortable but didn't respond.

"I don't care about your history," I interjected as I eyed Tallis and wondered why he was putting up with Alaire in the first place. Tallis didn't strike me as a man who did anything he didn't want to do, which made the whole visit even stranger.

"For someone who very nearly found herself in hot water after the deaths of two of my employees, you speak with great conviction, Ms. Harper," Alaire barked at me, his harsh expression revealing his irritation.

"That situation was handled by Afterlife Enterprises," I spat back at him. I wasn't able to keep the anger from my tone even though I started to quake with nerves on the inside. Maybe I was right all along—maybe Alaire's whole purpose for this meeting was to avenge the deaths of Ragur and Kipur. Perhaps he was just playing a game of cat and mouse until he was ready to kill me.

I wasn't sure exactly when I lost track, but when I next looked down at the pool table, I realized Alaire had only one striped ball left, number 14, which he sunk almost as quickly as I'd recognized it was the last one. After he announced which pocket he would sink the black "8" ball in, he did exactly that. He stood up straight and turned to face Tallis with a broad smile. "Good game," he announced before looking at me again. "My dear Ms. Harper," he started and I felt my teeth gnashing together, hating the sound of my name on his tongue. "When next you visit my humble city, I do hope you will grant me the honor of being my guest for dinner."

I felt my eyes growing wide at the same time I saw Tallis and observed a frown marring his features. He gritted his teeth and his hands fisted at his sides. I glanced back at Alaire and shook my head. "No."

He shrugged as if "no" wasn't the answer he expected. "If you merely consent to dine with me, Ms. Harper, I will guarantee you safe passage in my city." Then he eyed Tallis. "As I am almost certain, the Bladesmith will not be available to travel with you during every one of your missions, be he your guardian or not." He said the last sentence with a slight laugh, insinuating that he didn't believe Tallis was truly my guardian.

"I would rather try my own luck," I said, my faith invested wholeheartedly in my words.

Alaire shrugged. "Very well, but in case you change your mind, please give me a call." He walked over to his desk and retrieved a business card, which he handed to me. It was black and glossy and the only thing written on it was three numbers: 666.

"Funny," I said without any semblance of humor.

"I do hope you will accept my invitation, Ms. Harper," Alaire continued. "As it would certainly upset me if I were to find you ripped to shreds by one of my watchful demons."

I swallowed hard because I couldn't help it. But I didn't say anything more.

"Very well," Alaire finished as he clapped his hands together like he was ready to take his leave. "The car downstairs will drive you to the gates of the Underground, thereby allowing you to avoid any of my least pleasant citizens."

I nodded, but didn't comment. Instead, I started for the double doors of his office, now way beyond eager to get the hell away from him. I noticed Bill was right behind me. When I turned to inquire where Tallis was, he closed the gap between Alaire and himself and was now speaking in a hushed tone. I couldn't make out what Tallis's question was, but Alaire's response was loud. "I'm afraid the answer was no, Bladesmith," he said as he shook his head and pretended to seem compassionate. Then he shrugged. "I did try to argue for you, but alas, Afterlife Enterprises is the ultimate decision-maker on these sorts of things, aren't they?"

Tallis didn't reply, but I noticed his posture was again incredibly rigid. He simply turned around and retrieved his sword, which he slung over his neck, and stepped toward the door before Alaire stopped him. "Of course, there has been new … activity that has quite changed the scope of our original agreement," he continued with a glance up at me before raking me from head to toe. He faced Tallis again and smiled broadly. "Perhaps I can pull a few strings if you can manage to pull some of your own."

"Nae," Tallis responded immediately, turning on his heel as he approached us. Grabbing my arm and none too gently, he escorted me from Alaire's office.

"Envy and arrogance and avarice are the three
sparks that have all hearts enkindled."
– Dante's *Inferno*

# NINE

  Just as Alaire promised, we found the Jag
waiting for us outside his office building. As soon
as we climbed in, it drove us through the
Underground City, dropping us off at the gates
that would return us to the Dark Wood. None of us
said a word during the trip. Frankly, I wasn't sure
if the Jag was bugged, but I had a sneaking
suspicion that it must've been. So I decided to
postpone my questions for Tallis about everything
that went on in Alaire's office until we were far
away from any possible eavesdroppers. Since
Tallis wasn't much of a talker anyway, I couldn't
say his silence surprised me. Bill's reticence, on
the other hand, alarmed me until I concluded that
Bill was probably just as exhausted as Tallis and I.

  Once we crossed through the Underground
City's main gates and were "safely" ensconced in
the darkness of the haunted wood, I caught up
with Tallis. As usual, he had a good six-foot lead
on Bill and me. "So, what was that all about?" I
inquired, finding it difficult to keep up with him.
The path we were on wasn't really a path at all. It

was more like an obstacle course of dead tree limbs scattered here and there on the uneven terrain of the forest floor.

Tallis didn't reply right away. Instead, he kept his eyes trained on the ground until I wondered if he'd even heard my question at all. Or, for that matter, if he noticed that I was walking right beside him. In the bright light of the moon, which filtered through the dead branches and trunks of the skeletal trees, I could make out the redness of his cheeks. His jaw was still as tight as it was in Alaire's office. Any way I looked at him, Tallis had the overall appearance of a man who seemed extremely pissed off.

"Um, hello?" I continued, wanting, no, needing the answers to the questions that incessantly plagued me. First, I was dying to know about the hushed conversation I partially overheard between Tallis and Alaire. More specifically, what Alaire was talking about when he appeared to be making some sort of deal with Tallis concerning me.

"Whit was whit aboot?" the Bladesmith replied, never taking his eyes off the ground. I noticed his hands were balled up into fists at his sides and his knuckles were so white, the skin looked like a cadaver's. Yep, something was definitely rotten in the state of Denmark, or Tallis's head, whatever the case may have been.

"What just happened with Alaire!" I demanded impatiently, throwing my hands up into the air with frustration. "What else would I be talking about?"

Tallis shook his head and sighed before casting the briefest of glances my way. He'd been scowling for so long, the ghosts of frown lines remained on his forehead, despite his now neutral expression. "Naethin' happened with Alaire."

"Nothing?" I repeated, sounding unconvinced and possibly dumbfounded. Then I started to get angry because there was no way in hell Tallis could make me believe nothing happened with Alaire. However, I wanted to avoid offending Tallis and possibly destroying any chance of him actually telling me the truth, so I decided to rephrase my question. "May I ask what was Alaire talking about when he told you the 'answer was no'?" I inquired more politely.

"Ah dinnae care ta discoos it, lass," Tallis snapped at me with a shake of his head to convey that the subject was finished, apparently forgetting that I did understand English.

"Fine then," I answered, my chin protruding defensively, and of its own accord. "If you don't want to answer my question, that's up to you." It was his business, after all. "But you should tell me what Alaire meant when he said something about you pulling strings for him where I was concerned." I crossed my arms against my chest as I awaited his response.

"There is naethin' ta report regardin' that either," Tallis answered as he glanced over his right shoulder, then his left, as if he were looking for something. Maybe he was just scoping out the forest to keep us from being attacked by some horrible creature.

"There absolutely is!" I argued, my voice shaking with anger. It was now beyond obvious that Tallis was definitely hiding something from me. "Respect me enough to tell me the truth," I coaxed. But Tallis showed no signs of saying anything at all so I persisted. "I know Alaire was talking about me because he looked right at me when he said it."

"Alaire was taken with ye, lass," Tallis answered in a bored tone. "His comment was meanin'less. He simply fancied ye." Then he eyed me pointedly. "An' as yer guardian, Ah am tellin' ye, 'tis naethin' fer ye ta be concerned with."

"My guardian?" I repeated, shaking my head in disbelief. "Since when did you appoint yourself my guardian?"

"Since aboot twenty minutes ago," he responded. "An' as yer guardian, ye moost troost in meh an' troost Ah have yer best interests in mind. So when Ah tell ye that there is naethin' ta be concerned aboot with Alaire, ye shouldna concern yerself."

"You're impossible," I exclaimed, angry to be treated like I was all of five years old. Since arguing with Tallis was a dead end, I turned around, shaking my head with frustration while waiting for Bill to catch up with me. Sometimes, talking to Tallis was literally like extracting teeth.

He was the most frustrating and obstinate man I'd ever met.

"What's up?" Bill asked as he smiled at me almost sadly. His overall calmness was unusual, to say the least. Ordinarily, he was my lively, talkative, albeit slightly irritating, friend.

"Okay, who are you and what did you do with Bill?" I asked, hoping to get a smile from him as I shelved the frustrating conversation with Tallis into the back of my mind.

"Ha-ha," he answered, his mood still glum.

"What's up with you?" I continued, frowning at him. "You haven't said a word since we left Alaire's … Is everything okay?"

Bill exhaled a sigh that gave me the feeling everything was definitely not okay. "That Alaire guy freaked me out, Lil," he replied as he glanced up at me again and shook his head. "The way he was lookin' at you and talkin' to you … it was weird, you know?"

"He freaked me out too," I agreed with a nod. I was thinking to myself that "freaked out" didn't even really cover the half of it. "But that sort of goes along with the territory since Alaire is the head of the Underground City, you know? So it's not like we were expecting Mr. Rogers or something, right?"

"Yeah, that's a solid point, Lils, an' I know that, but still …" His words faded on his tongue, but when he faced me, I could tell there was more on his mind. "You know how I get those gut feelings sometimes? Like when something don't feel quite right to me, it's normally because it isn't?"

"Yes," I said as I nodded. Bill was right—he did have an almost uncanny ability to detect whenever impending doom lurked right around the corner.

"Well, I got me one o' them feelin's right now ..."

"About this forest?" I asked, my voice rising an octave.

"No, no, no," Bill replied as he waved his hand at me like I was way off base. "No, I'm talkin' about Alaire, nips. I'm sayin' I got a real weird vibe from him ... like the way he was lookin' at you, Lils ... It was like you were this big ol' vanilla, er," he paused briefly and glanced at my hair, "strawberry cake and he was like starvin' or some shit."

"I know what you mean," I said with a shiver when I remembered the particulars. There was no doubt about it, Alaire was definitely off-putting.

"I think we gotta be real careful about him an' the Underground in general," Bill announced, nodding his head as if he were trying to persuade himself. "I just got this really bad feelin' about it, ya know?"

I knew exactly what he was talking about and I nodded. There was something very strange about Alaire and his apparent fixation on me. Despite what Tallis said, or expected me to believe, I knew there was a lot more to the story than he was letting on.

Bill studied me for a few moments, with a pensive expression. "So, you weren't like … inta him, right?"

"Into him! Alaire?" I shouted in shock as my mouth dropped open in astonishment and a sense of mortification rushed through me. "Of course I wasn't! Are you nuts?"

Bill held up his hands, implying that he didn't mean anything by the comment, and I should calm down. "I'm not sayin' that I thought you were, Lils, so CTFD, yo." Then he took a deep breath before facing me again. "What I am sayin' is that I can see how some girls might get all giddy an' shit 'cause the dude's good lookin' and he comes off all Rico Suave an' shit."

"Well, those girls, if they even exist, aren't like me," I retorted, trying to suppress the slight I took from his comment. "There was nothing the least bit remotely attractive about Alaire in my opinion, Bill," I finished matter-of-factly.

"Good," Bill said with a nod. "Then you aren't plannin' on havin' dinner with him anytime soon, right?"

I'd temporarily forgotten about Alaire's dinner invitation. I shook my head. "No, I'm not." Then I sighed. "I'm not looking for any shortcuts with this soul-retrieving business, Bill. When I signed up, I knew what the risks were." I cocked my head to the side and reconsidered my statement. "Well, that's not entirely true, but had I known what we'd encounter, I would have made the same decision again. I would have chosen to live, even if that meant exactly what we're doing now." I took a deep breath and smiled at my friend. "Bill, you and I are in this together, through thick and thin. I'm not planning to search for the easy way out." I paused for a second as I further contemplated my point. "And Alaire isn't exactly the easy way out. Getting mixed up with him would, no doubt, be the biggest mistake I could ever make."

"Agreed, nips," Bill said as he reached over and grabbed me, pulling me into him and squeezing me hard. "I was real proud o' you with that crazy-ass, postal shit you pulled on Alaire back there. You were like 'Hi, I'm Nips, don't freak out 'cause my sword's up in your face or nothin'. Shit, the look on Alaire's face was flippin' priceless. I was sorta hopin' you were gonna de-nose him though—then there'd be freakin' blood everywhere like when Fabio was on that roller coaster and that duck flew into his face and he freakin' bled all over those Swedish chicks. You 'member that shit, nips?"

"Vaguely," I answered, amazed at how Bill's mind worked.

"Ya know something?" he continued.

"What?" I asked with a smile. Prying myself away from him, I tried not to choke on his rancid smell, which was a mixture between really rank BO and untreated sewage. I assumed I couldn't have smelled much better though.

"When I first met you, I knew we were gonna be besties for life," he said with a huge grin, that made me feel bad for being so prissy. "You were my friend at first sight."

"I wish I could say the same thing, Bill," I answered with a laugh. I remembered the first time he showed up at my door and how mortified I'd been when I learned that he was my guardian angel. "But when I first met you, you scared the shit out of me!"

"Ah, you said shit, Lils," he answered with a laugh. "You've come so far … 'Member how you wouldn't even say 'hell' when I met you?"

I nodded. "Yep, I guess you've successfully managed to corrupt me at least a little bit."

He flashed his eyebrows up and down in a funny gesture. Then the cartoonish antics in his features vanished and were replaced by a more serious expression. "I know this new life bullshit has been real hard on you, Lils," he started, "but you've settled in real good; an' I just want you to know … that I'm real proud of you." He sighed and his eyes started to shine with tears before he shook his head and looked embarrassed. "I'm not good at all with this emotional crap, nips, but I just want you to know that I'm real glad I was assigned to you."

I took his hand and squeezed it as I smiled warmly at him. "So am I, Bill. I thank my lucky stars every day that you're my angel."

"For reals?" he asked, wiping his eyes with the back of his hand.

"For reals," I answered resolutely.

He waved his hands in front of his face, which, I guessed was an attempt to stop himself from tearing up, "I hate it when I get all emotional," he said as he shook his head again. "I don't wanna start ugly cryin'," he squeaked as his voice broke. He squeezed his eyes shut tightly before opening them and wiping his tears away again. "Dammit, I even feel like givin' Tido a hate hug," he said as he eyed the very man, who was now nearly ten feet ahead of us.

"Um, that's probably a bad idea," I advised. I wrapped my arm around Bill's shoulder and glanced at Tallis whose posture was just as rigid as previously. No doubt about it, something was wrong with Tallis. And whatever it was, I had a feeling Alaire was probably at the center of it.

Almost as if he knew I was looking at him, Tallis suddenly stopped marching and turned around to confront us. His face was expressionless, as usual. Bill immediately cleared his throat and looked down, presumably so Tallis wouldn't notice he'd been crying.

"There is a waterin' hole not far from here," Tallis announced as he waited for us to catch up to him. "We can bathe there."

"That's music ta my ears," Bill exclaimed as he faced me. "I'm sick o' nips smellin' like shit." He beamed widely and I just shook my head. Then he looked back at Tallis. "So, Yeti, what you gonna do with that soul in the vial, anyway? Don't you gotta like give it some air so it don't die?"

Tallis shook his head. "Nae. The soul doesnae require air."

Bill nodded. "Okay, that's good, but what about my other question? You gonna set it free, or what?"

Tallis frowned at him. "Ye know naethin' 'bout this process, boot ye are employed by Afterlife Enterprises?"

"Yeah, so's what?" Bill retorted to Tallis's retreating back as the enormous Scotsman started working his way through the dead forest again. "It ain't like I've ever gone on a mission like this before anyway. Nips ain't the only newbie, so gimme a frickin' break, yo!"

"Ah will return the soul ta Afterlife Enterprises via Soul Mail," Tallis called over his shoulder.

"Soul mail?" I repeated curiously while facing Bill with a shrug.

He shrugged also, as if to say he had no idea what Soul Mail was either. Then he shook his head as he eyed Tallis's back. "Frickin' Shrek, man. Sometimes he is such a douche!" He started to glare at Tallis. "An' not only is he a total douche, but the dude's totally sufferin' from Gherkinson's Disease."

"He's suffering from what disease?" I asked while trying to figure out what Bill was trying to say.

"Gherkinson's," he responded as if repeating the name would give me the definition. "It's a condition what makes certain men overcompensate for their lack of manhood by overachievin' in areas such as…" he glanced up at Tallis again before facing me, "bodybuilding, for example."

"Gherkinson's Disease?" I repeated as I wondered how Bill came up with this stuff. "Tallis is acting a little bit weird," I admitted when my gaze fell on the Scotsman's broad back. As he moved, the tree tattoo on his back almost appeared as if it, too, were moving. It was an optical illusion, but the branches moved in time with his muscles. "Whatever happened back at Alaire's must've really bothered him, so much that he doesn't want to talk about it, or at least, that's what I'm thinking."

"Whatevs," Bill said as he shook his head and tried to appear as if he couldn't care less. "What happened at Alaire's bothered all of us an' you don't see me or you actin' like dickheads."

He had a point. "No, I guess we aren't."

"We'll stop here," Tallis declared before pulling his sword in its scabbard over his head and leaning it against a tree. Both Bill and I glanced around, looking for the promised waterhole.

"Um, I don't see no pool nowhere," Bill said before he looked at me. "Maybe Sparky's seein' a mirage or some shit?"

"'Tis right around the corner," Tallis said as he pointed to the skeletal remains of what was once an enormous tree on my right. Curious, I carefully made my way around the tree's exposed roots. When I reached the back of it, I saw the watering hole, which was about ten feet wide by twelve feet long. Large boulders and more skeletal trees surrounded it.

"Is it safe to go in?" I asked Tallis as I turned to face him.

He nodded and handed me a bar of what looked like handmade soap which he'd just taken from his sporran. The soap was the color of wheat and was maybe the size of my palm. There were all sorts of seeds and sprigs of various plants sticking out of it, which suggested the Bladesmith was not only a master ironworker, but also a good chemist. "Ye will go in first, lass, an' Ah will keep sentry fer ye," he said as he reached for his sword.

"You'll keep her what?" Bill inquired from where he sat at the bottom of a tree trunk about ten feet from me. He rubbed his back against the bark of the tree as if he itched and then closed his eyes.

"Sentry," I responded. "It means he's going to make sure nothing attacks me."

"That's good," Bill said, not bothering to open his eyes. "Just wake me when it's my turn. I'm gonna take an emotionap."

I figured that meant he needed a nap after his unexpected crying spell from earlier. I glanced at Tallis, while shaking my head, only to find he was already watching me. As soon as our eyes met, he dropped his gaze to the ground and looked flummoxed. Then he cleared his throat and eyed me again. "Are ye ready, lass?"

"Yes," I answered. I removed the scabbard which held my sword from around my chest and propped it against the large tree that I stood beneath. Then I took the last few steps around the tree, being careful not to trip over any of the exposed roots. When I reached the watering hole, I quickly looked down at myself and decided my clothes were beyond disgusting. They needed to be washed as much as my body did.

Tallis walked up to the largest boulder beside the still pool and leaned against it, taking his sword out of its sheath. His back was toward the water. "Is there anything in the water that I should be concerned about?" I asked.

Tallis didn't bother to turn around. "Nae," he answered while reaching into his sporran before producing a piece of iron, with which he started sharpening his sword. I figured that was my cue, and I took off my tennis shoes. I left them beside the large rock, pulling off my socks as I headed for the water. I stuck my toe in and was surprised by the tepid temperature of the water.

"It's warm," I exclaimed.

"Aye," Tallis responded. "There's volcanic activity in this section o' the wood. It heats oop the water."

Praying the volcano wouldn't go off anytime soon, I was extremely grateful for the warm water. I placed the bar of soap on a nearby rock and started undressing. When I was down to my sports bra and yoga pants, I kneeled down on my haunches and started washing my socks and sweatshirt with the soap. "So you make swords *and* soap," I commented.

"Aye," Tallis responded. I could hear him sharpening his blade.

"Not bad," I said. The soap's foam-ability was impressive. Once my sweatshirt and socks were nicely sudsy, I took a few more steps into the water and rinsed them out. Just as I did, my stomach started to grumble. "Are we going to eat anytime soon?" I inquired.

"Aye," Tallis responded.

"Is that the only thing you can say?" I prodded. I was well aware that he was in one of his anti-social moods, but I couldn't say I cared.

"Aye," Tallis said.

Frowning, I wrung out the sweatshirt and socks before spreading them out on top of a rock beside the pool. To my surprise, the rock was also warm. I hoped the warmth of the rock would dry my clothes more quickly.

Observing myself again, I realized I needed to take off the rest of my clothes in order to give them and myself a good washing. But I was very uncomfortable with the idea of getting naked while Tallis remained so close by. But, because he was completely occupied with sharpening his sword, I figured it was now or never. I took a few more hesitant steps into the water until it came up to my thighs. Unclasping my sports bra, I pulled it off my body, allowing my breasts to air out and breathe. I started washing the bra with the bar of soap and rinsed it out before placing it on the rock to dry.

With a deep breath, I started peeling my yoga pants off, having to bend over to pull them off my feet. That wasn't exactly an easy feat while in the water. Once I managed to free myself from them, I took another few hurried steps into the water until it came up to my waist. Then I started lathering my yoga pants, and rinsing them out again. After I wrung them out, I placed them beside my sports bra before I finally turned to washing my body.

Peering back at Tallis again, I noticed he was in exactly the same position as the last time I checked on him. Facing forward, I pulled my hair from its high ponytail and submerged my body down to my shoulders. I dropped my head back until my hair soaked up the water. Then, after rubbing the soap in my palms until I got a good lather, I started washing my hair. I rinsed it out and lathered it again, trying to eradicate every last drop of sewage water from it. Afterwards, I looped my hair back through my hair band, after washing the hair tie, of course, and stood up to start lathering my body. I relished cleaning away the filth from the Underground City. I couldn't remember a time a bath or shower had felt so good.

Once I was squeaky clean, I headed for the shallow end of the watering hole, where I'd first waded in, only after checking to be sure Tallis wasn't looking at me, of course. When I reached the rocks, I picked up my sports bra, and happily smiled as I declared, "My clothes are nearly dry!"

"Aye, the rocks are heated as well," Tallis replied, in a disinterested tone of voice.

I shook myself and tried to squeegee the remaining water from my arms and chest. Then I pulled my sports bra over my head and adjusted my breasts in the cups, before fastening it in the back. I took another few steps closer to the shore and squeegeed my legs before grabbing my yoga pants. They were just a bit wetter than my sports bra, but I hurriedly yanked them up my legs anyway. Once I was dressed again in clean clothes, I breathed a sigh of relief.

"Okay, I'm decent," I announced. Tallis didn't say anything or make any motion to move. I just shrugged, again at a loss in understanding the way the man's head worked. Instead, I went about my business: gathering up my socks, my sweatshirt, the bar of soap and my tennies. Once I collected everything, I walked over to Tallis and handed him the soap, which he silently accepted. I leaned against a rock adjacent to him and pulled my socks on. They were also completely dry. I shoved my feet into my tennis shoes and smiled at him. "I feel so much better."

"Ah'm glad fer it, lass," he answered in a monotone.

"I can be *your* sentry now," I said as I sat down next to him on the rock. He stood up and immediately shook his head.

"Ah dinnae need ye."

"But what if something tries to attack you?" I argued.

He adamantly shook his head. "Ah amnae worried. Ah can manage. Ye can return ta yer stookie angel an' take a nap. 'Tis another few hours' walk ta the tavern."

"The tavern?" I repeated without a clue of what he was talking about.

"Aye, Ah desire a warm meal an' a good whisky."

I felt my eyes widening because I didn't know Tallis drank hard liquor. That, and I was shocked that there was a restaurant in the Dark Wood in the first place. But the idea of a warm meal enticed me and I simply nodded and headed for our camp where I could see Bill snoozing against a tree. Not wanting to awaken him, I draped my nice, clean sweatshirt over one of the tree branches and reached for my sword before I sat down next to him. Instantly catching his horrible smell, I moved to another tree. I pulled my sword from its scabbard and admired the shiny steel. Running my fingers down the metal, I noticed how the lines on either side were perfectly symmetrical. Tallis truly was a master craftsman.

As soon as I thought of Tallis, I started to worry about him being in the water hole by himself without any protection. I knew enough about the haunted forest to suspect there were creatures inside it that would not hesitate to eat one of us for dinner. I wasn't sure what prompted it, but before I knew what I was doing, I was back on my feet, my sword in hand. I started for the watering hole, being very careful not to make any sounds because I knew how pissed Tallis would be if he caught me spying on him. But, it was a risk I was more than willing to take if it meant ensuring his safety.

"But when thou art again in the sweet world, I
pray thee to the mind of others bring me."
– Dante's *Inferno*

## TEN

When I made it around the tree, I noticed
Tallis was submerged up to his neck in the middle
of the pool and facing the opposite direction.
Grasping the opportunity to hide behind the same
large boulder he was sitting on when I was bathing,
I darted across the ten or more feet that separated
it from me. Then I sat down on the ground,
looking in the opposite direction as I asked myself
what in the hell I was doing. Peeking at Tallis
while he was naked? Had I lost my mind? I tried
to rationalize it by saying I was just looking out
for him, and being protective. But I honestly knew
that wasn't the full story. No, there was a side of
me that thrilled at the idea of seeing Tallis
completely in the buff. Although I didn't want to
admit it, that was the bare-faced truth.

I felt heat flooding my cheeks as I shook my
head and mentally berated myself. It wasn't right
for me to spy on Tallis, especially when he had no
idea I was there. But any attempt to talk myself
into returning to the sleeping Bill was futile. So,
with a deep breath, I turned around, and snuck a

peek behind the rock. Tallis was still in the water,
but now it was only up to his waist. He submerged
himself entirely before standing up again, and
throwing his head back while running his hands
through his hair to squeeze the water from it.

It wouldn't have surprised me to find myself
drooling. I just couldn't remember another
moment when Tallis appeared more breathtaking.
With his defined and sculpted chest, and the water
dripping down his face, sliding over his pecs and
abs, he could have been every woman's dream
come to life.

He shook his head more vigorously and the
water droplets flew left and right. Then he started
moving toward the shore. Realizing he was
planning to get out of the water, I immediately
ducked back down behind the rock and faced
forward. I started to panic when I thought about
how I was going to return to our campsite. If I
waited too long, Tallis would certainly see me
because I wasn't well hidden. I peeked around the
corner of the boulder again and watched him
wading through the water as it grew increasingly
shallower. Even though I knew I should take cover
again, I couldn't bring myself to. Instead, I silently
watched him, anticipating what I would see in
another few seconds. The idea of secretly
observing, and thereby experiencing, Tallis's nude
body thrilled me all the way down to my core.

I couldn't help the sharp gasp of breath I took
as soon as he stepped out of the water. He was
stunning to behold. His thighs were sculpted of

sinuous muscle; and the enormous creature that hung between his legs was, in a word, impressive. So much so, I couldn't pry my eyes from it. Despite my virginity, I'd seen naked men before—mainly in movies or on the Internet a time or two. But none of those men could hold a candle to Tallis. I couldn't tell if it was simply because he was right there in front of me, in all of his glorious, unclothed flesh, but my heart skipped a beat.

All at once, I grimly realized the predicament I was now in. Tallis was well on his way back to the rocks to retrieve his clothing, and here I sat. He would, no doubt, see me and that was for sure. With no time left to hightail it back to our makeshift camp, I knew I had to hide. Crouching low, I duck-walked away from my hiding place behind the boulder, seeking a better one. Spotting a few larger rocks down the way from the one I just left, I hurried to get to them. That was when I remembered my sword.

"Fuck!" I whispered inaudibly as my heart started thudding in my chest. Tallis would absolutely know I was there if he found my sword, so I instantly made up my mind to go back and retrieve it. I started crawling toward the boulder again, my heart lodged in my throat. My sword was right where I left it, innocently leaning against the face of the rock. I started to reach for it, but quickly thought I should probably check to see where Tallis was. If I were really lucky, he'd be facing the opposite direction, and I might be able to make a direct beeline for our campsite.

Silently lifting my head up from behind the rock, I found myself face-to-face with Tallis's bare thigh, and I squealed out loud.

After a few seconds, during which I wondered if my heart would simply give out, I craned my neck upward to face him. Of course, he was still completely naked; and as my gaze revisited *that* place, I told myself quite sternly to close my eyes or look away, but I did neither. Instead, I looked directly at it. *Right at it!* When my eyes finally reached Tallis's face, he was staring down at me, and he did not look amused.

As soon as we made eye contact, he reached down, clutching me by the back of the neck, and yanked me upward. I couldn't form a word in my mind as his intense gaze penetrated me, and his eyes narrowed in anger. I was so mortified, I couldn't even think. I just couldn't get past seeing Tallis's … unit when it was no more than three inches from my face. And like a total moron, all I'd been able to do was gawk at it.

Tallis didn't release his hold on me, but instead threw my head back when I tried to look away from him and break eye contact. As he thrust me backward onto the rough surface of the boulder, my breath caught in my throat as I wondered if he planned to do me in right there, to slit my throat just to be done with me. I dropped my eyes to the level of his pecs.

"Look at meh," he demanded.

Breathing deeply, I felt like I might pass out when my eyes met his again and I saw that his pupils were widely dilated. That was when I sensed he wasn't quite as angry as I'd originally imagined, but he appeared to be … rather … What? Excited? "Um," I started when I found my tongue and knew I had some 'splainin' to do if I were to extricate myself from this very odd and uncomfortable situation. "I … uh … um, I was only trying to protect you," I blurted out, my heart thumping in my chest.

"Dinnae speak," he replied and just stared at me, but released his grip on my neck. When he ran his fingers across my nape, over where his grasp had felt so hard, his fingers were much more tender.

"Tallis, please don't be upset with me," I pleaded, when my wits unexpectedly returned and brought along with them a severe case of diarrhea of the mouth. "I'm sorry I invaded your privacy ..."

He looked like he was about to say something before he clenched his teeth and stepped away. Turning to the rock next to him, he retrieved his kilt. I just stood there awkwardly, not knowing what to say or do, embarrassment flooding me. Actually, embarrassment didn't describe the half of it. Overcome by intense mortification and the sudden wish that the ground would open up and swallow me whole, I added, "I was worried about you." I felt obligated to explain my actions.

But Tallis didn't respond, and merely secured his kilt around his waist, before stepping into his sandals and retrieving his sword, snug inside its scabbard. He lifted the scabbard over his head and secured it in place against his chest, then turned to face me. When our eyes met again, his appeared more narrowed and angry. He didn't say a word when he started walking forward. With no other choice, I grabbed my own sword and obediently followed him.

"We will move oan ta the tavern," he announced.

He walked past Bill whom we found snoring against the tree trunk. I kicked Bill's foot to wake him, suddenly nervous that Tallis might just leave us. In fact, I was convinced that was exactly what would happen if Bill didn't wake up. "Bill!" I yelled when he made no sign or motion to open his eyes.

"What?" he asked as he jerked with a start and began scanning his surroundings, his eyes wide. "What's goin' on, nips?" he inquired when his gaze rested on me again.

"We've got to move," I announced, grabbing my sweatshirt and loosely tying it around my waist before starting forward. Tallis had already vanished beyond one of the trees directly in front of us.

"But I haven't bathed yet!" Bill protested in a whiny tone.

"I know," I replied and stopped walking for a moment as I glanced back at him. "But unless you want to be left all alone in this forest, my advice is to start walking now.'

"What the hell'd you do ta piss the Yeti off now?"

I shook my head at him and sighed. "You don't even know the half of it."

Bill grumbled something unintelligible as he rose to his feet. After trying to stifle a few yawns, he complied and started following me. I'd already made it past the tree where Tallis disappeared and now, I could just make out his body's outline as he walked around the base of a large hillside that was maybe twenty feet ahead of me.

"This is BS, man," Bill announced when he finally caught up with me.

"We're heading to a tavern and they might have baths there," I answered while increasing my pace, which, thankfully, Bill copied and kept up with me.

"A tavern?" Bill repeated as he scratched his head in obvious wonder. "Like a place where you drink alcohol an' find big-boobed wenches to motorboat?"

"I think that's probably the definition you'd find in Webster's Dictionary," I replied somewhat absently, since all of my attention was now centered on finding Tallis again. We were just approaching the hillside where I last saw him, but once we rounded it, Tallis was nowhere in sight.

"Dude, did the Yeti freakin' ditch us?" Bill asked as I broke into a run. My heart fluttered and I felt something lodge in my throat.

"I don't know!" I called over my shoulder. Looking to my right, and then to my left, I saw nothing besides the skeletal outline of charcoaled trees that populated the Dark Wood. I stopped running, when I realized it was utterly useless, and wheeled around in a full circle, trying to find any trace of Tallis. Bill caught up with me, and had to lean onto his thighs before he could catch his breath.

"If that prehistoric ape ditched us," he trailed off as he inhaled and exhaled deeply again, before coughing and trying to catch his breath.

"Hurry oop!" Tallis's voice suddenly roared from above us. Looking up, I noticed he was standing at the top of a steep cliff. It was probably a good forty feet high; and the cliff face was nothing but sheer, smooth rock.

"An' just how in the hell do you expect us ta get up there, He-Man?" Bill demanded with his hands on his hips. "Do we look like frickin' goats?"

"There is a trail 'round the bend," Tallis said in a monotone before disappearing from the top of the rock face, and presumably going the other way. I started around the bend of the mountain and noticed there was a narrow pathway that bisected the craggy rock face.

"We gotta hike up that?" Bill whined, clearly perturbed.

"Guess so," I answered as I started up the incline. My calves burned almost immediately, and moments later, the muscles in my thighs were blazing. But I didn't pause once, or bask in the luxury of feeling sorry for myself. Instead, I continued up the trail and ignored my over-fatigued muscles. The closer I got to the top, the worse the incline became. I had to ultimately pull myself up the last few steps by holding onto the rocks, which jutted from the face of the mountain.

Hoisting myself up and over the ledge of the cliff, I found a smiling Bill, who stood there with his hands on his hips and a smug look on his face. "Took ya long enough."

"Nice for you that angels can materialize," I grumbled as I dusted myself off. I soon noticed Tallis leaning against the remains of a large tree that was about twenty feet from us. He didn't say anything when he pushed away from the tree and continued down the pathway. I took another deep breath and Bill and I followed him.

Although a trail ran between the blackened trees, it was difficult to follow, given how dark the forest was. Speaking of the trees, the farther we walked, the larger they became. They were still dark with the color of death, their branches not having seen a leaf in who knew how long? But they were, nonetheless, immense. They dominated the never ending night sky. As we came around a bend in the path, a structure suddenly loomed before us.

"Is that the tavern?" Bill asked Tallis who was now ahead of us in his customary distance of only six feet.

"Aye," Tallis answered, his first words since starting this last trek of our tour.

The tavern looked like something you'd see in Shakespearean England. It was Tudor-style with a steeply pitched, thatched roof, and cobblestones covering the walls on the first floor. The second floor overhung the first and the black and white timber/plaster construction was reminiscent of Elizabeth I. The tall, mullioned windows and high chimney as well as the sign that hung over the front door which featured a carved glass of ale made it feel like we'd just traveled backward in time.

As soon as the image of the carved glass of ale registered with me, I turned to face Bill and glanced down at his wrist, focusing on his alcohol monitor. I wasn't exactly sure how the thing worked—if it alerted Afterlife Enterprises whenever Bill was simply around alcohol or if he actually had to ingest some. But what I did know was that I didn't care to find out.

"We are here," Tallis announced when he marched up to the front door, which was already slightly ajar. After pulling the door farther open and without waiting for us, Tallis walked inside.

"Time to get this show on the road," Bill announced with a big smile as he slapped his hands together and proceeded forward, looking excited.

"You realize, don't you, Bill, that you can't drink anything alcoholic?" I asked, as I followed him into the bizarre establishment.

Inside, it was nearly standing room only. Not being a huge place—maybe four hundred square feet in total, it was very much alive with people drinking, singing, and in general, appearing to have a good time. The floor was uneven cobblestones, but the ceiling boasted hardwood plank flooring that had to be at least a few hundred years old. There were roughly hewn pine tables and chairs set up around the perimeter of the room, although the center of the room was unoccupied. Well, with furniture anyway. It was peppered by a few couples "dancing," if you could call it that. Truthfully, all of them appeared to be at some level of inebriation, and the men kept clawing at the women, who I later decided were the tavern wenches. Their hiked-up skirts and plunging necklines, flashing their immense breasts, which were often hanging out, were my first clue.

Tallis was already seated at the bar at the far end of the tavern. Bill strode up to him and pulled out a wooden stool, while I was just a few steps behind. Once he was seated, Bill looked up at me and shook his head, appearing perturbed. "If I have just one drink, it ain't gonna be a big deal, Butter Nipples," he announced.

I shook my head and stood beside him because every other stool was already occupied. "If you drink anything, that monitor will go off," I said as I motioned to the slim, black band around his wrist.

"'Twill not work in here," Tallis stated as he held up his hand to get the bartender's attention.

"What do you mean, it won't work?" I inquired.

Tallis shrugged when the bartender, who was a stocky man with a bald head and thick glasses, approached him. "The sixteen-year-old Lagavulin," Tallis told him. The bartender didn't reply, but simply nodded and walked away. Tallis faced me and said, "We are oot o' range fer anythin' belongin' ta Afterlife Enterprises ta work."

"Snap!" Bill said as he nodded and grinned up at me. "So we've discovered one damned good thing about this crappy ass forest!"

But I shook my head at him. "I don't care," I said with a frown at Bill. "You're an alcoholic. You shouldn't even be in here." Scanning the room again and the myriad drunk people, I spotted one of the couples on the dance floor now caught in a heated embrace. The woman's loosely fitted blousy shirt fell off her right shoulder and exposed one of her large, but very droopy, breasts. I faced Bill again. "This is just a bad idea."

"Shit, you gotta live a little, nips," Bill responded, shaking his head in defiance. "We just went to hell an' back an' if that ain't cause for a drink, I don't know what is!"

Tallis nodded and the bartender returned. He handed Tallis a pewter cup, which was etched with all sorts of designs on the sides. The cup had two handles and inside it was a dark amber-colored liquid. Tallis nodded at the bartender in thanks as he reached inside his sporran, and placed a pound coin on the bar. The bartender then addressed Bill.

"Whaddya want, angel?" he asked, his accent thick and very English.

"You got any specials goin' in this joint?" Bill asked him and explained when the man frowned as if he didn't get Bill's gist. "Like you got any discounts on beer an' nachos or cheese fries or hot wings?"

The bartender shook his head as Bill sighed, long and hard. Then he turned around and faced me. "That's what I call an unhappy hour."

"Sir?" the bartender asked, clearly wanting Bill to order so he could tend to his other customers.

Bill glanced at the strange pewter cup Tallis was now lifting to his lips as he looked at the bartender again. "I'll have one o' those, I guess."

I was about to reprimand him but, not wanting to play the role of his mother, I decided Bill was an adult and should make his own decisions. That and maybe he did have a point—we were all far beyond stressed-out, owing to our last mission to the Underground. Maybe all we really needed was a little relaxation time—to enjoy one another and celebrate our escape from the Underground unscathed.

"And you, miss?" the bartender asked as he turned his heavily lidded eyes in my direction.

"What are you both drinking?" I asked, glancing first at Bill and then at Tallis. When it came to alcohol, I wasn't much of an imbiber. Frankly, I didn't have much experience with drinking alcoholic beverages in general.

"Whisky, lass," Tallis replied as he lifted the cup and took another swig of the amber liquid.

"Oh," I said, without a clue if I even liked whisky. Was that the one with the worm in the bottle? Hopefully not …

"Sweetcheeks will have one too," Bill piped up, facing the bartender. That was when I discovered that I'd failed to remember my purse on this little mission to the Underground. Therefore, I had no way of paying for anything.

"Actually, I'm okay," I said as I waved my hand dismissively before looking at Bill. "We don't have any money," I said in a low voice. I wasn't sure how we would pay for Bill's whisky, but figured Tallis would have to cover for Bill until I could pay him back.

Tallis tapped his hand against the counter to get the bartender's attention. "Bring the lass a whisky," he announced.

"But, Tallis," I started.

He shook his head, interrupting me, and faced the bartender again. "Dalwhinnie fer the lass," he said to the man. The bartender nodded and Tallis placed two more pounds on the bar. I figured the other pound was to pay for Bill's drink. The bartender took the money and approached the cash register. Moments later, he served two more pewter cups, handing the one filled with a darker amber liquid to Bill.

"Yo, I need a couple o' ice cubes," Bill said to the man as he pointed to his cup. "I like this shiznit on the rocks, if ya know what I mean?"

The bartender instantly frowned and Tallis shook his head. "Ye willnae deface the integrity o' Lagavulin by poisonin' it with ice," he growled as he lifted the cup to his lips. Moments later, after swallowing the last of it, he promptly ordered a refill.

"When in hell, I guess," Bill said with a shrug as he lifted the pewter cup to his mouth and took a large gulp before clutching his throat and coughing. "Disgusting!" he exclaimed as he looked at Tallis suspiciously. "What in the hell is that? Tastes like turpentine!" Then, addressing me, and still sputtering and choking, he said, "Don't drink it, Lils, I think it's poison! It's still burning my throat!"

Tallis just chuckled as the bartender took his pewter cup and refilled it when he returned momentarily. "Bludy Yank cannae handle his whisky," Tallis explained to the bartender, who chortled a response.

"You call that shit whisky?" Bill asked, shaking his head and clearly offended. "I call that liquid death!"

"Aye," Tallis answered with a chuckle as he downed another sip. "'Tis the smokiness ye cannae stomach, stookie angel," he declared before shaking his head with amusement.

"The peat moss," the bartender added with a nod before he glanced at me. "How 'bout yours, pretty lady?"

Now slightly nervous, I lifted the pewter mug to my mouth and inhaled deeply. The smell was acrid but pleasing at the same time. I took the smallest of sips and felt the alcohol burning as it slid down my throat. Shaking my head, I put the cup back on the bar. "Too strong!" I managed before my mouth salivated uncontrollably and my throat continued to burn.

Tallis laughed as the bartender shook his head. "The Dalwhinnie is the lightest o' the whiskies," he said.

"Aye," Tallis interrupted. "Coot it with water."

The bartender reached for a jug of water and poured what looked like two tablespoons worth into my whisky. I lifted it again and swirled it around, hoping the water would dilute most of the horrible taste. Bill stood up and patted his stool, intimating that I should sit there. The contents of his pewter cup were already gone. "I'm gonna go find out if this weird-ass place has a bath," he told me. "I can't deal with my own shit smell anymore." Sniffing his left armpit, he frowned and shook his head. "Save my seat, nips," he added.

"There are baths oopstairs," Tallis told him as he turned to face Bill. "Ask fer Katie oop at the front."

Bill nodded before working his way through the dancers in the center of the room as I faced forward again. I didn't look at Tallis, but at my pewter cup instead, forcing myself to take another sip. "Thanks for paying for the drinks," I said, still refusing to look at him. Truth be told, I was still far beyond embarrassed over everything that had recently passed between us.

"Aye," Tallis answered, downing the last of his whisky and motioning for the bartender to refill his cup.

"I didn't know you drank," I began as I wondered how well he could handle his alcohol. He was downing the whisky like he was afraid the distillery planned to stop distributing it to the Dark Wood.

"Aye," he said when he placed another pound on the bar top and the bartender happily took it.

"These drinks are pretty cheap," I commented, grasping for any topic of conversation that might interest him. I just couldn't sit there in silence since my mind reverted to the same thing it had been for the last couple of hours: Tallis's expression when he caught me staring at his penis.

"Och aye, inflation doesna exist in the Dark Wood," he replied. "So the cost o' everythin' is as it should be." Nodding, I lifted the cup to my mouth, feeling ill-at-ease under Tallis's meticulous scrutiny. "Do ye know what the coop yer drinkin' from is called, lass?" he asked.

I shook my head and tried not to cough. The whisky was still too potent although maybe not as much as before. The water reduced the acidity a bit. "No, what's it called?"

"A Quaich," he answered as he lifted it and admired the etched details. He pronounced the word: Kweich. "The Quaich goes all the way back ta medieval times," he continued, while still admiring it. "The Quaich would be filled with whisky ta offer welcomin' or farewell dram ta guests." He looked at me and added, "'Tis the way ye drink with friends."

"Oh," I said, inspecting my cup as I held my breath and took another sip. This time, the whisky didn't burn the back of my throat quite so much. Either I was getting used to it, or I was getting drunk.

"Well, well, well," I heard a deep but robust voice of a woman only seconds before she appeared in my line of sight. "If it isn't Tallis Black, the Bladesmith!" she finished before sashaying right up to the man in question and looping her arms around his neck as if he was her long lost love interest and she was his necklace.

"Katie," Tallis greeted her with a broad smile as he leaned in and hugged her in return. She boldly took a seat on his lap, which didn't appear to bother him in the least. It bothered me, however, until I convinced myself that it didn't. "Ah dinnae have ta ask whether ye met the stookie angel?"

Katie laughed in a high-pitched, grates-on-the-nerves voice. "Bill?" she asked as Tallis nodded. "I sure did. I got him all set up with a hot bath, an' afterwards could barely peel that boy off me!"

I believed it. With her voluptuous body, she was probably Bill's type to a perfect T. She wasn't exactly a small woman, but I couldn't call her overweight. She was rather curvaceous with enormous breasts, which she crammed into her red corset above a tiny waist and ample hips. Her platinum blond hair fell in ringlets to her waist and contrasted nicely against her tan skin. Her face was pretty, with high, pink cheekbones, big blue eyes, and a rosebud for a mouth.

"How long's it been, honey?" she asked him in a heavy Southern accent, not bothering to notice me or anyone else around her, for that matter.

"A loong time," Tallis answered before motioning to the bartender. Katie leaned over the bar to get the man's attention.

"You better be treatin' mah Bladesmith real nice, Patrick, ya hear?" she yelled. Then she giggled as she leaned back against Tallis. Patrick appeared moments later with another Quaich full of whisky for Tallis. When Tallis tried to pay him, he shook his head and smiled at Katie, tacitly indicating that a friend of Katie's was a friend of his. Katie, meanwhile, kept herself busy by drawing loopy designs all over Tallis's pecs with her index finger. I felt like I could vomit. "Tallis Black, I think it's been at least a few hundred years since you've shown your face round here," she pouted. "Did I scare ya off so easily?"

Concluding that I'd seen enough, I cleared my throat and stood up, leaving my now empty Quaich on the counter. Feeling slightly light-headed, I turned around and was about to make a quick exit when I felt Tallis's iron grip on my forearm. I rolled my eyes and inhaled deeply, disappointed that my escape attempt had just been foiled. He pulled me up next to him and smiled at

Katie. "This is Lily," he announced. "Though Ah call her Besom."

"And he's the only one who can," I added with a smile that hopefully conveyed, in no uncertain terms, that there was no way this Southern twit was allowed to call me "troublesome."

Katie eyed me up and down before plastering on the phoniest smile I'd ever seen. "An' how do the two of you know each other?" she inquired before she fluttered her eyelashes at Tallis so many times, it looked like she had a nervous tic.

"We jist returned from the Oonderground," Tallis answered with his eyes on me. "Ah am Lily's guardian."

Katie kept her eyes riveted on me. "What a lucky girl ta have such a guardian." Not knowing what to say or do, I just nodded and probably looked as uncomfortable as I felt. Katie then dripped off Tallis's lap and stood up, leaning into his ear as she whispered loudly, "I've gotta table that just opened up for you, Bladesmith."

"Verra good," Tallis responded as he finished his whisky and stood up to his full, impressive height. Katie grasped his hand and pulled him toward the center of the room. At the same time, Tallis gripped me around my waist and yanked me forward, indicating that I was to join them.

"You both probably have lots to catch up on," I said as I tried to extricate myself from his vise-like grasp.

"Nae, lass, ye are mah charge. Ah want ye where Ah can see ye."

Katie frowned at me when she led the way to our table, which was all alone in the back corner of the room. It was so remote that I hadn't even noticed it upon entering the tavern. Tallis slid into the booth seat, which was up against the wall on one side of the table. Of course, Katie took the open spot next to him while I sat down on the hard, wooden chair across the table from both of them. I wondered how much longer Bill would be in the bath. My second thought was that I couldn't just play third wheel forever. "So how do you both know each other?" I asked, trying to make polite conversation.

"We met right here," Katie piped up as she patted the table. I wasn't sure if she meant they met in the tavern, or at this very table. But I also didn't care enough to inquire about the details. "The Bladesmith used ta come visit me very often, and usually on his way back from the Underground." She practically purred as she rubbed herself against him. I couldn't tell if Tallis was interested in her or not. Actually, he seemed primarily interested in keeping his Quaich full.

"That's great," I said with a crocodile smile as I inwardly harangued myself for trying to be polite with them to begin with. I should have pretended that I was so thoroughly inebriated, I could no longer understand English. Or maybe if I developed Tourette syndrome, Tallis would be

less insistent about me remaining with them. Hmm
… that wasn't a half bad idea.

"Lily Harper?" I heard a man's voice and
turned around to find Saxon standing in front of
me, wearing a large smile. He might as well have
been backlit by a bright, white light and a choir,
singing "Hallelujah" because he was such a
godsend. He held his arms out like he wanted to
hug me so I promptly stood up and wrapped my
arms around him. I thanked my lucky stars that
he'd just randomly happened to show up. "You on
your way to a mission; or back from one?" he
asked.

"We're on our way back from a mission in the
Underground," I answered. "Directly from
Cerberus and the sewers."

"Ew, I don't envy you that one," Saxon said
with another broad grin. I noticed that he didn't
release me right away; and when he did, he kept
his hand on the small of my back. I couldn't say it
bothered me, however.

"Who's yer friend?" Tallis suddenly
demanded, eyeing me narrowly before he glared at
Saxon and gave him the once-over, looking none
too friendly.

"Apologies," Saxon responded with a smile.
He offered his hand to Tallis, who didn't bother
taking it. "I'm Saxon," he said with a shrug as he
dropped his hand. Looking back at me again, he
smiled, as if to say he wasn't bothered by Tallis's
obvious deficiency in proper courtesy or manners.

"This is Tallis Black," I interrupted when I realized Tallis had no intention of introducing himself. "And this is Katie," I added while inclining my head in the twit's direction.

"I'm already familiar with Katie," Saxon said with a small smile toward the woman. I had a feeling every man in the tavern was familiar with Katie.

"How you doin', sugar?" Katie responded. She was sitting so close to Tallis, she could have been his conjoined twin.

"Good, good," Saxon replied.

"Pull up a chair," I said with a sigh of relief that I wouldn't have to be subjected to Katie and Tallis by myself anymore. Nope, now that Saxon was here, he could deal with them as well. Saxon reached for a wobbly looking wooden chair from the table beside us, not bothering to ask the table's occupants if they needed it or not. Straddling the chair, he sat down and set his huge cup of ale on the table in front of him. Meanwhile, Katie began a secret conversation with Tallis, filled with whispers and giggles behind her plump little hands.

"How did ye meet Lily?" Tallis rudely asked Saxon as he lifted his Quaich and finished the remainder of his Lagavulin in a gulp. After losing count of how many times the bartender refilled it, I had the uncanny feeling that it would take quite a bit to get Tallis tipsy. If such was even possible.

"We met at Ael's," I replied for Saxon before giving Tallis an expression that tacitly warned him not to scare Saxon off by being his usual, abrasive self. Without waiting for Tallis's response, I turned to Saxon and asked, "So, are you on your way to or from the Underground?"

"Back from the Underground," he answered as he took a swig of his ale and plopped it back onto the table. "I was in Circle Four."

"Which one is that?" I asked.

"The toy shop," Saxon answered with a sigh as shook his head. "It's my least favorite of all the levels."

I nodded. "I can't say that I'll ever look forward to visiting the Underground again, in general, no matter the level."

"Well, since you're so new and you probably don't know all the ins and outs and shortcuts and all that good stuff, why don't I give you my number?" Saxon asked. "Feel free to call me whenever you want."

"Ah am the lass's guardian," Tallis suddenly piped up, his voice slightly sounding a bit drunk. "Ah know all the shortcoots."

Saxon glanced at Tallis with a hesitant smile before his gaze settled on me. I frowned at Tallis and looked at Saxon. "Yes, thank you, Saxon. I would really appreciate that. It would definitely be nice to have a friend to call on whenever I have questions."

I could feel Tallis's gaze burning right into me, but I refused to look at him. Saxon reached inside his pocket and produced a folded-up piece of paper, which he ripped in half. Not having a pen or pencil, though, Saxon stood up and approached Patrick. I watched him, refusing to even glance in Tallis's direction because of the weight in his unblinking stare. Although Katie continued whispering to him and giggling, it didn't seem to take his attention away from me.

When Saxon returned, he handed me the piece of paper. I thanked him and slipped it inside the waistline of my yoga pants, underneath the elastic band. Then I addressed Tallis and smiled broadly. "Maybe I will have another of those Dalwhinnies, after all." Tallis continued to scowl at me, but I wouldn't let his foul temper ruin my mood. "I believe I have become a true whisky drinker, as it turns out!"

"No more I tell thee and no more I answer."
– Dante's *Inferno*

## ELEVEN

"Ah dinnae like him," Tallis said of Saxon, his jaw set stubbornly.

"Well, who asked you?" I replied as I couldn't help smiling at the grumpy Bladesmith. Saxon had left the table about an hour or so ago. He said he planned to return to his home, which was located in Boston. Katie only lasted another twenty minutes, at most, before finally abandoning any further attempts to seduce Tallis. So now it was just the two of us, Tallis and me, holding down the fort. Bill, meanwhile, was making his rounds and flirting outrageously with any and all women in the tavern.

"No one, Ah soppose," Tallis answered as he leaned back against the booth seat and regarded me with keen interest.

"Just how many whiskies have you had to drink so far?" I asked, amazed at his ability to hold alcohol. He was definitely inebriated; I could tell by the slow movement of his eyes, as well as his brogue, which became progressively thicker the more he drank. Since he wasn't throwing up, it seemed pretty obvious that his stomach had to be made of steel. After two whiskies, I was done and could feel the effects of both of them. I didn't feel nauseous, necessarily, but just mindless and carefree.

"Ah dinnae know," Tallis answered. He continued to study me with his usual poker face. "Ah have a question fer ye, lass."

After watching Bill strike out, yet again, I turned to face Tallis, and found it more than interesting that he was attempting to make conversation for once. "What?"

"Why were ye spyin' oan meh earlier?" he asked, eyeing me narrowly. I wasn't sure if his expression simmered with anger or curiosity. "At the waterin' hole," he added, as if I could forget!

I felt my cheeks heating up as soon as I recalled the image of him naked, and couldn't bring myself to look at him. Instead, I chose to outline the etchings on my Quaich, which sat in front of me, empty. "Um, I already told you why. I was worried about you."

Tallis cleared his throat. "Ah dinnae care ta have a conversation with ye starin' at yer Quaich, Besom," he told me. I looked up at him and forced myself to hold his gaze, but his eyes appeared very strange. The midnight blue was still visible, but the color seemed as if it were much darker somehow. "The way ye looked at meh, lass," he continued, scrutinizing me intently, "'twas as if ye desired meh."

Even though I knew how difficult this would be to admit, I also knew I couldn't lie to him. "I did," I said in a small voice. That wasn't the half of it! If Tallis had any idea how much the sight of him naked turned me on, he wouldn't have asked the question in the first place. Feeling suddenly like I was being interrogated, I began to fidget before adding, "Again, Tallis, I'm sorry for invading your privacy."

Tallis waved away my apology as if it were insignificant. "Ah knew ye were behind the rock as soon as ye hid there."

"Then why did you pretend not to know?" I demanded.

He shrugged, but his eyes kept mine captive. There was something about them that suggested a trace of anger. "Ah wanted ye ta see meh."

"You wanted me to see you naked?" I asked dubiously, becoming very ill at ease now that we were even having this conversation. Usually Tallis was so indifferent. Maybe it was just the whisky speaking. "Why?"

Cocking his head to the side, he studied me unapologetically. "Ah desire ye, lass, as Ah've told ye before." The way he said it was very matter of fact; and there was nothing in his delivery that even hinted of flirtatious playfulness. It just was.

"Right," I replied, unsure of how I felt about the whole conversation since it was completely bizarre. "But you also told me you would never act out those feelings."

Tallis nodded and eyed his Quaich. "Aye, boot that was then." He took the last swig of

Lagavulin and licked his upper lip salaciously as his eyes began to burn into mine again. "An' this is now."

I swallowed hard, unable to comprehend what he was trying to tell me. "What's changed?"

He held my gaze, and even though I wanted to do nothing but break his hold, I couldn't. It was almost as if his mind brainwashed my eyes to remain fastened on his. "Everythin'," he answered.

"Why?" I quickly fired back. "And what provoked this sudden change?"

He was quiet for a few seconds as he studied me and his eyes grew narrow while his jaw remained tight. "Alaire."

"Are you going to tell me what happened in Alaire's office?" I asked, staring at him even more intently. "Because if you aren't comfortable discussing it, then we need to change the subject."

Tallis glared at me momentarily as if he didn't approve of my ultimatum, but then nodded. "Ah will tell ye," he announced. He momentarily hesitated and his attention was suddenly centered on the table again as he gazed at his Quaich for another few seconds. Looking back at me, his eyes were very angry. "There exists a fine balance atween Afterlife Enterprises an' the Oonderground City," he started. "Never can a decision be made that doesnae involve them booth."

"Okay," I said.

"Ah am doin' penance, as ye know," Tallis continued.

"Right."

He didn't look up at me for a few seconds, but continued to stare at his Quaich as though the words he sought were etched upon it. Tightening his jaw and closing his eyes, I could tell he was clearly upset about something. When he opened his eyes again, the midnight blue had deepened substantially. "Ah have retrieved ova one thousand souls, lass."

"One thousand?!" I repeated, my mouth dropping open in obvious awe. "But, my agreement with Afterlife Enterprises said I only had to retrieve ten souls before I could go on to the kingdom," I replied. I wondered if I'd gotten the number wrong, or maybe Jason just changed it on me. Of course, he would do it without letting me know.

"Ye are different ta meh, lass," Tallis responded. "Ye dinnae carry the baggage Ah do."

"Okay," I said, unwilling to argue that point. "So you retrieved one thousand souls from the Underground City. How long did it take you?"

"Hoondreds o' years," he answered. His posture grew more rigid as he seemed to become more defensive the longer we discussed the topic.

"But Y2K just happened at the turn of the twenty-first century," I argued. "Jason told me that most of the souls that were lost or misplaced were due to an error in the computer system since Afterlife Enterprises wasn't prepared for the century change."

Tallis shook his head and said, "The century change oonly made the situation worse," then he looked down dejectedly. "Nae, there have been problems with Afterlife Enterprises from the getgoo an', consequently, souls have been misplaced fer centuries."

"Okay, so you've been retrieving souls for hundreds of years?" I asked, returning to his story since it was miraculously rare for him to open up. I didn't want him to suddenly change his mind and withdraw into the sullen Tallis again.

"Aye," he answered with a nod. "An' Ah also worked as a Bladesmith, creatin' swords fer other Retrievers, as ye know."

"Right."

"'Twas mah oonderstandin' that once Ah retrieved one thousand souls, Ah would be absolved o' mah sins an' the spirit o' Donnchadh would release meh."

"And if you were forgiven, what does that mean?" I asked, although I sort of knew the answer. The spirit of Donnchadh made Tallis immortal, so maybe it meant Tallis would be free to die?

"That mah time as a Retriever an' Bladesmith would be over," he answered almost immediately, like it was a promise he'd made to himself. "Twould mean Ah could move oan ta the valley o' the Kingdom an' be forgiven o' mah sins."

"And that's not what happened? You weren't forgiven?" I asked, feeling sorry for him, but at the same time, I had to admit, selfishly, I was happy he hadn't moved on to the Kingdom. The idea of Tallis no longer in my life saddened me, to say the least. Even though there were occasions when we had a hard time getting along, I never considered him as anything but a friend.

"Nae, 'tis not what happened," he repeated. "Ah wasnae forgiven even though Ah should've been."

"That's the question you asked Alaire when we were in his office, wasn't it?" I asked as the realization suddenly dawned on me. "Whether you could go on to the Kingdom now, since you'd retrieved your thousand souls?" Tallis nodded as I continued. "And Alaire said something about pleading your cause, but Afterlife Enterprises had the final word?"

"Aye," Tallis said as his lips grew tight. "Boot Ah dinnae believe fer a second that Alaire pled me case. An' as Afterlife Enterprises an' Alaire didnae keep their word ta meh, Ah amnae gonna continue keepin' mah word ta them."

"What do you mean?" I asked, staring at him pointedly. I worried that his response meant he was about to go AWOL or something worse.

"Ah was in repentance fer mah history, lass, these last few hoondred years," he started. "Ah havenae allowed mahself the benefit o' human company. Ah have lived alone in the Dark Wood with naethin' boot demons fer company. Ah have forgone the necessities o' a man in denyin' mahself a woman." His hands began fisting as his eyes narrowed. "Ah have paid mah penance an' still Alaire an' Jason Streethorn havenae kept their side o' the bargain."

"Um, so what does that mean?" I asked, my stomach now churning.

"It means Ah am done playin' by their rules," he announced with more conviction. His eyes bore into mine. "Now Ah play by mah own rules."

"Okay," I said as I nodded, feeling very nervous under his intense scrutiny. "I can see that you're pissed off and I agree with you: none of this is fair."

"Nae, it isnae fair!" he spat back, undeniably still outraged over the situation.

"Right, but do you think you should just throw away all the hard work you've done up until this point?" I asked. I shook my head to make it clear that I thought the answer to my question was a resounding no. "Maybe it's just a matter of retrieving a few more souls? Maybe you're almost there?" Actually, I had to admit I was a little bit leery about what Tallis meant when he said he was going to "play by his own rules." Did that mean he intended to go back to his old ways? Was he planning to take what he wanted, and damn the consequences?

But Tallis shook his head. "Ah know now that Ah was jist a pawn. Jason knew there was no one that could traverse the Oonderground as well as Ah, so he manipulated meh by offerin' meh absolution."

"How do you know the Underground City so well?" I asked, eyeing him warily. It was a question I always wondered about, but never asked because I didn't think he'd answer it.

"That is a soobject Ah dinnae wish ta discoos," he answered firmly.

"Okay, that's fair enough," I said with a nod and an encouraging smile. "So you think Jason just hired you because he knew that you were the best? And no one could retrieve more souls than you? And he never meant to grant you a pardon?"

Tallis nodded. "Aye, that is what Ah believe, lass."

"And you believe Alaire was in on it as well?"

"Aye, Alaire had ta sign off oan meh freedom, boot Jason had ta approve it first. An' neither happened," he finished, his voice dropping dejectedly as his jaw grew tight again.

"So where does that leave you now?"

He chuckled without humor. "Aye, where does that leave meh?" he repeated while his eyes zoned in on the Quaich before him again. When he glanced up at me, his eyes seemed hollow and empty somehow. "It leaves meh ta live mah life the way Ah see fit," he responded.

"Is that why we're here in this tavern?" I asked while closely examining him. "As part of your penance, you abstained from alcohol, didn't you?"

"Aye, Ah didnae allow mahself inebriants."

"So that's why you brought us here," I deduced. Apparently, whatever Tallis forbade himself in the past, he would now make up for in spades.

"Aye," he answered.

I sighed as the puzzle pieces began to fall into place. "And that's why you didn't stop me from looking at you when you were bathing. You wanted me to watch you because you wanted me to desire you!"

He didn't answer right away, but simply stared at me, making me feel like he could see right through me. And, really, he didn't have to reply to my question verbally because the answer was quite obvious in his eyes. *Tallis wanted to have sex with me.* A flurry of butterflies started up in my stomach as that stinging ache between my thighs returned. "Ye are quick-witted," he said as he continued to study me. "Boot Ah always knew that."

The image of Katie, fawning all over him, flashed in my mind. Unexpected feelings of jealousy bubbled up inside me, throwing me for a loop. "If you wanted to have sex so badly," I began, almost amazed that the words were actually coming from my own mouth, "why didn't you take Katie up on her offer? She was all over you like a case of the hives."

He shook his head vigorously and a scowl appeared on his face. "Katie isnae the woman fer meh, Besom."

"She would certainly have debated that with you," I said as I peered at him intently to judge whether or not he was lying to me.

"Aye," he responded without breaking eye contact. "Ah have taken Katie many a time."

A wave of jealousy crested inside my stomach and I started to feel sick. "Oh," I managed to reply as I forced the ugly feeling back down again. "So, then, clearly she is the ... woman for you."

A subtle smirk on his lips gave me the feeling that he was well aware of my jealousy, and worse, he liked it. "Ah man has physical needs."

"Well, that's so nice to know," I said as I stood up, quite finished with the conversation. "Are we sleeping here tonight? Or do we need to head out?"

"Ah cannae navigate the Dark Wood when Ah'm blootered," he responded. I assumed "blootered" meant he was drunk.

"Okay," I started, frowning at him. "Then we're sleeping here?"

He nodded. "Ye can inquire oopstairs as ta where yer accommodations are."

"Then they're ready for us?" I asked. "You already told them we're staying?"

"Aye, they have put aside three rooms," he answered. I didn't say anything else but decided I'd already said enough as it was. Instead, I longed to retire into the solitude of my makeshift bedroom so I could replay the conversation in my head. I couldn't decide what I thought about it, and more importantly, what I thought about Tallis. "Sleep well, lass," Tallis finished with a quick smile.

I half-smiled in response before leaving the room and making my way to the staircase. I caught a glimpse of Bill from the corner of my eye.

He was laughing and hanging onto a large brunette, so I figured he was fine without me. For now, I needed to focus on just myself. I needed to analyze how I felt about all of this most recent information. It was almost too much for me to digest at once. Tallis was suddenly not the person I believed he was. All of his convictions and everything that made him the repentant person he used to be were now flung out the window. Although I understood the logic behind this new route he was taking, I had a hard time figuring him out.

But that particular subject didn't have to be solved tonight. Tonight, sleep was all I cared about. The thought filled me with unsurpassed pleasure since I was long beyond exhausted. After climbing up the narrow flight of stairs, a young boy met me at the top.

"Are ye lookin' fer a room, lass?" he asked in a Scottish accent, which naturally reminded me of the large, brooding Scotsman I'd left downstairs.

"Yes," I answered immediately. "There should be three rooms under the name Tallis Black."

The little boy nodded and dug inside his pocket, producing a metal key, which he handed to me. "Yers is the third one down the row, miss," he said with a shy smile. "There's a warm bath waitin' fer ye too."

"Thank you," I answered, wondering how warm the bath could be since I'd been downstairs for so long. Even a cold bath sounded better than

nothing though. After all, I wasn't sure how clean the watering hole was.

When I reached the bedroom door, I poked the key into the hole and wiggled it back and forth before the door creaked and opened. Inside, an oil lamp burned in the far corner, giving the room a shadowy, yet cozy ambiance. The bath stood in the middle of the room. It was no more than a large, metal basin. I spotted a few glass bottles of what I hoped were shampoo and conditioner as well as a bar of soap. The curtains were drawn across the window, which suited me just fine. The last thing I wanted to do was look out into the Dark Wood.

I closed and locked the door behind me, allowing my eyes to adjust to the darkness in the room. Placing my sword and sheath against the wall closest to the bed, I sat down and pulled off my tennis shoes and socks. When I padded over to the bathtub and stuck my hand into the water, I was pleased to find the water still warm. There was a white, folded towel sitting on a chair beside the tub. I took off my sweatshirt and sports bra along with my yoga pants. When I turned around to step into the bath, I noticed a full-length mirror propped against the opposite wall. I had to remind myself that the reflection in the mirror was me. Once again, my new body was the part that I never could seem to get used to—the new, physical me. My naked body was beautiful. My breasts were full and perky; and my legs were long and supple while my stomach was incredibly flat.

Turning back toward the bathtub, I stepped in and sat down, languishing in the warm water as it engulfed me. I submerged myself all the way up to my neck and closed my eyes in sheer ecstasy. Although I tried very hard to relax, something inside of me refused to be put to bed. There was something burning, something that felt a lot like lust.

Tallis's naked body suddenly flashed before my closed eyes and my breath caught in my throat. An urge came from deep inside me and I knew it wouldn't desist until I appeased it. I reached down between my thighs and touched myself. At exactly the same time, I heard a strident knock on my door. With my heart in my throat, I sat bolt upright and leapt out of the bathtub, grabbing my towel. Still dripping wet, I wrapped the towel around myself as I plodded to the door.

"Who is it?" I asked in a low, timid voice.

"Meh," Tallis responded.

I opened the door only a few inches. "What's going on?"

"There was a mistake with the rooms," he answered. "There are oonly two reserved an' Ah willnae share with the stookie angel." With that, he pushed against the door and walked right in as I stood there, still trying to process what his words meant. I closed the door behind me and watched him turn to face me.

"Well, we can't share a room," I told him. Tallis didn't argue or say anything. Instead, he raked me from head to toe as I stood there, dripping wet, clad only in a very short towel. "Did you hear what I said?"

He narrowed his eyes. "Ye have nae choice."

"Um," I said, when he suddenly walked the few paces that separated us, and stared at me almost lecherously. Pausing in front of me only momentarily, he closed his eyes, dropping his head back and opening his mouth. He appeared to be panting. As I watched him, I realized he wasn't panting, but absorbing the scent of something in the air, similar to a cat. Bringing his eyes back to mine, the stinging sensation between my thighs grew into an all-out incendiary. That was when I knew Tallis was smelling me in the air. He could detect the scent of my lust.

Without a word, he simply reached forward and yanked the bottom of my towel, which immediately fell off. I stood there in front of him, completely naked. His gaze descended from my face to my breasts as he ogled them with obvious approval. Before I knew what he was doing, one of his hands grasped the nape of my neck while the other one cupped my right breast. His grip on my neck was firm, like he didn't intend to allow me any means of escape. His fingers clamped my breast and I felt their coarseness and calluses as they brushed the tip of my nipple. A combination of anxiety and wild excitement overcame me, only exacerbating the longing, urgent sensation between my thighs. His fingers continued to play with my nipple while his other hand held me firmly in place.

When I looked into his eyes, I swallowed hard at his expression. His eyes were solely trained on mine and a lilt on his lips suggested he was amused. "Ye enjoy mah touch," he announced, in a deep, sexy voice.

I couldn't respond in words. They were something that my sexually deluged mind just couldn't comprehend at the moment. Instead, my eyes closed on their own accord and a loud moan escaped me. As soon as I made the sound, Tallis's fingers slipped between my thighs.

Separating the folds of my lips, he pushed his finger against my nub, rubbing back and forth as I arched backwards with pleasure and closed my eyes. He chuckled, presumably at my reaction or because he felt how wet I was. I tried to keep my equilibrium even though I almost collapsed right there.

When I opened my eyes, he yanked my head back with the hand that wasn't wedged between my thighs. His lips were on mine in an instant, hungrily seeking my tongue as he lapped at me feverishly. He seemed like he couldn't get enough, like he wanted to devour my body from the inside out. I moaned involuntarily from the back of my throat.

"Ah am eager ta take what Ah want," he whispered into my ear.

I swallowed hard. "What do you want?"

He chuckled mirthlessly. "Ah believe that is plainly obvious, lass," he answered while pushing hard against me.

I gasped when I glanced up at him again, in shock at seeing his eyes. They were eclipsed with black again, which could only mean Donnchadh was at the helm of his body. At least, I guessed that was what it meant. Either way, something suddenly rebelled within me and I realized I didn't want my first sexual encounter to be like this. Especially since I wasn't even sure if Tallis was the one talking to, looking at, and touching me. For that matter, I had no way of knowing if the person I called Tallis was really the true Tallis at all.

With my palms on his chest, I pushed him away. "I don't want this," I whispered, despite my body's protests. Tallis narrowed his eyes, but didn't pull away. "Until I know who the real Tallis Black is, I don't want any of this," I repeated.

"Ah am mahself," he answered.

"The Tallis you were has changed," I argued, taking a few steps away from him and reaching for my yoga pants. He watched me, motionless, as I pulled them up my thighs. "You can sleep in here tonight," I said, reaching for my sweatshirt, before I yanked it over my head. "Bill and I will share the other room."

Then I grabbed my sword, socks and shoes, and my sports bra and started for the door. I rotated the doorknob and looked back at Tallis, but couldn't say anything more. Really, what more was there left to be said? The situation was what it was. I opened the door and closed it behind me.

Little did I know then that when I woke up in the morning, Tallis would be long gone.

"Let not thy fear harm thee; for any power that he may have shall not prevent thy going down this crag."
– Dante's *Inferno*

# TWELVE
## THREE WEEKS LATER

I was on my way to the Underground City again. But this time, my only companion was Bill. After waking up in the tavern in the Dark Wood, only to find Tallis's room vacant, I figured he'd either left during the evening or early in the morning. Since then, I hadn't seen nor heard from him. Now that he'd changed his way of thinking and was no longer interested in rescuing souls for Afterlife Enterprises, I figured he didn't see the reason for maintaining our friendship. That, or maybe he was just angry that I'd refused to have sex with him. Whatever the reason, I tried to talk myself out of constantly thinking about him, which was an errand I found exceedingly difficult. I just couldn't help but wonder where his life was headed now that he'd changed his mind about following the path toward redemption.

"Hey, Nerdlet, what are you gonna do if you start melting once we step into the Underground City like that wicked witch chick from that movie

*The Wizard of Aussie*?" Bill asked as we arrived at the gates of the Underground.

Glancing up at the imposing gates which were maybe twenty feet high, I couldn't help but gulp. They were just as I remembered them, comprised of bluish-grey iron and ancient bricks. The reliefs of animal and human faces were just as gruesome as I recalled. Inside the Underground City, the sky was still dominated by black clouds which appeared to be on fast forward, the light of the moon above, our only guide.

"I don't know," I answered honestly. "Hopefully I've still got enough of Tallis's blood inside me that I'll still be considered impure," I finished and then clutched my sword closer to me. It was just a matter of time before Tallis's blood would no longer keep me safe in the Underground, but I figured I'd deal with that crisis later. For now, I had a more urgent one, which was getting in and out of the Underground City unscathed.

I glanced down at the map of the Dark Wood and the Underground City which Saxon had sent me. Prior to this trip to the Underground, I'd called Saxon and grilled him with questions, including how I was supposed to find my way through the Dark Wood, where I was supposed to get the specialized vials used to retrieve souls (which, coincidentally, were available online), and how I was supposed to navigate the various levels of the Underground City in order to find level three, the prison. Luckily, I did still have the portal ripping device Tallis had given me because I'd used it to cut my path from my apartment in Edinburgh into the Dark Wood. I'd tried to cut a portal from the Underground City back to my apartment only to learn that I had to be twenty miles from the Underground City in order for the ripping device to work. That meant Bill and I were in for another two or so days of walking through the haunted wood.

Luckily for me, Saxon had also given me directions on how to locate Ael's gym, so I'd managed to maintain my daily physical training for the last three weeks. Well, as soon as I'd armed myself with a boatload of Air Jordans, that is. And although I no longer had Tallis or any other instructor to help me with my swordplay, there wasn't a day that went by when I didn't practice on my own.

"Okay, yoze, you ready ta get this shit over and done with?" Bill asked. "I dunno about you, but I'm thinkin' we're pretty damn crazy to even attempt this without Conan, namsay?" he finished as he glanced over at me and shook his head.

"We can do this, Bill," I answered steadfastly. "We don't need Tallis. We can make our own way." My pep talk was intended to bolster myself as much as Bill.

"You're right," Bill answered with a nod, but I could tell he was unconvinced and simply agreeing for my benefit.

"Okay then," I said with another nod as I started forward, and reaching into my fanny pack (hey, it was the closest thing to a sporran that I could find!) I gripped the key Saxon had duplicated for me. Then I unlocked the gate to the Underground City and pushed against it. The ancient metal creaked as it scraped against itself but it opened all the same. Taking a deep breath, and hoping this wouldn't mean my own destruction, I planted my toes down on the ground just inside the perimeter of the gate. Nothing happened. I released my pent up breath and took another full-footed step, balancing on one leg until I realized I was good to go. Then I glanced back at Bill and smiled. "I'm okay."

Bill let out a long sigh of relief and closed the gate behind him as he started forward. "What does the map say?" he asked as I pulled my sword out from its sheath, wanting to be prepared in case anything decided to waylay us.

"Level three is fairly close to the entrance of the Underground City," I responded, remembering the image of the map in my head. "We can take the subway which is just on the other side of those buildings," I said and pointed to the four or so skyscraper buildings that interrupted the horizon directly in front of us. "We would get off at the first stop."

"Let's do it," Bill answered.

We started down the paved road that wove between the buildings and I scanned my surroundings left and right to ensure that nothing suspicious was anywhere near us. The closer we ventured into the center of the city, the more Watchers walked by. They all seemed highly interested in us, although none of them ventured too close. Instead, they just studied us, cocking their heads from left to right like curious dogs.

"Think they're gonna tell Alaire we're here?" Bill asked nervously.

"I'm sure of it," I answered as I clutched my sword more tightly and told myself not to worry about whether Alaire knew we were here or not. "We take a right at the end of this street and the entrance to the subway should be on our left," I announced, not even needing to look at the map. Truth be told, I'd studied it every day since Saxon sent it to me—so much so that it was now imprinted in my memory.

Even though I knew what to expect when it came to the Underground City, since this was our third trip here, I was still put off by the utter lack of life. The absence of foliage, birds singing, and the hum of insects was unsettling to say the least. Nothing quite like the chaos of silence to unravel your mind. Even though the temperature in the Underground City was always cold, as in never rising above 40 degrees, I couldn't feel it. Probably because my nerves were set for full steam ahead.

"There it is," Bill announced as we turned a bend in the road and saw the staircase leading down into the subway. "You think the subway is like its own level in the Underground?"

"No," I answered. "I think it's just a subway."

"Oh," Bill replied as we took the stairs that led beneath the city. The subway station was barely lit, but the dim light emanating from the tunnel just beside the platform was blue. It bathed the entire place in a ghostly, sapphire hue. There wasn't anyone or anything waiting for the subway at our stop, which was a relief, in and of itself. Instead, the subway platform looked similar to any other platform—and the concrete floor suggested centuries of wear and tear. The white subway tiles lining the concave ceiling were blackish in some areas, probably due to leaks.

After another few seconds, I heard the sounds of the subway train as it rolled through the tunnel and shook the walls, sounding almost like an earthquake. The subway train was also bathed in a blue light, probably owing to the reflection of its blue headlights or taillights on the ceiling. It stopped directly in front of us and the automatic doors slid open almost immediately. There wasn't anyone inside the subway car. "Go, Bill," I said as he nodded and darted forward, nearly tripping over the curb of the train. He took a seat on the plastic bench farthest from the door. I decided to stand. I gripped the metal pole that extended from the floor to the ceiling with one hand, holding my sword with the other.

The doors slid shut and with the hiss of the brake release, we were off. The train rolled over the track, its wheels shrieking in time with the twists and turns of the track. We entered another tunnel and as soon as the lights dimmed in the interior of the train, that was when I saw "her." It was a split second that my stomach dropped down

229

to my feet as my heart started racing and I screamed. She was sitting directly next to Bill. As soon as he looked to his left, his mouth dropped open in horror and he screamed even louder than I had. He was on his feet in a split second, the same time it took me to get into fighting stance, holding my sword high above my head.

"What the hell shit is that?" Bill squawked.

The spirit or whatever she was simply glanced at Bill disinterestedly and then faced forward again, making no motion to do anything. She was a cloud of translucence beneath her chin. Above it, though, she appeared as three dimensional as Bill or me. She wore a dark hood that somewhat covered her black hair, but it was her face that scared the hell out of me. Her skin was the color of overcooked peas and her eyes were the same green. Her lips were a purplish black and the deep lines in her face pointed to the fact that she was old. A dark, circular mark appeared on her right cheek.

As soon as we emerged from the tunnel, the ghost woman vanished just as quickly as she'd appeared. The train began to slow until the hissing of the brake sounded again. Moments later, the doors slid open and I'd never seen Bill move faster than when he jumped down onto the platform. I was just behind him, and seconds later, the train departed.

Bill glanced at me, shaking his head, as if to say he was still too scared to talk. I smiled at him and, trying to look on the bright side, said: "One spooky ghost woman down and the prison left to go. Things are looking up."

Bill immediately frowned. "Said no one ever."

I continued to smile at him, figuring an uplifting attitude would help us both. But, really, I was just trying to keep my own cool. Getting scared and panicked would do us no good. Instead, I needed to be calm and ready for whatever the Underground City threw at me next. "We just go up these stairs and the prison should be on our left," I finished.

"TGIAO," Bill responded.

"Thank God it's almost," I started.

"Over," he finished for me.

"Amen to that," I responded with a sigh as I started up the steps leading out of the subway station, Bill just beside me. When we reached the street level, I turned to my left. Directly in front of us was the prison.

An immense and imposing Gothic stone structure, it had turrets, flying buttresses and battlements, and looked like a castle or maybe an ancient cathedral you'd find in Europe. The clock at the top of the three-story structure reminded me of the clock tower in *Back to the Future.* From my vantage point in front of the prison, I could tell the prison yard inside was in the shape of a parallelogram. It was enclosed by a stone wall approximately eight feet tall. At each corner of the wall stood a large turret, which I imagined was occupied by the prison guards; well, if there were any. At the top of each turret was a stone demon gargoyle with its wings spread out. One of its arms was extended in front with the fingers wide open as if reaching for any passersby who happened to walk beneath it.

"Hey, Nips, what did Dante say about this level?" Bill asked as his eyes settled on the gargoyles, his voice low and clearly frightened.

"This is the level of avarice and prodigality," I responded, my attention riveted on the front doors of the prison. Hopefully we wouldn't need a key to gain entrance, because I didn't have one.

"Come again?" Bill asked, spearing me with a frown. "English please. None o' them big words."

"It's the level reserved for the greedy and the wasteful. Dante says we'll find those who lived their lives insatiably or who hoarded their fortunes, not sharing anything."

Bill nodded and then cocked his head to the side as if he were considering my statement carefully. "Sharing *is* caring."

I looked at him and took a deep breath. "I don't want to waste any time. Where's your phone?" Bill handed his phone to me and I flipped it open, immediately spotting our soul on the map which Jason had texted to us. The misplaced soul was in the center of the prison, apparently on the top floor. "Here's hoping we don't run into Plutus," I said and started forward.

"Who or what the hell's that?"

"Dante describes him as a wolf-like demon," I answered as I took the stairs leading into the prison two at a time. Each of the prison windows was reinforced with thick iron bars that were bolted to the stone walls. When we reached the entryway, I pushed against the thick wood doors and found, to my surprise, that they opened without any trouble.

Inside, the prison appeared to be ill maintained. The uneven concrete walkway was buckling in places and worn down in others. The walls featured peeling paint and most of the windows were either broken or boarded up with crude pieces of wood. The doors leading into the various rooms were splintered and damaged, most hanging freely from their hinges.

I glanced down at Bill's phone and noticed the soul was to our left. "This way," I said in a small voice as I held my sword above my head and proceeded cautiously. My heart was thumping in time with my footsteps but I refused to allow myself to feel fear for even one second. If I gave into my own feelings of panic and anxiety, I'd be doomed. Instead, I maintained my good posture and focused on my surroundings, sizing up everything around me.

We passed by a few of the prison rooms which were tiny—maybe ten feet long by eight feet wide. They were also empty of any inmates. The paint inside the rooms was peeling even worse than it was in the hallway, revealing the dark brown of the rock walls. There were a few ancient metal bed frames randomly discarded in some of the rooms, their mattresses long gone.

"It's too freakin' quiet in here," Bill whispered.

"Yep," I answered, never prying my eyes from my surroundings. When we reached the end of the hallway, I stopped alongside the wall and checked the map. We were supposed to continue forward and then take a right turn. Glancing down the hallway, I realized that the open double doors at the end of the hall demarcated the end of this building. That meant we were venturing into another section of the prison. I started forward, and quickly noticed that when we reached the end of the hall, the walkway became uneven cobblestones. We were supposed to make a right turn and then walk underneath the arched walkway directly in front of us. The path continued under the archway before leading left, from where an orange light emanated. With a look at Bill's phone again, I realized we were headed right for the orange light.

"I gotta real bad feelin' about this," Bill said from where he stood right behind me.

"We don't have a choice," I responded as I started forward, forcing any fear into the back of my mind. I had a job to do and I would do it. End of story.

When we reached the end of the hallway, I scaled the wall and noted that directly in front of us was an open area that I assumed was the prison yard. Inside were the souls of the damned. They formed a ditch that was in the shape of a large circle. Within this ring, two groups of souls pushed stone wheels, but in opposite directions. The stone wheels were probably six or seven feet tall and each group of souls completed a semicircle before they crashed into one another and had to turn around again, pushing their heavy wheels back in the other direction once more. A few of the souls tripped, and dropped to the ground, but the stone wheels just rolled right over them despite their cries of pain.

Surrounding the souls were creatures I first mistook for dogs standing on two feet. But upon closer inspection, I realized they were more like wolf men. Standing up, they were immense, maybe seven or eight feet tall. And their bodies were just as massive, comprised of bulbous muscle covered in coarse, pitch black skin. Their heads appeared almost ape-like, with their eyes deeply recessed. They all had snub noses and large, pointed ears with wide mouths and enormous fangs. The only splash of color on their bodies was in their orange, quill-like hair, which grew on their heads, their jawlines and their chests.

Even though they walked on two legs, they were hunched over with misshapen backs and lumpy, overdeveloped muscles. Their calves weren't at all human in appearance, looking more like the legs of a hooved beast. Observing them silently, I watched as they moved swiftly, running after the souls of the damned, using their hands and feet, and sinking their teeth or sharp talons into the woeful spirits who wailed with agony.

"After these last two trips to the Underground, I'm never gonna even consider gettin' a dog," Bill whispered as I counted the wolf-men in front of us.

"There are six of them in total," I said and nodded as if to suggest we were fully prepared to take on six monstrous demons. Looking down at Bill's phone again, I added, "We've got to get across the prison yard and then we have to go back into the prison."

"Are you sure there's no other way to get to the other side of the prison?" Bill asked. "'Cause I gotta feelin' that these ugly SOBs aren't gonna be too happy with us interruptin' their little tea party."

I again referred to the map before looking at Bill. "It appears like the part of the prison that we need to access is separate from the rest of the prison. That, and the map is telling us to go this way; so I'm thinking we need to follow the map's directions, namsay?"

"Cute, nips, real cute," Bill replied with a frown.

"Once we reach the other side of the prison, we go up to the third floor and our soul should be there waiting for us," I finished.

"Yeah, but who's gonna be waitin' for us with the soul?" Bill grumbled. "That's what I wanna know."

"I guess we'll find out."

With a deep breath, and a mental reminder not to give in to the feelings of panic and terror that were now merely a breath away, I held my sword above my head. Eyeing Bill with an expression that said I was ready, I stepped into the prison yard. I could detect Bill's presence beside me from the corner of my left eye, but all of my attention was centered on the creatures before me. Only two of the wolf men noticed us at first. They seemed dumbstruck to see us which gave me the idea that they didn't get very many visitors. We continued forward until we were separated from them by about ten feet. A few more turned to face us, and one of them bared its myriad teeth, emitting a low growl, before they all did.

"We are on Afterlife Enterprises business!" I called out, my voice unwavering. "We do not want any trouble."

The wolf men continued to growl at us and I wondered if they were capable of understanding language and, if so, if English was among their qualifications. I could only hope so. They made no move to attack us as we continued forward, but instead, watched us from narrowed eyes that glowed white. Once we were halfway across the yard, I whispered to Bill, "Get behind me so my back is covered." He immediately fell in line and brought up the rear. "You need to be my eyes," I explained.

A few of the wolf men began approaching us, and I learned I was way off regarding their height. It was probably more accurate to say that they were closer to nine feet tall. "We are on a mission under the authority of Jason Streethorn!" I yelled at the wolf man now closest to us who continued coming even closer. I watched him kneel down on his haunches with his arms spread wide before him and his palms flat against the ground. His crouching position meant one thing. "He's going to attack!" I yelled to Bill as I faced forward, my feet shoulder-width apart. I braced myself with my sword held high.

The wolf man leapt at us and, with my legs still spread, I slid across the ground, moving to my right, and narrowly missing him as he landed on all fours only a foot or so away from me. Facing him, I stood up straight, with my chest and torso aimed slightly forward to maintain my balance. While the creature snorted and pawed the ground, I quickly took stock of my surroundings. The other five wolf men were standing behind this one, but none were in crouching attack positions, although a few of them were coming closer.

"If the other three attack, you've gotta do something to attract their attention," I whispered to Bill who stood to my left.

"Got it," he responded.

The wolf man directly in front of me continued to stare as it resumed its crouched position before launching itself high into the air with its claws poised to rip apart whatever it happened to land on. Bill jumped out of the way at the same time that I circled around and sliced my sword through the air, with the creature at the bottom of the sword's trajectory. I felt the blade catching in the demon's arm. The thing yelped and jumped backward as black goo began bubbling up from its wound, a wound which was far from fatal.

Gripping my sword with all my might, I stood stock-still, my feet again shoulder-width apart as I faced the demon. After seeing its attack-style, I concluded that it wasn't highly skilled, but probably accustomed to intimidating its adversaries just by its mere enormity. It was boastful in its attacks, which was the demon's fatal weakness: something Tallis taught me to look for.

I maintained my fighting stance, but rather than going on the offensive, I took Tallis's advice and waited for the creature to come at me. It, meanwhile, paced back and forth, never taking its eyes off me. It appeared to be debating whether to attack me again or return to its post and harass the souls of the damned. When it got down onto its haunches for the third time, however, I knew its intentions.

"Come on, you ugly asshole," I whispered. I was so focused on the demon, I had no idea where Bill was or what he was doing. But he couldn't be killed so I wasn't going to worry about him. I kept my elbows bent and close to my sides as the creature leapt high into the air again, at an almost vertical arc. Realizing I was dead center in its path, I decided to do something very risky. In a split second, I knelt down onto my knees and rotated my sword so that the hilt was directly in line with my belly button and the blade was facing directly up and away from me.

I felt the swoosh in the air as the demon landed on top of me, my blade piercing it through the stomach and coming out through its back. It screamed a high-pitched wail that lasted for a second or two before its body went slack. I tried to roll out of the way but was too late and the dead creature pinned me to the ground. The weight of its impact drove my breath right out of my lungs. After a few seconds, I cleared the stars from my vision, but strained against the thing's oppressive, mammoth body, and had to use every ounce of adrenalin I could muster to push it off me.

"Are you okay?" Bill asked as he helped to pull the enormous creature away from me. His eyes were wide with concern.

"Where are the other ones?" I demanded, very well aware that now would be the best opportunity for the other demons to attack us.

"They all backed away," Bill answered as he gave me a hand up. Taking it, I sucked in a few deep breaths before assessing the situation around me again. The remaining five wolf men had retreated and were now busying themselves by growling and snarling at the souls of the damned who continued to push their stone wheels around incessantly.

Assessing my injuries a few seconds later, I happily discovered I was unscathed. Walking over to the now dead demon, I stepped on its chest with one foot while I reached down and gripped the hilt of my sword. I had to pull up on it as hard as I could. The demon's ribs snapped as my sword emerged. It was a horrible sound I knew I wouldn't forget any time soon.

I took another few breaths, allowing the adrenaline that was piquing inside me to dissipate so my heartbeat could return to normal. I needed to constantly maintain my own sense of cool so I wouldn't lose it and become a hysterical mess.

I glanced back at the wolf-man pack again just to make sure they were, in fact, attending to their own business. Affirming that they were, I turned to face Bill. "Let's go get our soul."

He nodded as we both jogged the remaining distance of the prison yard. Reaching the double doors that led up to the third floor, Bill pulled one open, ducking his head inside to make sure the coast was clear. He nodded to me and I walked through the doors into the hallway, Bill right behind me.

"That was like Matrix worthy shit, Lils," Bill suddenly burst out. "You were like a freakin' ninja." Then he karate chopped the air a few times as I checked his phone to make sure we were still going in the right direction. "Fuck that was crazy cool!" he finished with a large grin.

"Okay, Bill, we need to concentrate now," I said, knowing that anything could still be lying in wait for us. "This mission is far from over," I finished as we located the staircase leading to the second floor. Bill took the lead, apparently wanting to scout out the situation for me before I got there, which was fine by me.

"All clear," he said once he reached the second floor. I pulled his phone out of my fanny pack and glanced down at the screen. Our soul was located directly above us, but the staircase to the third floor was on the opposite end of the hallway. Bill started down the hall, ahead of me, poking his head into each prison cell. When he reached the end of the hall, he paused at the bottom of the staircase leading to the third floor. With a nod at me, he let me know I was good to follow him. I ran the length of the hallway and stopped at the base of the stairs, watching as Bill started up the staircase. When he reached the top, he craned his neck down the hallway and turned around to face me, waving me up the stairs.

I took the stairs two at a time and when I reached the top, I followed Bill back down the hall, allowing him to keep a ten-foot lead on me so he could look inside each room and make sure nothing was going to attack us.

We were nearly at the end of the hallway when the sound of a woman's scream pierced the otherwise still air. Bill and I immediately stopped walking and then just stood there. I held my sword high above my head and took a few steps toward Bill, as we both continued to listen for another sound. Moments later, it sounded like something large and possibly wooden shattered against the wall in the room at the end of the hall, which was maybe twenty feet from us. I stood stock-still, continuing to hold my sword above me in a defensive stance.

"Our soul is in that room," I whispered to Bill. "We have to go in there."

"Maybe we'll be lucky and it'll just be ghosts screaming and throwing furniture around," Bill said nervously.

I raised both of my eyebrows in an expression that said who knew what we would find and followed Bill as he started taking baby steps toward the room. He was careful about not making any sounds, which was a good idea, since we didn't want to alert whoever or whatever was in the room that we were out here.

I sidled along the wall a few steps behind Bill, moving swiftly and almost silently. When we reached the end of the hallway, I heard another loud bang and the sound of a woman whimpering that came from the room directly in front of us. I stood behind Bill, now only two feet from the closed door. I motioned to Bill to open the door on the count of three.

He frowned, but shaking his head, took a few steps forward and gripped the doorknob. Then he looked back at me as I mouthed: One, two, three! On three, he forced the door open at the same time that I rushed it, only to find myself up close and personal with a wide-eyed, terror-stricken girl. She darted out the door and I didn't have time to find out where she went. Before I knew it, I was straining to look up at the most enormous creature I'd ever seen. It had to stoop down to walk through the doorway, and once it did, it looked down the hallway, presumably for the girl, before it then returned its attention to me. I held my sword in a defensive position and, amazingly, found the gumption to speak.

"I am on Afterlife Enterprises business," I said in a steely voice which wavered with the fear I was doing my best to suppress. "I'm here to retrieve a soul and I don't want any trouble."

The immense creature laughed a horrible sound that reminded me of nails on a chalkboard. It made shivers rush down my spine. "Another one?" the creature asked, presumably implying that the woman who'd just escaped was also a Retriever on Afterlife Enterprises business.

While I would have categorized this creature as a wolf-man also, it appeared different to the others. Its face much more closely resembled a wolf's with its incredibly long and shaggy dark hair, its pointed ears that stuck straight out of its head, and its canine snout. Chains dangled from each of its wrists and looked like they had, at one time, been appointed to restrain this creature. Something which clearly hadn't worked. The creature's body was much more like that of a man's than the other demons had been, but this creature was even taller and broader than they were. If I'd had to guess, I would've said it was ten feet tall.

"I don't want any trouble," I repeated.

"Are you the one who killed one of my wolves, Retriever?" the creature demanded, its voice loud as it echoed through the hall.

I didn't know whether or not to answer the question honestly, but decided in the end that honesty was the best policy. "Yes," I said as I tightened my grip on my sword. The creature glanced down at it and seemed to examine it closely.

"The mark of the bladesmith," it announced before its red eyes centered on me again. "How is it that you have possession of this sword?"

I was surprised that the creature was able to detect that Tallis had made my sword and even more so, that he was questioning me about it, but I saw no reason not to answer. "The bladesmith made it for me."

The creature didn't seem very pleased with this information and its posture became more rigid. It studied me for a few moments, its chest rising and falling with its increased breathing. I wasn't sure whether it was deciding to kill me or let me go. Either way, the fact that I carried Tallis's blade had certainly made some sort of impact on it.

"I am here to retrieve the soul I was sent for," I said, clenching my teeth just to keep them from chattering. I couldn't remember a moment when I was more terrified.

The creature didn't say anything, but took another few steps towards me until barely six inches of air separated us. I could feel its hot breath consuming my entire body with a foul smell that reminded me of rotting flesh. "Alaire will be informed of your transgression," the creature stated.

"That's fine," I answered resolutely. "I wouldn't have attacked your wolf if he hadn't attacked me first. I was only defending myself."

The demon narrowed its eyes at me and continued to study me. "You tell the bladesmith that Plutus released you," he continued. "You tell him I no longer owe him any favors."

"I will tell him," I responded. "Now where is my soul?"

Plutus opened one of his clawed hands which was the size of my head. When he extended his fingers, I could see the little glowing ball of light hopping around on his palm as if it were a Mexican jumping bean.

"Bill!" I called out, not taking my eyes from Plutus and maintaining my hold on my sword.

"Aw, come on," Bill responded as he realized what his job was going to be. He didn't say anything else, though, and simply walked up to me, unzipped the fanny pack, and produced a clear vial. Then he turned around and faced Plutus. "Even though I ain't carrying his sword, the bladesmith's mah boy, and he's real fond o' me. Got it, Pluto?"

The demon glared at Bill silently. Bill sighed as he approached the demon before standing as far away from the creature as he could. He leaned forward and extended his arm out, holding the vial to Plutus's hand. The soul beelined for the vial as Bill capped it and returned to my side before placing the captured soul back into my fanny pack.

"Thank you," I said to Plutus as I took a step backward.

"Wait!" a woman's voice sounded from beside me. I didn't dare take my attention from Plutus but continued to stare at him as the woman approached us. "I … I'm supposed to retrieve my soul too," she said, her voice wavering.

"Plutus, where is the other soul?" I asked the demon.

"That is not part of our bargain," he responded.

"Release the soul to this Retriever," I announced. "Then we will all be on our way and your debt to the bladesmith will be erased."

Plutus didn't respond right away, but moments later, he opened his other palm. Another ball of light appeared between his fingers.

"Bill!" I called to the angel who was right beside me.

"Ah, shit balls," he grumbled as he unzipped my fanny pack again and pulled the vial out. Then he walked up to Plutus, pulled the cap off the vial and allowed the soul to join the other one. He pulled back from Plutus and returned the vial to my fanny pack before directly starting for the stairs, calling over his shoulder, "Bill Angel's had enough o' this crap! I'm out!"

"Go," I whispered to the woman beside me who immediately followed Bill down the stairs. I backed up slowly, my eyes fastened on Plutus and my sword still held high. I took the stairs slowly since I was walking backwards. Plutus, meanwhile, just stood there, making no motion to follow me. But that wasn't any insurance he wouldn't change his mind and attack me as soon as I reached the steps. Once I got to the bottom of the stairs, I figured it was now or never, and turned around, running like hell for the front doors to the prison. Bill pushed the right door open and we all hurried outside, slamming the door behind us.

Then I faced the prison yard, and taking a deep breath, was about to start running for it when a hand on my arm stopped me. "Wait!" the woman cried, and pulling what looked like a piece of white chalk from her pocket, she kneeled down in front of the stone wall surrounding the prison yard. She immediately began drawing an arc, starting where the stone wall met the ground and then coming up about five feet before finishing the arc by coming back down again. "This will cut a portal to the other side," she announced.

Sure enough, the inside of the half oval she drew suddenly looked transparent almost. She didn't waste any time but threw herself through the opening. I could see her come out on the other side.

"After you, nips," Bill said.

I nodded and tucking my sword into my body, I pushed through the portal. It took me a split second to find myself on the other side. Then moments later, Bill arrived right behind me. The woman immediately approached the stone wall, then, and drew a giant "X" through the half oval, thereby immediately canceling the portal.

"You know, nips," Bill started with a frown as he threw his hands on his hips. "It would've been nice if you'd asked Saxon for a piece of get-me-the-fuck-outta-Dodge chalk!"

"Unto the foot of a tower we came at last."
– Dante's *Inferno*

# THIRTEEN

"I'm Delilah Crespo, but you can call me Dee," the woman Retriever announced, offering me her hand with a wide smile. "Thanks for saving me back there."

Physically, Delilah was a very pretty girl who stood about five foot four inches, and looked like she was probably in her late twenties. She had a slight figure, coupled with a very curvaceous butt that I couldn't help noticing Bill couldn't help noticing. Her hair was a wavy, chocolate brown that barely dusted the tops of her shoulders. Her large, dark brown eyes hinted of Hispanic heritage. She wore black, horn-rimmed glasses that framed her perfectly arched eyebrows, giving her a retro, yet very hip sort of look. When she smiled, her whole face lit up, courtesy of her dimples and her dark reddish-pink lipstick.

I shook her hand and returned the smile. "I'm Lily Harper and this is my guardian angel, Bill," I said as I eyed the angel and gave him a nudge.

"Nice ta meetcha," he said as he looked her up and down. I was sure he appreciated her booty-hugging jeans and tight, purple sweater. "An' no probs on savin' you back there. Not a big deal, ya know?" he finished as he pointed at her and winked obnoxiously. Never mind the fact that if anyone saved her, it was me …

After the three of us made it through the Underground City, we were, once again, ensconced in the Dark Wood, and on our way back home, which raised a good question. "Delilah, er, Dee, where are you headed to?" I asked.

"Oh," she began, although a little discombobulated. Of course, the threat of getting eaten by a giant wolf-man is probably known for having exactly that effect. "I live in Barcelona," she said at last before she started inhaling and exhaling much more deeply. When she bent down unexpectedly and put her hands on her knees, I wasn't sure if she would pass out or throw up. Her skin was pale and rather clammy.

I walked up to her and placed my hand on her back. "You're fine, Dee, everything's fine," I said as I rubbed her back. I knew exactly how she felt after experiencing it … What? Three times now! "You're out of the Underground City now and everything will be okay."

She took another deep breath as she stood up and smiled, shaking her head. "I'm sorry … I'm just still in shock." There were unshed tears glimmering in her eyes and I could tell she was struggling to keep herself together. Even though she was obviously in deep, over her head, she was strong. "I thought for sure I was a goner back there."

"It's totally normal for you to still be in shock, after what you just went through," I reassured her. "Just take your time. If you want to sit down, that's fine too."

She paused for a second and took another few deep breaths. She was obviously trying to deal with nearly losing her life, and most likely, the second time around, or so I assumed. "Do you mind if we just sit here for a minute or two?" she asked.

"Not at all," I answered. I watched her drop down to the ground as she leaned against the hulled out remains of a tree behind her. She closed her eyes and tried to slow down and regulate her breathing, in and out. Bill sat down beside her and reached for her knee, giving it a hearty pat. She opened her eyes and glanced at him warily, but he just nodded with a quick smile. It was his way of letting her know that she would be fine.

Propping his arms behind his head, he leaned back against the tree stump, and stretched his stocky legs out in front of him, appearing as comfortable as a cat in front of a warm fire. I didn't sit down, but stood beside Bill with my sword suddenly feeling much too heavy in my hands. I carefully scanned my surroundings again, especially the perimeter of the forest directly in front of us. I was looking for anything that might mean trouble. Bill, however, had his eyes closed and looked like he was ready to take another emotionap.

"How long have you been a Retriever?" I asked Delilah, thinking it was a good idea to focus on anything besides her run-in with Plutus.

Delilah sighed as she opened her eyes and looked at me. "Not long," she said as she stretched her arms above her head before leaning forward, and crossing her arms over her legs. She glanced up at me again and added: "I think ... maybe a week."

I'd already noticed that she wasn't carrying a weapon. "Where's your sword?"

"That demon back in the prison broke it in half over his knee!" she said, her eyes going wide. "You called him Plutus, right?"

I nodded as I imagined Plutus breaking her sword in half. "Did you get your sword from the bladesmith in the Dark Wood?" I asked. I couldn't imagine that one of Tallis's finely crafted blades would break so easily.

Delilah shook her head. "*I* didn't get it at all. Afterlife Enterprises shipped it to me a few days ago, right before I was sent on this mission."

I could only imagine they'd gotten the sword elsewhere. Moreover, Plutus probably wouldn't have tried to kill her if he saw Tallis's mark on her sword. He most likely would have had the same strange reaction to her as he did with me.

But as to Delilah, she was as ill-prepared as I was when Jason first appointed me to my new position. "So, that was your first trip to the

Underground City?" I asked and she just nodded. "Did Afterlife Enterprises prepare you for your mission at all?"

"Um, I don't really know," she answered as she leaned back against the tree again, pulling her legs into her chest. She continued to breathe more deeply. "I mean, they gave me a goody bag. That included the portal-cutting chalk, and another portal ripping device that allows me to enter the Dark Wood directly from my apartment in Spain. I also got a key to the Underground City's front gate and a map of the Underground City and the Dark Wood. Other than those things, no, I received no further preparation at all."

"Shit, you got more goodies than we did," Bill exclaimed, opening one eye to study her. "We got a whole lot o' jack."

"Afterlife Enterprises didn't send you Dante's *Inferno*?" I asked. It puzzled me because it made no sense that I received certain items that she didn't, and vice versa.

Delilah studied me for a moment, looking as perplexed as I. "What? The book that everyone has to read in high school English class?" she asked. When I nodded, she shook her head. "No, I never received any book."

"They sent me the *Inferno* to use as a guide in the Underground," I explained. "Apparently, Dante toured the Underground City in the fourteenth century and wrote all about it. Now, Afterlife Enterprises uses the book to help

Retrievers navigate and find their way through the various levels of the Underground."

"Oh," Delilah answered with a nod, although she didn't look especially interested. The color in her cheeks had returned, although her pupils were still wide and dilated. Apparently it wasn't easy to lose the stamp of terror you receive after going through hell and back.

"Not that Dante really knew what the hell he was talkin' about," Bill piped up, shrugging. He didn't bother opening his eyes when he added, "Half the time, the frickin' thing's wrong!"

Delilah smiled at him uneasily before eyeing me again.

"And where's your guardian angel?" I asked. I tried to comprehend what the people who worked for Afterlife Enterprises were thinking when they sent this poor girl out with no angel and no preparations. How did they expect any of us to succeed as Soul Retrievers when they provided absolutely no support or training? If not for Tallis, I was more than sure my first mission to the Underground would have been my last. And now, if not for us, Delilah would, most likely, have met her demise.

She studied Bill before shrugging. "I don't know. I don't even know if I have one. I mean, if I do, I've never been introduced to him or her."

That brought up another interesting fact in my mind—the only other two Retrievers I'd met thus far were Saxon and Sherita. We encountered Sherita during our first trek to the Underground

City. The thing that struck me as most curious was the glaring absence of a guardian angel in attendance with Saxon or Sherita. I looked at Bill and frowned with confusion. "Why am I the only Retriever with an angel in tow?" I asked him.

He shrugged. "Got me, nips," he replied before feigning a keen interest in the mustard stain on his Metallica T-shirt.

"Bill?" I demanded, more than aware that anytime Bill actually mentioned his own slovenliness, it was usually because he was trying to avoid something else. "Why do I detect that there's much more to this story than you're letting on?"

He was quiet for a few seconds before he broke out into a big smile. "Ah, what the hell? I'll tell ya." Then he cleared his throat and addressed both Delilah and me. "Just so you got the background, D-girl," he said to Delilah, who appeared surprised at her new nickname, "I have a slightly tarnished reputation at Afterlife Enterprises," he started and I sighed. I could only imagine how much this story was about to be blown out of proportion because exaggeration and Bill were the best of friends. "So here's the deal, I'm real popular with the ladies and I'm kinda the life o' the party an' shit like that. So, naturally, lots of other, less awesome and more douchy angels aren't down with how cool Angel Bill is, right?" Without waiting for either of us to respond, he added, "Right. It's called jealousy."

"Okay," Delilah said with an expression of complete bewilderment.

"Right, so I'm like this accidental Jedi, you know?" Bill continued. By this point, he'd already lost both of us. "Like everything I do is super-Jedi; like even though I'm not aware I'm even doin' it." He stared at Delilah and his eyebrows reached for the sky. "That's how cool I am."

"Oh," Delilah said while nodding to let him know she was paying close attention, or so I figured.

"So, I get inta some deep water 'cause I'm partying a little too hard, and overall, just bein' a little too awesome for all the other angels ta handle," Bill explained. Glancing up at me, he said, "Hence your little accident, nips."

"Great," I muttered, but I wasn't really angry. Actually, I was intrigued as to where his story was going.

"Anyhoo," Bill resumed the rambling narrative, "so, ya know, Jason Skeletorhorn has ta like make an example of me 'cause he don't want any o' the other angels suddenly growin' some balls an' actin' as cool as Bill, namsay?"

"That means 'know what I'm saying?'" I translated for Delilah.

"Oh," she said before facing Bill again. "I know what you're saying," she added with a little smile.

Good," he answered. "So, tryin' ta make an example of Angel Bill, Skeletor decides to put me on cafeteria lunch duty."

"What?" I demanded. I had no idea where his story came from, much less where it was going, and how it even got there.

"Right?!" Bill asked me while shaking his head. "Freakin' Skeletor turned me into the goddamned Lunch Lady!" I shook my head like he couldn't be serious. "So, I'm like hatin' this new job 'cause it's so freakin' lame, ya know?" Delilah nodded again. "So one day, they're servin' up this crap that looks like Godzilla ate the Swamp Creature an' then took a big ol' shit right into one o' my servin' dishes! An' I'm like, dude, I can't do this no more, ya know?"

Delilah nodded. "I know."

"So I rebelled," Bill finished, throwing his hands up into the air. He acted like we were supposed to guess the rest.

"What do you mean you 'rebelled'?" I inquired.

"I wouldn't let the man drag me down no more," he continued. "They already tried ta ruin my reputation by turnin' me into the lunch lady, an' finally, I just had enough. No more Mr. Nice Angel."

"So what did you do?" I asked patiently. My palm was beginning to ache from clutching my sword so tightly in my hand. Thinking it was probably all right to resheath it, since we hadn't encountered anything too concerning, I removed the scabbard from around my chest. Then I slid my sword inside it and replaced it on my person before turning to face Bill. I was anxious to hear the rest of his odd story.

"I frickin' set up about twenty plastic spoons along the edge of my counter before I loaded them with Godzilla shit. Then I unleashed the fury that was Angel Bill's retaliation and shot as many freakin' yokels as I could with that nasty, green dinosaur excrement." He started laughing hysterically and slapping his thigh. "It was freakin' awesome!"

"So you … what? Started a food fight?" I asked, frowning. I was slowly figuring out exactly how Bill arrived on my doorstep that fateful morning a few months back. After being kicked out of his position as a guardian angel for basically allowing me to die prematurely, Afterlife Enterprises demoted him to the cafeteria staff. It was just another job which he clearly couldn't handle. So, with no other place for him to go, and at a loss over what else to do with him, they sent him to me.

*Fabulous.*

"No, it wasn't a fight, nips. A fight implies that the other side retaliated. No sir, baby, this was complete annihilation, a blitz, a premeditated act of destruction aimed at all yokels and dumbasses by Angel Bill. Never was there such a full-scale food slaughter waged so deftly, and never shall there be again." He nodded with satisfaction and fell silent for a few seconds. "Amen to that," he finished … at last.

Delilah had a look of concern on her face, but she didn't say anything as Bill eyed us again, his smug smile freshly renewed. "So after that, Skeletor asked me what more he should do with me. Dude! I was like, send me to nips!" Bill grinned up at me warmly. "And here I am. The rest is ancient history."

"And on that cheerful note, are you both ready to start moving again?" I asked, mostly addressing Delilah to see if she was feeling okay.

She smiled at me and nodded before getting on her feet. "Do you know what we're supposed to do with the souls in the vial?" she asked as I fished through my fanny pack until I located the map of the Dark Wood.

I nodded but wasn't exactly sure where the Soul Mail drop was. Saxon kindly circled it for me on the map, however, so I replied, "According to the map, we should spot a river once we make it past this hill." Glancing down at the map and then up at the horizon before us, I saw that the hill dropped off about forty feet from where we stood.

"Cool," Delilah said and she and Bill began to lead the way. I brought up the rear, which was fine by me.

"So Delilah, huh?" Bill asked and she responded by looking at him with a curious expression on her face. "That's a real interestin' name," he said before facing her and singing. "Hey there, Delilah, what's it like in the Underground City?"

Delilah immediately started laughing at Bill with a wide grin. "I'm sure Plain White T's would love hearing your unique rendition of their song," she remarked before laughing again.

I shook my head, but couldn't keep from smiling too. Sometimes, Bill was pretty funny; I had to admit. I continued to walk in silence, and watched the two of them as they laughed together. I had the strangest feeling of contentment. It just sort of blossomed inside me from nowhere. I was thankful for the brief moments of "alone time" whenever I could find it. It was the first opportunity for me to really contemplate our last mission to the Underground City.

Without boasting or tooting my own horn, I had to admit I was way beyond proud of myself. I not only explored the Underground, but also managed to defend us against demons, and all by myself. That was an incredible feeling. All of my hard training, combined with the physical and emotional tolls, were well worth it. I achieved the goals I set and became the woman I always strove to be. I was brave and strong.

All of a sudden I had an epiphany. I basically wasted my former life by constantly trying to fix what I believed was wrong with me; but in reality, nothing ever was. The old me never learned that morsel of wisdom. Instead, I tried to change everything about myself until I wasn't even living my own life. If I worried that I needed to be more outgoing, I read a self-help book about it. If I thought I should be funnier, or more confident, or more easy-going, or more of this and less of that, I could always find a book on the subject. And I read them, all of them. I basically spent most of my adult life reading self-help books. But all they managed to do was keep me from experiencing my own life, and my own feelings, and living how I saw fit. That was probably the biggest lesson I could take from my experience in the Underground. When your life is right on the line, there really is no time but the present.

One thing I knew for sure was that I never could have accomplished what I did in such a short amount of time without the help and guidance of Tallis

*Tallis.*

Suddenly, I got a strange and intense desire to touch the blade of my sword. It was like a craving or a need that just welled up and exploded inside of me that came out of nowhere. I gripped the hilt of my sword in its scabbard and pulled it out slightly, until the metal blade shone in the moonlight. Then I brought my fingers to the blade. The results of my action nearly knocked me over as a flood of images instantly started flashing before my eyes. I had to stop walking when the images became more real than the forest surrounding me.

I saw a castle, and recognized it was Fergus Castle. The sky was stormy with grey clouds and the water that splashed around the castle moat was the same color as Tallis's eyes. It was the same castle I saw the first time I touched my sword.

That was when Tallis said the sword had identified me as its mistress. Fergus Castle had been in Tallis's family for centuries.

The castle slowly faded away and I was overcome with the perception that Tallis needed me. I wasn't sure why, much less how, but I felt sure my sword was trying to impart that information to me. Even though it was nothing but a hunch, and an intuitive feeling, it grew so powerful and resolute, I couldn't ignore it.

"There it is!" Hearing Bill's voice made the thoughts inside me vanish in an instant. He started running down the other side of the hill, toward the river, which lay on our right-hand side. It was really more like a creek than a river.

I took a deep breath when my sword ceased giving me any other strange images or feelings. I slid it back down into the scabbard as I tried to make sense of what happened. I knew it was some sort of sign, but what I was supposed to do next, or where I was supposed to go, eluded me.

"Lils, what do we do now?" Bill asked me.

Paying more attention to the immediate task in front of me, I glanced down at the map and noticed we were in the right place. I followed Delilah down to the creek bed. Pulling out the vial with the two souls in it, I reached for a permanent marker in my pack, and wrote on the outside of the vial:

*Two Souls retrieved by Delilah Crespo and Lily Harper.*

I wanted to make sure we both received our due credit for retrieving the souls. I handed the vial to Delilah, who seemed startled at first, but she accepted it all the same. "So do I just drop it into the water?" she asked and I nodded, remembering the instructions Saxon gave me over the phone. "Okay, here goes," she said as she released the vial into the water and we watched it disappear downstream. Neither of us said anything. When she looked back at me, her eyes were watering as she smiled. "Thank you for helping me retrieve my first soul."

I nodded and returned her smile. "Two souls down and eight more to go," I announced.

Delilah's grin was warm and happy. "One soul down and nine more to go."

Just then, Bill reached into his pocket for his phone, which was vibrating with an incoming text message. He flipped the top of the phone open and started reading before glancing up at me with a frown. "Um, Lils, looks like Alaire is looking for you."

"What?" I asked incredulously as I reached for his phone, which he gladly handed to me.

"I have no clue how the devil got my phone number," he said as he scratched his head.

"It's a company phone, Bill," I answered, my stomach already abuzz with new anxiety. "Jason probably gave it to him."

"True dat," Bill replied as I read the text message.

*My Dear Ms. Harper,*

*Having just been informed of the death of one of my employees in the prison realm, I learned from Plutus that you are responsible for this tragic event. If you do not wish to have this incident reported to Afterlife Enterprises, please agree to meet me at the gates of the Underground City next Tuesday evening, 8:00 pm, your time. We can discuss the particulars over dinner.*

*P.S. If you do not respond to this message by tomorrow at 10:00 pm, your time, or if you refuse to meet me, I will have no choice but to alert Afterlife Enterprises about the unfortunate incident. They will proceed with their own investigation into the matter. Let me also remind you that two infractions buy you a ticket on the nearest train to Shade.*

*It is a shame we missed one another during your time here. I do hope you enjoyed your stay.*

*Fondly,*

*Alaire*

"Ugh," I said as I shook my head and tried to control the anger now pounding through me.

"What did it say?" Bill inquired.

I looked at him and then at Delilah before coming to terms with what I had to do. "It looks like I have a date with the devil," I said, taking a deep breath. Then the images my sword displayed in my mind and the suffocating feeling that something was wrong with Tallis returned.

Well, Alaire would have to wait for our dinner date. If Tallis needed me, he was my number one priority.

I only hoped I wasn't too late.

To be continued…

Also Available From HP Mallory:

# ONE

It's not every day you see a ghost.

On this particular day, I'd been minding my own business, tidying up the shop for the night while listening to *Girls Just Wanna Have Fun* (guilty as charged). It was late—maybe 9:00 p.m. A light bulb had burnt out in my tarot reading room a few days ago, and I still hadn't changed it. I have a tendency to overlook the menial details of life. Now, a small red bulb fought against the otherwise pitch darkness of the room, lending it a certain macabre feel.

In search of a replacement bulb, I attempted to sort through my "if it doesn't have a home, put it in here" box when I heard the front door open. Odd—I could've sworn I'd locked it.

"We're closed," I yelled.

I didn't hear the door closing, so I put Cyndi Lauper on mute and strolled out to inquire. The streetlamps reflected through the shop windows, the glare so intense, I had to remind myself they were just lights and not some alien spacecraft come to whisk me away.

The room was empty.

Considering the possibility that someone might be hiding, I swallowed the dread climbing up my throat. Glancing around, I searched for something to protect myself with in case said breaker-and-enterer decided to attack. My eyes rested on a solitary broom standing in the corner of the Spartan room. The broom was maybe two steps from me. That might not sound like much, but my fear had me by the ankles and wouldn't let go.

*Jolie, get the damned broom.*

Thank God for that little internal voice of sensibility that always seems to visit at just the right time.

Freeing my feet from the fear tar, I grabbed the broom and neared my desk. It was a good place for someone to hide—well, really, the only place to hide. When it comes to furnishings, I'm a minimalist.

I jammed the broom under the desk and swept vigorously.

Nothing. The hairs on my neck stood to attention as a shiver of unease coursed through me. I couldn't shake the feeling and after deciding no one was in the room, I persuaded myself it must've been kids. But kids or not, I would've heard the door close.

I didn't discard the broom.

Like a breath from the arctic, a chill crept up the back of my neck.

I glanced up and there he was, floating a foot or so above me. Stunned, I took a step back, my heart beating like a frantic bird in a small cage.

"Holy crap."

The ghost drifted toward me until he and I were eye level. My mind was such a muddle, I wasn't sure if I wanted to run or bat at him with the broom. Fear cemented me in place, and I did neither, just stood gaping at him.

Thinking the Mexican standoff couldn't last forever, I replayed every fact I'd ever learned about ghosts: they have unfinished business, they're stuck on a different plane of existence, they're here to tell us something, and most importantly, they're just energy.

Energy couldn't hurt me.

My heartbeat started regulating, and I returned my gaze to the ectoplasm before me. There was no emotion on his face; he just watched me as if waiting for me to come to my senses.

"Hello," I said, thinking how stupid I sounded—treating him like every Tom, Dick, or Harry who ventured through my door. Then I felt stupid that I felt stupid—what was wrong with greeting a ghost? Even the dead deserve standard propriety.

He wavered a bit, as if someone had turned a blow dryer on him, but didn't say anything. He was young, maybe in his twenties. His double-breasted suit looked like it was right out of *The Untouchables*, from the 1930s if I had to guess.

## HP MALLORY

His hair was on the blond side, sort of an ash blond. It was hard to tell because he was standing, er floating, in front of a wooden door that showed through him. Wooden door or not, his face was broad and he had a crooked nose—maybe it'd been broken in a fight. He was a good-looking ghost as ghosts go.

"Can you speak?" I asked, still in disbelief that I was attempting to converse with the dead. Well, I'd never thought I could, and I guess the day had come to prove me wrong. Still he said nothing, so I decided to continue my line of questioning.

"Do you have a message from someone?"

He shook his head. "No."

His voice sounded like someone talking underwater.

Hmm. Well, I imagined he wasn't here to get his future told—seeing as how he didn't have a future. Maybe he was passing through? Going toward the light? Come to haunt my shop?

"Are you on your way somewhere?" I had so many questions for this spirit but didn't know where to start, so all the stupid ones came out first.

"I was sent here," he managed, and in his ghostly way, I think he smiled. Yeah, not a bad looking ghost.

"Who sent you?" It seemed the logical thing to ask.

He said nothing and like that, vanished, leaving me to wonder if I'd had something bad to eat at lunch.

Indigestion can be a bitch.

~

"So no more encounters?" Christa, my best friend and only employee, asked while leaning against the desk in our front office.

I shook my head and pooled into a chair by the door. "Maybe if you hadn't left early to go on your date, I wouldn't have had a visit at all."

"Well, one of us needs to be dating," she said, knowing full well I hadn't had any dates for the past six months. An image of my last date fell into my head like a bomb. Let's just say I'd never try the Internet dating route again. It wasn't that the guy had been bad looking—he'd looked like his photo, but what I hadn't been betting on was that he'd get wasted and proceed to tell me how he was separated from his wife and had three kids. Not even divorced! Yeah, that hadn't been on his *match.com* profile.

"Let's not get into this again …"

"Jolie, you need to get out. You're almost thirty …"

"Two years from it, thank you very much."

"Whatever … you're going to end up old and alone. You're way too pretty, and you have such a great personality, you can't end up like that. Don't let one bad date ruin it." Her voice reached a crescendo. Christa has a tendency towards the dramatic.

"I've had a string of bad dates, Chris." I didn't know what else to say—I was terminally single. It came down to the fact that I'd rather spend time with my cat or Christa rather than face another stream of losers.

As for being attractive, Christa insisted I was pretty, but I wasn't convinced. It's one thing when your best friend says you're pretty, but it's entirely different when a man says it.

And I couldn't remember the last time a man had said it.

I caught my reflection in the glass of the desk and studied myself while Christa rambled on about all the reasons I should be dating. I supposed my face was pleasant enough—a pert nose, cornflower blue eyes and plump lips. A spattering of freckles across the bridge of my nose interrupts an otherwise pale landscape of skin, and my shoulder length blond hair always finds itself drawn into a ponytail.

Head-turning doubtful, girl-next-door probable.

As for Christa, she doesn't look like me at all. For one thing, she's pretty tall and leggy, about five-eight, and four inches taller than I am. She has dark hair the color of mahogany, green eyes, and pinkish cheeks. She's classically pretty—like cameo pretty. She's rail skinny and has no boobs. I have a tendency to gain weight if I eat too much, I have a definite butt, and the twins are pretty ample as well. Maybe that made me sound like I'm fat—I'm not fat, but I could stand to lose five pounds.

"Are you even listening to me?" Christa asked.

Shaking my head, I entered the reading room, thinking I'd left my glasses there.

I heard the door open.

"Well, hello to you," Christa said in a high-pitched, sickening-sweet and non-Christa voice.

"Afternoon." The deep timbre of his voice echoed through the room, my ears mistaking his baritone for music.

"I'm here for a reading, but I don't have an appointment ..."

"Oh, that's cool," Christa interrupted and from the saccharin tone of her voice, it was pretty apparent this guy had to be eye candy.

Giving up on finding my reading glasses, I headed out in order to introduce myself to our stranger. Upon seeing him, I couldn't contain the gasp that escaped my throat. It wasn't his Greek God, Sean-Connery-would-be-envious good looks that grabbed me first or his considerable height.

It was his aura.

I've been able to see auras since before I can remember, but I'd never seen anything like his. It radiated out of him as if it had a life of its own and the color! Usually auras are pinkish or violet in healthy people, yellowish or orange in those unhealthy. His was the most vibrant blue I've ever seen—the color of the sky after a storm when the sun's rays bask everything in glory.

It emanated out of him like electricity.

"Hi, I'm Jolie," I said, remembering myself.

"How do you do?" And to make me drool even more than I already was, he had an accent, a British one. Ergh.

I glanced at Christa as I invited him into the reading room. Her mouth dropped open like a fish.

My sentiments exactly.

## HP MALLORY

His navy blue sweater stretched to its capacity while attempting to span a pair of broad shoulders and a wide chest. The broad shoulders and spacious chest in question tapered to a trim waist and finished in a finale of long legs. The white shirt peeking from underneath his sweater contrasted against his tanned complexion and made me consider my own fair skin with dismay.

The stillness of the room did nothing to allay my nerves. I took a seat, shuffled the tarot cards, and handed him the deck. "Please choose five cards and lay them face up on the table."

He took a seat across from me, stretching his legs and rested his hands on his thighs. I chanced a look at him and took in his chocolate hair and darker eyes. His face was angular, and his Roman nose lent him a certain Paul Newman-esque quality. The beginnings of shadow did nothing to hide the definite cleft in his strong chin.

He didn't take the cards and instead, just smiled, revealing pearly whites and a set of grade A dimples.

"You did come for a reading?" I asked.

He nodded and covered my hand with his own. What felt like lightning ricocheted up my arm, and I swear my heart stopped for a second. The lone red bulb blinked a few times then continued to grow brighter until I thought it might explode. My gaze moved from his hand, up his arm and settled on his dark brown eyes. With the red light reflecting against him, he looked like the devil come to barter for my soul.

"I came for a reading, yes, but not with the cards. I'd like you to read … me." His rumbling baritone was hypnotic, and I fought the need to pull my hand from his warm grip.

I set the stack of cards aside, focusing on him again. I was so nervous I doubted if any of my visions would come. They were about as reliable as the weather anchors you see on TV.

After several long uncomfortable moments, I gave up. "I can't read you, I'm sorry," I said, my voice breaking. I shifted the eucalyptus-scented incense I'd lit to the farthest corner of the table, and waved my hands in front of my face, dispersing the smoke that seemed intent on wafting directly into my eyes. It swirled and danced in the air, as if indifferent to the fact that I couldn't help this stranger.

He removed his hand but stayed seated. I thought he'd leave, but he made no motion to do anything of the sort.

"Take your time."

Take my time? I was a nervous wreck and had no visions whatsoever. I just wanted this handsome stranger to leave, so my habitual life could return to normal.

But it appeared that was not in the cards.

The silence pounded against the walls, echoing the pulse of blood in my veins. Still, my companion said nothing. I'd had enough. "I don't know what to tell you."

He smiled again. "What do you see when you look at me?"

Adonis.

No, I couldn't say that. Maybe he'd like to hear about his aura? I didn't have any other cards up my sleeve ... "I can see your aura," I almost whispered, fearing his ridicule.

His brows drew together. "What does it look like?"

"It isn't like anyone's I've ever seen before. It's bright blue, and it flares out of you ... almost like electricity."

His smile disappeared, and he leaned forward. "Can you see everyone's auras?"

The incense dared to assault my eyes again, so I put it out and dumped it in the trashcan.

"Yes. Most people have much fainter glows to them—more often than not in the pink or orange family. I've never seen blue."

He chewed on that for a moment. "What do you suppose it is you're looking at—someone's soul?"

I shook my head. "I don't know. I do know, though, if someone's ailing, I can see it. Their aura goes a bit yellow." He nodded, and I added, "You're healthy."

He laughed, and I felt silly for saying it. He stood up, his imposing height making me feel all of three inches tall. Not enjoying the feel of him staring down at me, I stood and watched him pull out his wallet. I guess he'd heard enough and thought I was full of it. He set a one hundred dollar bill on the table in front of me. My hourly rate was fifty dollars, and we'd been maybe twenty minutes.

"I'd like to come see you for the next three Tuesdays at 4:00 p.m. Please don't schedule anyone after me. I'll compensate you for the entire afternoon."

I was shocked—what in the world would he want to come back for?

"Jolie, it was a pleasure meeting you, and I look forward to our next session." He turned to walk out of the room when I remembered myself.

"Wait, what name should I put in the appointment book?"

He turned and faced me. "Rand."

Then he walked out of the shop.

~

By the time Tuesday rolled around, I hadn't had much of a busy week. No more visits from ghosts, spirits, or whatever the PC term is for them. I'd had a few walk-ins, but that was about it. It was strange. October in Los Angeles was normally a busy time.

"Ten minutes to four," Christa said with a smile, leaning against the front desk and looking up from a stack of photos—her latest bout into photography.

"I wonder if he'll come," I mumbled.

Taking the top four photos off the stack, she arranged them against the desk as if they were puzzle pieces. I walked up behind her, only too pleased to find an outlet for my anxiety, my nerves skittish with the pending arrival of one very handsome man.

The photo in the middle caught my attention first. It was a landscape of the Malibu coastline, the intense blue of the ocean mirrored by the sky and interrupted only by the green of the hillside.

"Wow, that's a great one, Chris." I picked the photo up. "Can you frame it? I'd love to hang it in the store."

"Sure." She nodded and continued inspecting her photos, as if trying to find a fault in the angle or maybe the subject. Christa had aspirations of being a photographer and she had the eye for it. I admired her artistic ability—I, myself, hadn't been in line when God was handing out creativity.

She glanced at the clock again. "Five minutes to four."

I shrugged, feigning an indifference I didn't feel. "I'm just glad you're here. Rand strikes me as weird. Something's off ..."

She laughed. "Oh, Jules, you don't trust your own mother."

I snorted at the comment and collapsed into the chair behind her, propping my feet on the corner of our mesh waste bin. So I didn't trust people—I think I had a better understanding of the human condition than most people did. That reminded me, I hadn't called my mom in at least a week. Note to self: be a better daughter.

The cuckoo clock on the wall announced it was 4:00 p.m. with a tinny rendition of Edelweiss while the two resident wooden figures did a polka. I'd never much liked the clock, but Christa wouldn't let me get rid of it.

The door opened, and I jumped to my feet, my heart jack hammering. I wasn't sure why I was so flustered, but as soon as I met the heat of Rand's dark eyes, it all made sense. He was here again even though I couldn't tell him anything important last time, and did I fail to mention he was gorgeous? His looks were enough to play with any girl's heartstrings.

"Good afternoon," he said, giving me a brisk nod.

He was dressed in black—black slacks, black collared shirt, and a black suit jacket. He looked like he'd just come from a funeral, but somehow I didn't think such was the case.

"Hi, Rand," Christa said, her gaze raking his statuesque body.

"How has your day been?" he answered as his eyes rested on me.

"Sorta slow," Christa responded before I could. He didn't even turn to notice her, and she frowned, obviously miffed. I smiled to myself and headed for the reading room, Rand on my heels.

I closed the door, and by the time I turned around, he'd already seated himself at the table. As I took my seat across from him, a heady scent of something unfamiliar hit me. It had notes of mint and cinnamon or maybe cardamom. The foreign scent was so captivating, I fought to refocus my attention.

"You fixed the light," he said with a smirk. "Much better."

I nodded and focused on my lap. "I didn't get a chance last time to ask you why you wanted to come back." I figured it was best to get it out in the open. I didn't think I'd do any better reading him this time.

"Well, I'm here for the same reason anyone else is."

I lifted my gaze and watched him lean back in the chair. He regarded me with amusement—raised eyebrows and a slight smirk pulling at his full lips.

I shook my head. "You aren't interested in a card reading, and I couldn't tell you anything … substantial in our last meeting …"

His throaty chuckle interrupted me. "You aren't much of a businesswoman, Jolie; it sounds like you're trying to get rid of me and my cold, hard cash."

Enough was enough. I'm not the type of person to beat around the bush, and he owed me an explanation. "So are you here to get a date with Christa?" I forced my gaze to hold his. He seemed taken aback, cocking his head while his shoulders bounced with surprise.

"Lovely though you both are, I'm afraid my visit leans more toward business than pleasure."

"I don't understand." I hoped my cheeks weren't as red as I imagined them. I guess I deserved it for being so bold.

He leaned forward, and I pulled back. "All in good time. Now, why don't you try to read me again?"

I motioned for his hands—sometimes touching the person in question helps generate my visions. As it had last time, his touch sent a jolt of electricity through me, and I had to fight not to lose my composure. There was something odd about this man.

I closed my eyes and exhaled, trying to focus while millions of bees warred with each other in my stomach. After driving my thoughts from all the questions I had regarding Rand, I was more comfortable.

At first nothing came.

I opened my eyes to find Rand staring at me. Just as I closed them again, a vision came—one that was piecemeal and none too clear.

"A man," I said, and my voice sounded like a foghorn in the quiet room. "He has dark hair and blue eyes, and there's something different about him. I can't quite pinpoint it ... it seems he's hired you for something ..."

My voice started to trail as the vision grew blurry. I tried to weave through the images, but they were too inconsistent. Once I got a hold of one, it wafted out of my grasp, and another indistinct one took its place.

"Go on," Rand prodded.

The vision was gone at this point, but I was still receiving emotional feedback. Sometimes I'll just get a vision and other times a vision with feelings. "The job's dangerous. I don't think you should take it."

And just like that, the feeling disappeared. I knew it was all I was going to get and I was frustrated, as it hadn't been my best work. Most of the time my feelings and visions are much clearer, but these were more like fragments—almost like short dream vignettes you can't interpret.

I let go of Rand's hands, and my own felt cold. I put them in my lap, hoping to warm them up again, but somehow my warmth didn't quite compare to his.

## HP MALLORY

Rand seemed to be weighing what I'd told him—he strummed his fingers against his chin and chewed on his lip. "Can you tell me more about this man?"

"I couldn't see him in comparison to anyone else, so as far as height goes, I don't know. Dark hair and blue eyes, the hair was a little bit longish, maybe not a stylish haircut. He's white with no facial hair. That's about all I could see. He had something otherworldly about him. Maybe he was a psychic? I'm not sure."

"Dark hair and blue eyes you say?"

"Yes. He's a handsome man. I feel as if he's very old though he looked young. Maybe in his early thirties." I shrugged. "Sometimes my visions don't make much sense." Hey, I was just the middleman. It was up to him to interpret the message.

"You like the tall, dark, and handsome types then?"

Taken aback, I didn't know how to respond. "He had a nice face."

"You aren't receiving anything else?"

I shook my head. "I'm afraid not."

He stood. "Very good. I'm content with our meeting today. Do you have me scheduled for next week?"

I nodded and stood. The silence in the room pounded against me, and I fought to find something to say, but Rand beat me to it.

"Jolie, you need to have more confidence."

The closeness of the comment irritated me—who was this man who thought he could waltz into my shop and tell me I needed more confidence? Granted, he had a point, but damn it all if I were to tell him that!

Now, I was even more embarrassed, and I'm sure my face was the color of a bad sunburn. "I don't think you're here to discuss me."

"As a matter of fact, that's precisely the reason I'm …"

Rand didn't get a chance to finish when Christa came bounding through the door.

Christa hasn't quite grasped the whole customer service thing.

## HP MALLORY

"Sorry to interrupt, but there was a car accident right outside the shop! This one car totally just plowed into the other one. I think everyone's alright, but how crazy is that?"

My attention found Rand's as Christa continued to describe the accident in minute detail. I couldn't help but wonder what he'd been about to say. It had sounded like he was here to discuss me ... something that settled in my stomach like a big rock.

When Christa finished her accident report, Rand made his way to the door. I was on the verge of demanding he finish what he'd been about to say, but I couldn't summon the nerve.

"Cheers," he said and walked out.

**AVAILABLE NOW**

Also Available From HP Mallory:

# ONE

There was no way in hell I was looking in the mirror.

I knew it was bad when I glanced down. My stomach, if that's what you wanted to call it, was five times its usual size and exploded around me in a mass of jelly-like fat. To make matters worse, it was the color of overcooked peas—that certain jaundiced yellow.

"Wow, Dulce, you look like crap," Sam said.

I tried to give her my best "don't piss me off" look, but I wasn't sure my face complied because I had no clue what my face looked like. If it was anything like my stomach, it had to be canned-pea green and covered with raised bumps. The bumps in question weren't small like what you'd see on a toad—more like the size of dinner plates. Inside each bump, my skin was a darker green. And the texture … it was like running your finger across the tops of your teeth—jagged with valleys and mountains.

"Can you fix it?" I asked, my voice coming out monster-deep. I shouldn't have been surprised—I was a good seven feet tall now. And with the substantial body mass, my voice could only be deep.

"Yeah, I think I can." Sam's voice didn't waver which was a good sign.

I turned to avoid the sun's rays as they broke through the window, the sunlight not feeling too great against my boils.

I glanced at Sam's perfect sitting room, complete with a sofa, love seat and two armchairs all in a soothing beige, the de facto color for inoffensive furniture. Better Homes and Gardens sat unattended on Sam's coffee table—opened at an article about how beautiful drought resistant plants can be.

"You have nine eyes," Sam said.

At least they focused as one. I couldn't imagine having them all space cadetting out. Talk about a headache.

Turning my attention from her happy sitting room, I forced my nine eyes on her, hoping the extra seven would be all the more penetrating. "Can you focus please?" I snapped.

Sam held her hands up. "Okay, okay. Sheesh, I guess getting changed into a gigantic booger put you into a crappy mood."

"Gee, you think?" My legs ached with the weight of my body. I had no idea if I had two legs or more or maybe a stump—my stomach covered them completely. I groaned and leaned against the wall, waiting for Sam to put on her glasses and figure out how to reverse the spell.

Sam was a witch and a pretty damned good one at that. I'd give her twenty minutes—then I'd be back to my old self. "Was it Fabian who boogered you?" she asked.

The mention of the little bastard set my anger ablaze. I had to count to five before the rage simmered out of me like a water balloon with a leak. I peeled myself off the wall and noticed a long spindle of green slime still stuck to the plaster; it reached out as if afraid to part with me.

"Ew!" Sam said, taking a step back from me. "You are so cleaning that wall."

"Fine. Just get me back to normal. I'm going to murder Fabian when I see him again."

Fabian was a warlock, a master of witchcraft. The little cretin hadn't taken it well when I'd come to his dark arts store to observe his latest truckload delivery. I knew the little rat was importing illegal potions (love potions, revenge potions, lust potions … the list went on) and it was my job to stop it. I'm a Regulator, someone who monitors the creatures of the Netherworld to ensure they're not breaking any rules. Think law enforcement. And Fabian clearly was breaking some rule. Otherwise, he wouldn't have turned me into a walking phlegm pile.

Sam turned and faced a sheet of chocolate chip cookie mounds. "Hold on a second, I gotta put these in the oven."

She sashayed to the kitchen and I couldn't help but think what an odd picture we made: Sam, looking like the quintessential housewife with her apron, paisley dress and Stepford withe smile, and me, looking like an alien there to abduct her.

She slid the cookies in, shut the oven door and offered me a cheery grin. "Now, where was I? Ah yes, let me just whip something together."

Kneeling down, she opened a cupboard door beneath the kitchen island and grabbed two clay bowls, three glass jars and a metal whisk. One jar was filled with a pink powder, the next with a liquid that looked like molasses, and the third with a sugary-type powder.

"Sam, I don't have time to watch you make more cookies."

"Stop being so cranky! I'm stirring a potion to figure out how the heck I'm going to help you. I have no idea what spell that little creep put on you."

I frowned, or thought I did.

Sam opened a jar and took a pinch of the pink powder between her fingers. She dropped it in the bowl and whisked. Then she spooned one tablespoon of the molasses-looking stuff into the bowl and whisked again. Dumping half the white powder in with the rest, she paused and then dumped in the remainder.

Then she studied me, biting her lip. It was a look I knew too well—one that wouldn't lead to anything good.

"What?" I demanded.

"I need some part of your body. But it doesn't look like you have any hair. Hmm, do you have fingernails?"

I went to move my arm and four came up. But even with four arms, I didn't have a single fingernail—just webbed hands that looked like duck feet. I bet I was a good swimmer.

"Sorry, no fingernails."

"Well, this might hurt then."

She turned around and pulled a butcher knife from the knife block before approaching me like a stealthy cat. Even with my enormous body, I was up and out of her way instantly.

"Hold on a second! Keep that thing away from me!"

"I need something from your body to make the potion work right. I won't take much, just a tiny piece of flesh."

I felt like adding "and not a drop of blood," but was too pre-occupied with protecting myself. I glanced at the wall and eyed the snotty globule, still attached to the plaster as if it had a right to be there. "What about that stuff?"

Sam grimaced but stopped advancing. "I'm not touching that."

"Okay, fine. How about some spit then?"

"Yeah, that might do."

My entire body breathed a sigh of relief which, given the size of me, was a pretty big breath. She put the knife back, and I made my way over to her slowly—not convinced she wasn't going to Sweeney Todd on me again.

She held out the bowl. "Spit."

I wasn't sure if my body was capable of spitting, but I leaned over and gave it a shot. Something slid up my throat, and I watched a blob of yellow land in her bowl.

It was moving. Gross.

It continued to vacillate as it interacted with the mixture, sprawling this way and that like it was having a seizure.

"Yuck," Sam said, holding the bowl as far away from her as possible. She returned it to the counter as the timer went off. Facing the oven, she grabbed a mitt that said "Kiss me, I'm Wiccan," pulled open the oven door and grabbed hold of the cookie sheet, placing them on the counter.

My stomach growled, sounding like an angry wolf, and unable to stop myself, I lumbered toward the cookies. I grabbed the sheet, not feeling the heat of the tin on my webbed hand. Sam watched me, her mouth hanging open as I lifted the sheet of cookies and emptied every last one into my mouth, swallowing them whole.

Sam's brows furrowed with anger, giving her normally angelic face a little attitude. "I was saving those to bring to work on Monday, thank you very much!"

Sam didn't wear angry well. She was too pretty—dark brown shoulder length hair, perfect skin, perfect teeth, and big brown eyes.

"Come on, Sam," I pleaded, my mouth brimming with gooey chocolate. "You know I didn't do it on purpose. I don't even like sweets."

Something slimy and pink escaped my mouth and ran itself over my lips. It took me a second to realize it was my tongue. Rather than curling back into my mouth, it hesitated on my lip as I focused on a stray chocolate chip lounging against the counter. Instantly, my tongue lurched out and grabbed hold of the chip, recoiling into my mouth like a spent cobra.

Sam quirked a less-than-amused brow and ran her palms down her paisley apron, as though composing herself. I have to count to ten, twenty sometimes. Otherwise, my temper is an ugly son of a bitch.

"Besides, none of the guys at work deserve them anyway." I knew because I worked with Sam.

She appeared to be in the process of forgiving me, a slight smile playing with the ends of her lips. I turned to the potion sitting in the bowl. The yellow ball of spit was still shivering. I nearly gagged when Sam stabbed it with the whisk and continued stirring.

I peered over her shoulder and watched the potion change colors—going from a pale brown to red then deepening into flame orange. "What's it doing?"

Sam nodded as if she were watching a movie, knew the ending, and was just dying to tell someone what happens. "Ah, of course, I should've known. The little devil put a *Hemmen* on you."

"A what?"

"It's a short-term shape-shifting charm. You'll be back to normal in about five hours or so."

"Five hours? Look at me! Can't you get rid of it sooner?"

Sam shook her head. "Would take lots of herbs and potions I don't have. I'd probably have to get them at Fabian's." She laughed. "How ironic is that? Just hang tight. It'll go away, I promise."

It figures the little bastard would've put a short-term spell on me. Currently, there weren't any laws against turning someone into a hideous creature if it would wear off after a day. And even if he had turned me into this creature long term, he'd probably only get a slap on the wrists. The Netherworld wasn't exactly good with doling out punishments.

I was working on making it better.

"You're sure?" I asked.

She nodded. "One hundred percent. Let's just watch a couple movies to keep your mind off it."

She hurried to her entertainment center and scanned through the numerous titles, using her index finger to guide her. "Dirty Dancing? Bridget Jones?"

"The first or second Bridget?"

"I have both," she said with a triumphant smile.

"I like the first one better."

With a nod of agreement, Sam pulled the DVD out and gingerly placed it into the player.

I wasn't really sure what to do with myself. I couldn't fit on her couch, and with my slime ball still suspended on the wall, sitting was out.

Sam pointed a finger in my general direction. "How did Fabian catch you unaware enough to change you into … that?"

I sighed—which came out as a grunt.

"Well?" she asked while skipping into the kitchen to microwave a packet of popcorn.

I couldn't quite meet her eyes and, instead, focused on drawing slimy lines on her counter top with one of my eight index fingers.

This was the part of the story I was least excited about. Fabian never should've caught me with my guard down. I'm a fairy. We're renowned for being extremely quick, and we've got more magic in our little finger … well, you get it.

"My back was to him," I mumbled. "I know, I know … super dumb."

Sam's eyebrows reached for the ceiling. "That doesn't sound like you at all, Dulce. Why was your back to him?"

If I wasn't excited about that last part of the story, this part excited me even less. "There was someone in his shop—a guy I've never seen before."

Sam laughed and quirked a knowing brow. "So let me make sure I've got this right."

She plopped her hands on her hips and paused for a good three seconds. Maybe she was getting me back for the cookies. "You, one of the strongest fairies around, turned your back on a known dark arts practitioner because he had a hot guy in his store?"

"No, it wasn't that at all. I'd never seen him before, and I couldn't figure out what he was."

As a fairy, I have the innate ability to decipher a creature as soon as I see one. I can tell a warlock from a vampire from a gorgon in seconds. I don't get paid the big bucks for nothing.

Sam's face took on a definite look of surprise, her eyes wide, her lips twitching. "You couldn't tell what he was? Wow, that's a first."

I nodded my bulbous head. "Exactly. And if he's here permanently, he never checked in with me or Headquarters."

Any new creature who hoped to settle in Splendor, California, needed to contact Headquarters, otherwise known as the A.N.C (Association for Netherworld Creatures). And more pointedly, they had to register with me. This new stranger had done neither. Maybe he'd gotten lost when coming over. It wasn't rare for a creature to come through the passage from the Netherworld to Earth and somehow get lost along the way. You'll find the directionally challenged everywhere.

"Maybe you should talk to Bram," Sam said. "He always seems to know what's going on."

It wasn't a bad idea, actually. Bram was a vampire (I know, how cliché …) who ran a nightclub called No Regrets. No Regrets was in the middle of the city and was the biggest hangout for creatures of the Netherworld. If something was going down, Bram was always among the first to know.

"Yeah, not a bad idea," I said.

First things first, I'd pay a visit to Fabian and let him know how much I didn't appreciate his little prank. Then, if he couldn't give me any info on his strange visitor, I'd try Bram. My third choice was Dagan, a demon who ran an S&M club called Payne that wasn't far from No Regrets. Dagan was always my last resort—I hated going to Payne. I'd seen things there that had scarred me for life.

So it looked like my plans for the weekend were shot. Not like I had much planned—just editing chapters of my romance novel, *Captain Slade's Bounty*. I'd been looking forward to a quiet weekend, so I could focus on Captain Slade and his ladylove, Clementine. Now, it looked like I'd be working the streets of Splendor instead.

Big goddammit.

### ###

Six hours later, and with Bridget Jones one and two, Dirty Dancing and four bowls of popcorn under my belt, I was home and back to myself. I felt like hell considering I'd eaten more in one evening than I usually ate in a day.

I headed through my sparse living room and straight to my bathroom. I threw off the clothes Sam had lent me (the mass I'd been turned into had shredded my outfit) and turned on the shower full force. I was back to myself, but still disgusting—covered in a layer of what looked like clear snot, like I'd just dropped out of God's nose.

I tested the water, waiting for it to warm. Then I turned to face myself in the mirror. I'm not a vain person but I was very happy to see my small and slender self reflected back at me. I pulled my mane of honey-gold hair from behind my back and inspected it. If I was narcissistic about anything, it was my hair. It was long—right down to my lower back and it looked like it had fared well in the metamorphosis. Except for the slime.

I keep my hair long because I'm not thrilled with my ears. As a fairy, my ears come to points at the tops. Think Spock. Other than that, I look like a human. And no, I don't have wings.

I checked the water again; it was warm enough. I lived in a pretty crappy apartment and the pipes in the wall screamed every time I turned the hot water on—they'd just pound if I wanted cold. I know I mentioned earlier that I make a good living, and I do. The crap apartment is due to the fact that I'm saving all my money to retire from the A.N.C. Then I can focus on my writing full time.

It might sound strange that one as magical as I would need to work nine-to-five weekdays and some weekends, but there it is. There are strict laws that disallow those of us who can, to create money out of thin air. I guess the powers that be thought about it and realized all creatures who can create something from nothing—fairies, witches and warlocks, just to name a few—certainly would be at the top of the food chain ... something bad for the less fortunate creatures and humans, too.

That, and money created from magic turns to dust after a few days anyway.

So I have to work. I've accepted it.

I stepped under the less-than-strong flow of water, which was more like a little boy peeing on my head, and grabbed my gardenia-scented soap, lathering my entire body. I repeated the process four more times before I could actually say I felt any semblance of clean.

After toweling myself off, I plodded into the living room with a towel wrapped around my head and body. Then I noticed the blinking red light on the answering machine beckoning to me. I had three new messages.

I hit play. Bram's alto voice, the pitch reminiscent of his English roots, filled my living room.

"Ah, I've missed you, Sweet. Come by the club. I have information for you."

The arrogant bastard—he never bothered saying, "It's Bram." As to the information he had … that could be meaningless. Bram had been trying to get into my pants since I became a Regulator—about two years ago. And just because he had my home phone number didn't mean he'd succeeded—I used to be listed in the phone book.

I deleted the message. I'd have to pay him a visit tomorrow. The next message was from my dry cleaners—my clothes were ready to be picked up. The third message was from my boss.

"Dulce, it's Quillan, Sam told me what Fabian did to you. Just calling to make sure you're okay. Give me a call when you get in."

I hit delete. Quillan was a good boss; he was the big wig of Headquarters, and an elf.

Elves are nothing like you're imagining them, although they are magical. Whereas I have the innate ability to create something from nothing (all it takes is a little fairy dust), Quillan is magical in his own way. He can cast spells, control his own aging and he's got the strength of a giant. Fairies and elves are like distant cousins—sprung from the same magical family tree but separated by lots of branches.

Quillan is tallish—maybe five-ten or so, slim, and has a certain regality to him. He's got a head of curly blond hair that would make Cupid envious, bronze skin, and eyes the color of amber. And he's also the muse for the hero in my romance novel. But he doesn't know that.

I wasn't in the mood to call Quillan back. I'd add him to my long list of visits for tomorrow. Even though it was Saturday, it looked like I'd be working.

Sometimes working law enforcement for the Netherworld is a real bitch.

**AVAILABLE NOW!**

**H. P. Mallory** is the author of the Jolie Wilkins series, the Dulcie O'Neil series, the Lily Harper series and the Peyton Clark series.

She began her writing career as a self-published author and after reaching a tremendous amount of success, decided to become a traditionally published author and hasn't looked back since.

H. P. Mallory lives in Southern California with her husband and son, where she is at work on her next book.

If you are interested in receiving emails when she releases new books, please sign up for her email distribution list by visiting her website and clicking the "contact" tab: www.hpmallory.com

Be sure to join HP's online Facebook community where you will find pictures of the characters from both series and lots of other fun stuff including an online book club!

Facebook: https://www.facebook.com/hpmallory

Find H.P. Mallory Online:
www.hpmallory.com
http://twitter.com/hpmallory
https://www.facebook.com/hpmallory

**Also by H.P. Mallory:**

## THE JOLIE WILKINS SERIES:

## THE DULCIE O'NEIL SERIES:

## THE LILY HARPER SERIES:

## THE PEYTON CLARK SERIES:

Made in the USA
San Bernardino, CA
17 May 2014